Helene Wiggin was born in Bolton, of Scottish
parents, and graduated from Leeds University to
become a teacher in the Midlands. She has worked as
a literacy tutor, market trader, café proprietor and
health worker in the NHS. She now lives with her
husband in a village in the Yorkshire Dales and has
four children.

Also by Helene Wiggin

Dancing at the Victory Cafe

Days of Bread and Roses

Helene Wiggin

For Jenny with love and thanks.

First published in 1996 by Hodder & Stoughton
A division of Hodder Headline PLC
A Coronet paperback original

10 9 8 7 6 5 4 3 2 1

Wiggin, Helene
Days of bread & roses
1. English fiction – 20th century
I.Title
823.9'14[F]

ISBN 0 340 65820 7

Printed and bound in Great Britain by
Cox and Wyman Ltd, Reading

Hodder and Stoughton Ltd
A Division of Hodder Headline PLC
338 Euston Road
London NW1 3BH

'We want bread and roses too!' –

Slogan of striking women at a Massachusetts factory

'Only friends will tell you the truths you need to hear
to make your life bearable!' –

Francine Du Plessix Gray

Author's Note

Women began campaigning for a vote in the nineteenth century. Suffrage societies in the textile towns of the North of England joined together in 1897 to form the National Union of Women's Suffrage Societies (N.U.W.S.S.). Their colours were red, white and green. Activities were low key, ladylike and law abiding, delivering many tons of petitions to Parliament, raising awareness amongst all political parties about the many injustices against womenkind. This peaceful approach was inevitably slow to progress.

In 1903 impatient members, such as Emmeline Pankhurst and her three daughters broke away with their supporters to form the Women's Social and Political Union (W.S.P.U.). Their colours were purple, green and white and their motto, 'Deeds Not Words'. They attracted wide support around the country and moved their base to London. Nicknamed 'suffragettes' by the *Daily Mail* in 1906, they took a more militant approach which was high profile, daring and used civil disobedience as a weapon.

The split between the law-abiding suffragists and these 'Panks' was bitter and long term, especially when the press lumped them all under the same contemptuous title of 'suffragettes'.

Some Useful Dates

1903 Mrs Emmeline Pankhurst forms the Women's Social and Political Union at her home in Nelson Street, Manchester.

1905 Demonstration in the Free Trade Hall in Manchester. Arrest of Christabel Pankhurst and Annie Kenney.

1906 General Election with new Liberal Government. Beginning of split between the militant 'Panks' and the 'Suffs'.

1908 Anti-Suffragist, Lord Asquith becomes Prime Minister. W.S.P.U. steps up militant campaign.

1909 Hunger strikes and forcible feeding of Suffragettes begins. Winston Churchill campaigns in Bolton, Preston and Lancashire in run up to General Election of 1910. W.S.P.U. organise demonstrations.

1910 Liberals are returned. The Conciliation Bill is defeated. Militants resume violence, resulting in Black Friday assault and arrests after clashes with Police at Westminster.

1911 Coronation Processions and truce. Second Conciliation Bill is defeated. W.S.P.U. responds with outbreak of window smashing.

1912 National Union of Women's Suffrage supports pro Labour Candidates at by election.

Contents

The Bread and Roses Society. 1887   1

Votes for Women. 1901 – 4   53

Deeds Not Words. 1904 – 9   111

Stone Walls Do Not A Prison Make. 1909   169

A Bitter Harvest. 1910   215

Into the Fire. 1910   271

Postscript. 1971   317

Plain and Fancy: Recipes from the Lancashire
Suffrage Cookbook   325

Acknowledgements

I am indebted to Jill Liddington and Jill Norris's excellent research in the Virago History Series' *One Hand Tied Behind Us*. Here I was introduced to some of the Lancashire women who worked for Women's Suffrage and inspired this story: Selina Cooper, Ada Neild Chew, Harriet Mitchell, Cissie Foley, Sarah Reddish, Esther Roper, *et al*.

The story is entirely fictitious but many of the events described are not. The Pankhurst family and Edith Rigby make brief and imaginary entrances into my narrative but they were present during the campaign against Winston Churchill in Lancashire during his 1909 visits to Preston and Bolton.

Once again I am indebted to Jill Sandiford for opening up the world of computer technology to me. I am grateful for information gleaned from Bolton Central Library Archives on local Suffrage Societies. The Bolton I describe but never name is from a landscape of memory and the heart.

The recipes in the *Cookbook* have been gleaned from my own collection of charity cookbooks.

I am aware that my generation owes much to Suffrage workers of all persuasions who sacrificed their time, their health and sometimes their life to achieve for women the right to vote. I hope we never take our hard-won franchise for granted or become casual in exercising this precious right.

My story comes from a personal discovery of these amazing women. Most of all I was struck by the power and joy of their friendships. In any campaign to make change happen, suffering is only made bearable by loyal and courageous support. Without such friendships life can become a stale crust indeed.

The Bread and Roses Society

Society

1887

Chapter One

'Go on! Dare you, Seddon,' sniggered the lads. 'Give us a flash of your drawers!' The aisle of St Anselm's, Plover Street, stretched out before them like a hopscotch board of gaudy tiles. The Vicar was late and Standard Five was bored. The girl hesitated. 'Cowardy cowardy custard, yer face'll turn to mustard!' the taunts continued.

She spun herself expertly down the aisle with ten cartwheels to the chancel steps and the class cheered. The Reverend Rowland Thompson chose that moment to emerge from the vestry behind his young daughter who carried a vase of garden roses. A flying clog caught the girl's hand, sending the whole display into the air. A gobsmacked hush descended upon the congregation, followed by the crash of shattered crystal on the terracotta-tiled steps. The two girls collided together, falling in a tangled heap, pink-faced and breathless. The culprit scrabbled across the tiles, desperately hoping to undo the damage, picking up the shards of glass with raw fingers.

'Here, let me help,' whispered the Vicar's girl as she knelt down beside her: a girl of her own age with bluebell eyes and golden plaited braids hanging over her shoulders. 'Don't worry, it's only a vase. Plenty more in the vestry.'

The Vicar stood over the proceedings like an avenging angel, booming, 'You stupid girl! Desecrating God's holy temple with such horseplay. Grace dear, leave her be! Let this creature clear up her own mess. What's your name, girl?'

'Phia, sir,' spluttered the girl, close to tears.

'Fire? What sort of name is that? None that I've baptised!'

'It's Sophia, sir, Sophia Seddon.'

'Well, that's not on my register, either. A Wesleyan, are we?'

'No, sir, me dad don't believe in it, sir!' piped the girl, silencing any chatter.

'Unbaptised, uncatechised . . . What will happen to you if you die? Has your father thought about that?'

Phia stood her ground. 'Yes, Reverend Thompson. He don't hold with any of it . . . says it's rubbish, all of it. We've a bad enough time here without it going on for ever and ever, he says.'

Out popped Wilf Seddon's heresies like bullets from a gun. She was for it now.

The Vicar plumped up his ruffled feathers and addressed the congregation. 'Behold a little heathen in our midst, a product of free thinking and Socialism, a defiler of God's Temple. Is this what we breed in Plover Street School? Is this what Miss Norris teaches Standard Five? Who need plough the Mission field when such a harvest is at our door?

'So, Miss Sophia Seddon, how do you intend to make reparation for this destruction?'

'Yer what?' replied Sophia, blood dripping from her fingers on to the grubby pinafore skirt of her cotton overall. 'Sorry, Vicar.'

'So you should be, silly girl. I want to see you in church every Sunday in Lent or I will pay your father a visit and ask him for a replacement crystal vase.'

'But, Papa, she's bleeding. Come with me,' ordered his daughter, grabbing Phia by the wrist and dragging her into the vestry parlour to clean her fingers under the tap. It was a musty-smelling, panelled room, dark and cluttered with vestments hanging eerily on hooks.

To Phia's untutored eye, the only brightness shone from Grace Thompson, dressed like a picture-book princess, straight from the pages of *Girls' Own*. Her cream calico dress hung loosely from a dropped waist and box-pleated skirt to mid-calf, and from under it peeped white cotton socks and the shiniest patent leather ankle-strapped shoes. Not for her Cissie's clomping hand-me-downs, scuffed and shabby. These were delicate shoes from an expensive catalogue. It was worth torn fingers to be so close to this creature from another world; a world where roses bloomed in the high-walled Vicarage garden instead of being nicked from the park and stuck in a jam jar.

'Thank you, miss,' said Sophia.

'Thank you for cheering up the Catechism class.'

'Are you being confirmed then?'

'I expect so. Will you come to church?'

'I might. What's it like?'

'Come and see,' replied Grace Thompson as she rummaged under her skirt for a handkerchief, winding it tightly around the cut fingers. 'There, that'll see you home. Your mama can bandage them properly then.'

'I haven't got a mother. She died when Ethel were born . . . but there's my dad, Gran and Cissie, Jack, Walter and Ethel.'

'Goodness! How do you all fit in? There is only Papa and I in the Vicarage but Aunt Calvert comes to stay in the holidays.'

'So you've got no mam either?'

Grace shook her head. 'She was ill. I don't remember . . . It was a long time ago.'

'Grace, hurry up, child, and join the class!' The Vicar stood at the door, glowering.

'See you on Sunday then, Phia?' The two girls smiled as he unlocked the vestry door and half-pushed the culprit out into the weak sunshine of a February afternoon.

'Now, Grace, I don't want you mixing in the street,' he said, turning back to his daughter. 'That girl spells trouble!'

'But, Papa, I thought you wanted me to be a missionary?' she said, smiling sweetly as she placed the roses in another vase.

Phia sped along the sunless side of the street, past the regiments of red-brick terraced houses flanking the cobbled road, saluting St Anselm's Parish Church as it rose from their ranks like an over-decorated general. She was too excited even to leap over the bogeymen lurking under the cracks in the flagstones.

Grace . . . Grace Thompson. I bet she has two Christian names . . . Grace was such a beautiful name, not rough like the names on the Board School register. All the Bessies, Berthas, Aggies and Ellens: names fit for cart horses. Grace sounded so refined, so dignified, so inspiring. She was going to need a bit of inspiration herself to get to see Grace Thompson again.

Sophia dawdled down the back entry to number nine, pausing to watch puffs of blue smoke drifting from behind a loose brick in the privy. Dad was home early, locked in the lav for a quiet smoke. He knew the score on baking days. If he put his pipe across the doorstep, Gran would yell, 'Get that filthy thing out of my clean house, Wilf Seddon . . . We've enough fumes from that load of dust, what Mr Higson carts round on his wagon as coal.'

This was the only order Dad obeyed. Mam had never liked the smell of baccy either. Still it was Friday night and that meant billiards and darts at The Spindlemaker's Arms so he would be in a good mood. The girl loitered in the yard.

'Dad?'

'Yes, our Phia.'

'Why did you call me Sophia?'

Wilfred Seddon sucked on his pipe and smiled to himself. 'I thowt you'd need some sense, being a lass. As I

7

recall the name's summat to do wi' being wise . . . What's brought all this on?'

'Dad,' she continued, 'can I join the Sunday School?'

'What the hell do you want to go God-botherin' for? Haven't I told you it's a load of tripe?'

'Yes, I know that, but I'm not getting much schooling, what with mindin' Ethel and helpin' Gran on wash days. I hear they do reading and writing there as well. I could do wi' some practice. And you do say never miss a chance of free learning, don't you, Dad?'

Silence from the throne.

'Aye . . . well, go on then,' he replied. 'Reckon I named thee right enough.'

Sophia grinned to herself. That was the first hurdle over. Now to tackle the second.

The smells wafted through the yard, better than Warburton's bakery. The table was laden with trays of currant buns, railway slice and Eccles cakes (fly cemeteries, Jack called them, to put you off your share); a mouth-watering display of untouchables. In the side oven the first of the barm cakes and over bottom bread tortured nostrils and belly.

Bun Gran drew up her wrinkled face into one of her stringbag looks of disapproval. 'Where've you bin till this time, lady? Park larkin'? Look at you, like Madge Wildfire! I needed you to take Ethel out of my hair. She's twined all afternoon, Phia. How've you got blood all over yer pinny? And you can get yer thievin' fingers off my bakin'. Stop pickin'!'

'Sorry, Gran, but I got in a bit of bother in the Vicar's class.' Sophia held up her fingers for sympathy. 'Look, the Vicar's daughter bound them up with her hanky. Can I wash this for Sunday Church? See, it's real lace with her initial embroidered in the corner. "G" is for Grace. She was ever so kind.'

'Is she yon pale-faced stick o' a lass, the one as looks as if she needs a square meal inside her? I'm surprised Parson lets her mix with Board School kiddies. 'Er who cleans up at the Vicarage says she's right chesty and he don't want her pickin' up germs and thick vowels. She goes to some fancy school up town, away from all the smoke and fumes of the iron foundry.'

'She's goin' to be my friend so I must get this washed.'

'Well, soak it in a pan with cold water and salt to get the blood stain off. You can boil it up later if there's enough fire left. I'm not puttin' no copper to boil for one lace hanky. It can wait while Monday when we do the wash, and you can collect Walter and Ethel from next-door's yard. You'll 'ave to mind her bairns tomorrow.'

Millie Walker, affectionately nicknamed 'Bun Gran', wiped her floury brow and pitched into her last batch of dough with sturdy arms, bending her cottage loaf shape, with its round bosom and ample hips, to the task. When her daughter had died in childbirth she'd come to the rescue, leaving her own hearth to keep house for them all. Now she was feeling every one of her sixty-five years.

'Can I knock back the bread for you?' Sophia loved punching her fists into the warmth and stickiness of the dough and sitting by the fender turning the bowl. Bread was mysterious, rising secretly under its cloth, lumpen and lifeless at first then puffed up ready to bake.

'Not with them fingers, you can't. Beat the rag rug or donkey stone the front doorstep. We'll not have anyone in Plover Street say I keep a dirty house. Not like them slopers next door. I don't think she cleans her nets from one spring to the next.' Gran bashed into the dough. 'Mind on, our Phia, you don't get good bread without a hard knockin' back. The more you bash, the higher it rises. So work hard at yer lessons, young lady, and perhaps you'll rise like bread!'

'Got top marks again for composition. Miss Norris says my essays are a revelation. Can I stay on . . . do proper lessons? Miss Norris says I could be a Pupil Monitor. I don't want to go into Berisford's Mill, I want to be a teacher like Miss Norris.'

'Ada Norris has no right to put ideas into yer head. It's all right for her, being an only child and no oil painting either. Her dad could afford to give her an education. She'll not tempt any curate with yon squashed face of hers! But education's not for the likes of us in Plover Street, and certainly not for a harum-scarum flibberty-gibbet like you, so don't get yer hopes up. Any road, it's yer dad who decides. Berisford's Cotton Mill is good enough for Cissie. Why should you be different, my lady?'

''Cos I'm a clever clogs, so sharp I'll cut myself! You've told me that a hundred times. It's not fair to shove me in the mill. I'll shrivel up with boredom.'

'Boredom? Where do you get such words? No one is ever bored in a mill. Just ask Cissie. She'll soon put you straight.' Gran sniffed the range and flung back the black-leaded door in a flurry. 'Look! Your day dreams nearly burnt the bread.'

'Just like King Alfred,' came the reply.

'Enough of your uppity nonsense. People like us are here to keep the numbers up, so no more fancy notions. Make yerself useful for a change.'

Phia slipped a bun deftly into her pocket and skipped out into the back yard with a grin. On Sunday she intended to meet Grace Thompson properly.

'All dolled up like a dish of tripe' was the verdict on Sophia's Sunday appearance. She curled the frills around her best cotton smock with the goffering iron, polished her clogs above their station, tortured her thick brown hair into rag-rollered corkscrews. Cissie gave her a piece of pretty off-cut ribbon to tie back her curls in the fashion of the Royal Princesses, as stamped on their biscuit tin.

'You'll do,' said Bun Gran grudgingly, reluctant to admit that the girl paid for dressing up, with her raisin-coloured eyes, glossy chestnut mane and square little body, just like her poor departed mam's. 'You know I don't hold with all them smells and bells! Religion should be plain, not fancy. St Anselm's is definitely fancy. That Reverend Thompson is a right one for dressing up the church and himself, and not above poaching from the Wesleyans given half a chance! But mind you behave yerself. We may be working folk but the Seddons can hold their head up to anyone in this street.'

The girl stuffed the lace hanky into her pocket and headed out of the front door, listening to the five-minute bell tolling from the soot-blackened church tower. She took her place amongst the rows of scholars penned in pews by the side of the Lady Chapel, swinging their legs, bashing the oak panels, poking their noses and wiping off snot on the hassocks. She scanned the pews for the out-line of Grace Thompson and saw her sitting on the front row.

A shaft of dusty sunlight bathed Grace's head like a halo; a band of silk flowers was swathed around her bonnet and cascades of blue satin ribbon tumbled nonchalantly down her back. Miss Grace Thompson looked just perfect. Phia recognised the satin ribbon from the trimmings stall in the open market. Even if she minded all the kids in the street for a week to pay for a yard or two, it would never look smart on her bashed up straw hat. Only its shabbiness would be enhanced.

The service was boring. What a relief when they were turfed out before the sermon, row by row. A truculent toddler refused to budge from the front pew and Sophia could see Grace struggling to cajole the child and subdue its wails. She shot forward and grabbed the toddler. 'Give her here, miss . . . Annie Thornber's a right pain.'

'Thank you,' said the other girl with relief. 'So you came after all?'

'Yep. Thowt I'd give it the once over. What do I do next?' she whispered, conscious they were holding up the other children.

'Well, you go to Bible Study in the Church Institute room.' Grace pointed to the building tucked in a corner behind the school yard. 'I have to look after the tinies in the Infants' Hall with the other ladies till we go back in again . . .'

'Back in again?' gulped Sophia.

'Yes, of course, for Communion. We just bow our heads for the Blessing until we're confirmed.'

Sophia knew all about Confirmation Sunday. That was when the ones who had stuck out the classes were draped in borrowed lawn veils and white frocks, swanking their finery along the street like fairy queens. Not that they were as grand as the Catholic girls from St Peter and Paul's who paraded in long bridal dresses, necks adorned with gold crucifixes, and covered from head to toe in cobweb lace. Now *they* were something to gawp at. Even Kitty Kelly, who was a right cow, looked like a Vestal Virgin from a distance. Gran said that the Kellys went hungry for weeks, pawning their souls to see Kitty done up properly. No, a St Anselm's confirmation was a poor second and Bun Gran certainly wouldn't abide any dressing up.

As they walked slowly to the vestibule door and the parting of their ways, Sophia took a deep breath. 'Do you need an extra hand in there? Annie can be a tartar when she's got a mood on.'

'Are you sure? It's awfully kind of you to offer. I'm not very good with them.'

'Don't you bother. I know them all and can soon sort them out. I push them out in the washday cart often enough, Miss Thompson.'

'Do call me Grace.' She held out her hand formally.

'And I'm Sophia . . . Seddon.' Phia was not going to give her street name. It was so common. 'It's a bit stiff and starchy.'

'Then I'll call you Sophie, if you like? Don't you think it sounds soft round the edge – soft as kitten fur?' said Grace with a smile.

'Suits me nicely.' Sophie almost purred with pleasure. She watched the young children sitting on diminutive chairs whilst the pianist, Miss Bowker, played hymns. An offering bag was handed round to relieve them of any coins, but little was plopped into the velvet pouch. Sophie felt a beetroot blush rising from her neck. No one had warned her about a collection. The pouch bobbed closer.

'Don't worry about the Offering,' said Grace as she whipped up the bag, plunging it into the next row. All too soon the class was dismissed towards the porch. 'We can skip the next bit, if you like. Nobody will notice.' The Vicar's daughter pointed towards the cemetery gate.

'Come and see my favourite graves. I collect names. Come on, hurry!'

They scampered over the turfed mounds, picking out weathered lettering from the lichen-encrusted headstones.

'Look! My favourite . . . "In Memory of Christmas Day and his beloved wife, Mary". Isn't that romantic, to be called Christmas?'

'Not if they read the school register every day. I bet he got teased summat rotten,' Sophie argued.

'Do you really think so? I never thought about that.'

'I didn't mean to spoil it for you,' she replied. 'Let's find some more. I think my mam is buried here but it's hard to tell now.' Sophie found herself talking about Mam and all the chores she herself now had to perform.

The other girl nodded encouragingly. 'My mama died when I was little. I can't remember her very well but Papa says she's an angel in Heaven now, watching over me. Do you think she's watching us now?' Grace moved closer. 'Aunt Calvert is kind but ever so strict.'

'So's my gran.' They both giggled.

'You know, you ought to get your brothers to help you do your jobs,' said Grace thoughtfully.

'Never! They'd never . . .'

'If they were my brothers, I'd make them. Otherwise it's not fair!' Grace leaned forward with a new intensity behind those blue eyes; so deep, so determined. Sophie, in all of her eleven years, had never considered whether it was fair that she should have to darn socks while Jack and Walter went out to play in the street. This creature from behind the Vicarage wall was indeed remarkable.

'I'll see you next week then. I'll show you the owl's nest in my garden,' ordered Grace as they strolled on to the path where the congregation lingered by the porch, talking to a tall woman in a beaded black cape who eyed them both keenly.

'Where have you been, Grace dear? Loitering in the damp? You missed the Blessing.'

'I felt a bit faint again and we thought the fresh air might help. Didn't we?' Sophie bowed her head.

'Who is this?' Aunt Calvert asked.

'My new friend, Sophie Seddon,' came the reply.

'Do you think that's wise, dear?' her widowed aunt sighed. 'I'm not sure your father . . .'

'Oh, but I do. And can she come for tea?'

Chapter Two

'Take your feet off the wall and walk on yer hands like me!'

'Look, I'm doing it!' Grace yelled back to Sophie as she launched herself off the privy wall, out into the cobbled back street. Her flannelette and lace-edged petticoats, tucked decorously into her garter tops, soon flopped over her face, blinding her bulging eyes, distracting her from her efforts to catch up with Sophie's own flotilla of grubby cottons sailing up the alley.

Life had taken a topsy-turvy turn for the better since Sophie Seddon had cartwheeled into her sedate existence. Plover Street was no longer a drab forbidden territory but an exciting wonderland of back ginnels and snickets, winding around the dark mysterious monolith of Berisford's Mill which they had christened 'Dragon Castle'.

If Aunt Calvert ever guessed what she got up to these days . . . How she sneaked out of the garden through a gap in the laurel hedge, conveniently widened and disguised. How she raced through the recreation ground, along dusty cinder paths, to meet her friend after school and share a ha'porth of chips in a newspaper parcel; squidgy chips, piping hot, doused with vinegar and salt. Afterwards the grease coated her fingers for hours with the sweet memory of this disobedience. Eating in public was unheard of in Vicarage polite society, a punishable offence. Yet, doing so hidden under rows of flapping washing, listening to the Seddon goings on at number nine, planning assaults on Dragon Castle, was the highlight of her week.

Sophie was always dreaming up some scheme like fishing for sticklebacks in the canal or hunting for frog's spawn whilst pushing a truckload of washday orphans, all curious to poke their fingers into the gooey jelly. The babies went home that day soaked through but happy and still in one piece. And now they had plotted their most daring escapade: to explore Dragon Castle, storm the Dragon's belching chimney lair and rescue the fair Cecily Seddon from her weaving loom!

'Piece of cake!' bluffed Sophie, her mind racing ahead to the perils of the porter's gate or Hellfire Corner, afterwards avoiding the engine rooms with their Dragon's breath and sussing out the warren of stone-flagged steps to the carding rooms and spinning mules, warp rooms, and finally the weaving sheds with their jagged-tooth rooftops. Cissie's description of the place was drawn on a hanky like a secret map. For the captain of such a daring enterprise, Sophie was still vague as to her sister's actual whereabouts amongst the hundreds of women working there, but undeterred by such minor details. The mission was their grandest scheme so far and Grace was happy to tag along.

'I'm not goin' to go and work in the mill and you certainly won't, so why not have a secret recce just to see what it's like? Miss Norris says we should always investigate matters. Investigate . . . is that one of them Latin words you learn?'

Grace rested her leg against a wall; her hands were filthy and pitted with blue-black cinders. 'I'm not sure. I've only got as far as *amo, amas, amat*. I love, you love, he loves.'

Sophie wobbled as she walked on her hands. '*Amo . . . amas . . . amat . . .* I'm goin' to learn Latin and French when I'm a teacher. Miss Norris knows Latin. She says Latin words are a better class of word. Our reccy ground is from Latin . . . recreation ground . . . and so are omnibuses. I bet there's even Latin in the mill so we have to investigate.'

'What if we get caught?' asked Grace.

'Not on your Nelly! Who'll notice two more in a thousand? Any road, we'll be in disguise.'

Grace's hands gave way and she flopped on to the cobbles. 'A disguise. How exciting!'

'Wait here and I'll get them. Don't get too steamed up. We can't go as pirates but this is the next best thing.'

Sophie uncurled herself, and once upright darted through the back gate into the whitewashed privy with its two wooden seats, scattering a cloud of buzzing flies as she pulled out a bundle of clothes stuffed behind the door. 'I borrowed these from our Jack and Walter. They're a bit big but who'll notice? Try them on.'

'I can't wear these!' Grace sniffed the oily, sweaty breeches covered in foundry dust, dropping them with disgust on to the cobbles.

'Well, you can't storm the citadel dressed in a blue serge skirt, cream blouse and school tie. A right advertisement for the High School if ever I saw one! Don't be a spoil-sport. Get yerself breeched up. I will . . . see!' Sophie pulled off her skirt and flannel petticoat, tucking the old shirt into stiff trousers and loosening her wool stockings, drawing her garters down under her knees.

Reluctantly, Grace peeled off her uniform, folding it neatly into a pile. 'What about my hair?'

'Just tuck it under the flat cap. Hurry up, we've not got all day. Come on, you blushing rose!' said Sophie impatiently.

'Shut up, barm cake!' giggled Grace, using their secret nicknames. 'You should be the blooming rose. I'm only plain bread.'

'Aye, a right white bloomer we have 'ere!' Sophie pointed at her fine cotton drawers. They fell on to the two lavvy seats at the mention of bloomers, pounding each other and roaring with laughter.

'Roses and bread – what a combination,' gasped Grace.

'Who said anything about combinations!' More raucous giggling as they emerged dressed as lads from the privy, linking arms in anticipation of their great adventure. 'Bread and roses, roses and bread . . . What does it matter so long as we're friends?'

At the sight of the soot-blackened chimney towering into the clouds and the wrought-iron mill gates, Grace felt her courage fail and her heart tremble. They joined the hundreds of men and women returning for the afternoon shift. Mill girls in straw boaters, their aprons hidden under long woollen shawls, gathered in groups along the street like a clattering army on the march.

Perhaps this was not a good way to spend her extra school holiday, donated by the Governors of the High School for the Queen's Jubilee, thought Grace. But it was the only chance both girls had to meet on a weekday and roam the streets before the big celebrations began in earnest; all the processions and choral concerts, parades, fun fairs, sports competitions and parties.

The mill flags hung limply and already the shop fronts in the streets were bedecked with bunting and loyal pictures of Her Majesty, looking stern and sad. The Girls' High School had been practising choral anthems for the massed choir festival in the Queen's Park. Papa would be walking his parish faithful along the streets to join the massed Sunday School parades with their patronal banners held high, Grace imagined, feeling the clogs chafing the backs of her heels and the scratchy breeches pricking her skin. How could people endure such coarse cloth? The two girls lurked at the corner shop, eyeing the black hands of the mill clock, waiting for the familiar hooter to summon the workers back to the den. When a gaggle of lads passed them by without comment, it felt safe to tag on behind. Under this cover they sauntered casually through the gates, deep in conversation, drifting in the same general direction as the boys. Then Sophie surreptitiously pulled out the map and squinted closely, turning it this way and that to get a sense of direction.

'I hope you know where we're supposed to go?' whispered Grace as the huge wooden gates closed behind them, shutting out the latecomers with a bang, sending those on the other side scurrying to the small porter's gate, to the penny hole, to have their pay docked.

'It's bigger than I thowt, that's all. I think we go through that door and up some stairs. We'll give Cissie a right turn when she sees us togged up as errand boys!' Sophie beckoned excitedly to a hesitant Grace. 'Don't dawdle. We must stick together! In here, in here!'

The minute she pushed open the door she smelt the stench of oily rags and knew her mistake. The vast room shook with the whirling of spinning mules; the force of the steam heat took her breath away for a second. There were bare-chested men sweating at their tasks, slithering barefoot across an oily wet floor. Grace stood awestruck at the sight of giant rollers winding the huge bobbins of yarn, and pushed them both forward to get a closer look at this vision from hell.

Sophie pushed her back, mouthing as loud as she could. 'Get back, quick, it's the wrong place! Let's get out before we're spotted by the overseer.' She had noticed a giant of a man with a grimy chest, wearing only stained white fustian breeches and a neckerchief, giving orders to a group of small boys who crawled barefoot like shiny black cockroaches, scrubbing under the machinery. He turned and caught a glimpse of them, striding forward immediately. The girls stood staring, transfixed by the sight of his greasy moustache, dripping with sweat.

'Now then, tiddlers, looking for a job? Bit on the small side but you'll do, lad. Get under that machine and clean up the gubbins. You'll get yerself a gobful of cotton if yer keep yer jaw gawpin' like that. Sharp on!' He pushed the stunned Grace, taller by a head than her mate, down to the floor. 'New, are we? Get stuck in under there – and mind yer head!'

Grace recoiled from him, frozen with fear.

'Cat got yer tongue? Lads do men's work in my place. Don't be a girl's blouse! Do you want my boot up yer backside? Shift yer arse!'

'Let me do it, mister.' Sophie yanked the brush from his hand and made for the gap under the machine, quickly removing her clogs.

'Bugger off! This one'll show me what it's made of.' He dragged Grace over the floor, white-faced and trembling, and shoved her under the machine. 'Do what yer bloody well told or I'll bray yer, right here! These half-timers have it soft these days . . . a dose of nimby-pimbies!'

Sophie watched in horror as her friend bravely brushed away the oily cotton fluff, crawling further under the whirling machinery with tears rolling down her cheeks. 'Stop the machines! Stop them at once! It's all my fault. You mustn't make her go in there. She's got a bad chest,' Sophie yelled at the overseer.

He stared in disbelief as the lad's cap caught on the machinery and snagged the whole process. A stream of golden hair fell down the child's back, revealing her disguise. He ordered a boy in ragged breeches to drag her out.

'What the hell are you playing at?'

He grabbed them both and shook them roughly as he marched them out of the door, up stone-flagged steps to a mahogany door. He knocked on this and shoved them through. 'A right set of silly interlopers we 'ave here, sir. Just look at them – a couple of lassies larking about in t'mill. Tell Mr Berisford just what you've been doin'.'

At a leather-topped desk sat a man with a bulbous head and bushy whiskers of the purest white down each side of his pink cheeks. He peered over his half-moon spectacles, looking at them sternly like Moses before the Egyptians in Grace's *Illustrated Bible*.

'It was my daft idea,' snivelled Sophie.

'Shut up . . . I'll do the talking,' commanded Grace. 'We had an idea it might be fun to explore Dragon Castle . . . your mill . . . to see what it's all about. We only meant to look round . . .'

'To investigate,' chirped Sophie, using her best word.

'I am sorry we have wasted your time. We do apologise,' added Grace politely.

'I see. And just who has been doing this investigation of Dragon . . . er, my mill?'

'I am Grace Margaret Thompson from St Anselm's Vicarage, and this is my friend, Sophia Seddon, from Plover Street.'

'Number nine,' piped Sophie.

'Ah-hah! One of the illustrious Seddon clan. I'd better be careful. Kick one of them and they all squeal. So I have before me the Vicar's lass and her accomplice. I wonder what our Parson will have to say about that, young lady?' replied Jairus Berisford, trying not to smile.

'You could have been scalped, maimed for life, child! How dare you disgrace us with such behaviour? I blame that Seddon girl. I said it was an unholy alliance. I told you no good would come out of it, Maude, didn't I?' Rowland Thompson wiped his forehead and shook his head at his daughter, standing on the Persian rug, shuffling her calf-skin boots over the intricate patterns.

'Don't get overheated, Rowland. The girls have apologised and Mr Berisford has decided not to take it any further. They are at that silly age, neither fish nor fowl. Girls like to be chummy. If you will do Mission work in a poor parish, who is there suitable for Grace to consort with? You can't cage her in the Vicarage all day.' Aunt Calvert poked a needle into her tapestry with a sigh.

'I know this is not an ideal place in which to raise a motherless daughter, but I do my best. Never in my wildest dreams did I think a child of the cloth would demean

25

herself in breeches and parade herself on my own doorstep – fouling the nest in such a brazen manner! Well, what have you to say for yourself?'

'We just wanted to see inside the mill, if only to know how lucky we are not to have to work there and to understand those who must. I am to be a missionary and Sophie a school teacher. We had to storm Dragon Castle . . . it's a dreadful place, Papa. Children like us slave under machines like blind dogs in filth. They have to submit to bad language and horrible tasks. I saw it all for myself . . .'

'Is this Socialist talk I'm hearing? Wilf Seddon's brood are well indoctrinated! We are all given a station in life by the Almighty in His wisdom. He allots us our sphere and our span. Do not query his justice or judgement, my girl. With privilege comes responsibility and that is a burden in itself. You have the burden of your late mama's legacy to account for. That could lead to danger. Many will envy you such riches. Let us thank Him for His mercy in showing me the subversion to which I am exposing you in this parish. Needless to say, there will be no more contact with the Seddon brat!'

'But, Papa . . .'

'Silence, Grace! You shame your mother's sacred memory by your disobedience. If this defiance is a foretaste of what I must expect from you, then I must take steps to amend my lenience. Confine yourself indoors as a punishment. You will not be attending the Jubilee Celebrations. You must learn discipline and decorum, not jeopardise my parish work by hobnobbing with street riff-raff. Do you understand?'

'No, Papa. Sophie is my friend. We meant no harm. Why must we be separated?'

'Stick to your own class. I will not have her near the place. Aunt Calvert and I will find you some more suitable companions. Go to your room now and meditate on your condition.'

Grace sat on the window ledge overlooking the recreation ground, peering through the stained and leaded glass to watch all the fun of the Sports Day races on the grass beyond the Vicarage garden. Plover Street was bedecked with bunting and trestle tables lined the cobbles for a children's party. Aunt Calvert had hinted that Papa would request a transfer from the Bishop if Grace's bad behaviour continued; to a parish farther out of town, away from the forest of chimneys and sooty streets she now called home. He would use her wheezy chest as an excuse to terminate his ministry here.

Suddenly she saw Sophie waving a handkerchief, the signal for her to creep down to the back garden fence and squeeze through the gap. They sat on a sunny bench in the municipal rose garden, admiring the half-moon beds of rosebuds almost in bloom. Grace hugged her knees to her chest alongside her sad secret while Sophie fingered the pretty muslin of her afternoon dress admiringly. 'Thank God you won't have to go into the mill, Soph. I couldn't bear to think of you stuck in such a terrible place,' said Grace at last.

But for once Sophie was silent and stared straight ahead, a clout from Wilf Seddon still ringing in her ears.

'You stupid besom! Have you stewed yer brains? You nearly got our Cissie the sack! And I thowt you'd more than cotton fluff in yer head . . . Gettin' above oursel' with that stuck up Thompson lass, are we? It won't last. She'll get shut of you in no time. Whatever put such a crackpot idea in yer head?'

'We just wanted to see what it were like.'

'Well, now you know. And the sooner you get half-time, the better.'

'But I'm not goin' in no mill, am I, Gran? Miss Morris says I can be a pupil teacher.'

'Oh, she does, does she? Then someone'll have to put her straight, won't they? You'll go into the mill like yer sister, and Ethel when her turn comes. Think on. This is Plover Street. You can't live off dreams. They don't make bread and butter! We need yer wage in this house, same as all the rest.'

'Oh, yes . . . so you can flush them all down the lav at The Spindlemaker's Arms every Sat'day night!'

The side-winding blow stung her ear. 'Get out o' my bloody sight, cheeky brat! Who do you think you are? Gettin' above yer station, that's for sure. A week in the mill'll soon sort yon nonsense. I don't want you turnin' into a shrivelled up old prune like Ada Norris. Book-learnin' has done nothing for her looks. Education's not for women. What can you do wi' it but get wed and read to bairns?'

'Bun Gran, tell him, please, how good I am at school! Miss Norris sent my composition to a competition for the Jubilee Prize.'

Wilf Seddon's jaw set firm and his cheeks twitched at her challenge.

'This 's nowt to do wi' her. Yer gran has a job to make ends meet as it is, without wasting time on book-learnin'.'

'You promised,' pleaded the girl as her sister Ethel stood watching wide-eyed.

'Phia, I never promised you owt. It's all bin in yer head. However did you think you could escape the mill?'

'But it's not what I want!' she cried as the snivels dripped from her nose.

'Who care's a monkey's curse what you want, lass? You do as yer told or you'll taste the back of my leather belt on yer backside. Think on!' Her father puffed on his empty pipe, sucking in air noisily.

'I hate you all!' she screamed, racing up the wooden stairs to fling herself on the bed, the springs creaking in protest as she bounced and kicked, sniffing into the coal-dusty tang of the patchwork quilt, beating her fists against the bolster. 'It's just not fair!'

The girls stared silently as the shadows of late-afternoon crept over the crescent-shaped shrub beds, each nursing a secret from the other with a heavy heart. 'You will be my always friend, won't you?' whispered Grace, breaking the spell. 'No matter what . . .'

'We'll be the Bread and Roses Society, like the Co-op . . . with just two members, right?'

'And this will be our secret badge.' Grace leaped from the bench and plucked two pink rosebuds from the floribunda bushes. 'One for you and one for me. Let's press them into our Prayer Books for ever.'

A voice from the park keeper's cottage yelled and a man waved a fork in their direction. 'Just you get off them flower beds, lassie, before I have your guts for garters! Don't you dare trespass! Can't you read them bye-laws . . . children is forbidden in here. Gertcha!'

They scuttled like mice into the undergrowth through a well-beaten track and out on to the playing field where the last of the Jubilee Races gathered a crowd of onlookers.

'Spoilsport!' grumbled Sophie, puffing up with fury. Why did grown ups always have to throw mud over her dreams?

Chapter Three

'Phia! Wake up!' A voice forced its way into her sleep, tugging at her sleeve. She woke with a start. A hand nudged her again. Where was she? Dozing at her desk again. The droning of a Standard Five spelling chant had lulled her off to sleep. She looked up sheepishly at the teacher's familiar face.

'Sorry, Miss Norris.'

'The first few weeks are always the worst, Sophia.'

'Yes, Miss Norris.'

'You'll get used to going part-time.' The mistress sighed as she returned to her high desk overlooking rows of bog-eyed half-timers, sent back from Berisford's after the lunch break to continue their futile studies. Sleep was what they needed, not instruction, these pale faces wizened before their time; faces which never saw the daylight or fresh air; children who supplemented the family income by a precious half-a-crown a week. If it was up to her they

31

would be left alone to sleep off their weariness, but since the last impromptu visit of the new Chairman of School Managers (who'd caught four poor souls snoring) she must toe the line or else risk a reprimand from the governing body who relied on regular inspections to keep their teachers up to scratch.

The classroom itself did not encourage diligence with its dark walls and depressing aspect overlooking tarmacadam yards at either side, the building penned in by iron railings and high brick walls. The rooms were large, containing row upon row of desks and benches. There was little leaven in the dough of formal instruction. Fates were sealed for these children long before they gulped their first breath. Mines or foundry work for the boys. Mills or service for the girls. On her desk was the prize book token awarded the Seddon child for her Jubilee essay. Sophia Seddon and Annie Pilling were the only two bright sparks in the class, eager to learn despite their tiredness. She had pleaded in vain with the Headmaster to make an exception, persuade the father to let Sophia stay in school. 'We ought to do something for our prize-winner. It's not often that St Anselm's gets a recommended pupil. She ought not to be wasted on a Lancashire loom!'

'Now then, Miss Norris. I know you mean well but you mustn't get too involved. We answer to our managers and to Jairus Berisford, our Chairman. So long as she passes the medical and gains an attendance certificate, it's none of your concern where she goes.'

'But she would make an excellent Pupil Monitor . . .'

'That's as may be but your duty, young woman, is to drum the rudiments into your charges, whether conscious or not.' He laughed at his own feeble joke. 'How's your poor mother?'

'Not one of her good weeks, Mr Grundy. She is getting very forgetful.'

'Did I hear that the Constable had to escort her back from the Market Hall last week?'

Trust him to have heard of their disgrace! How Mother had managed to walk three miles into the town and fill a basket with nonsense from the stalls she did not know, thought the teacher, blushing with embarrassment.

'You make a splendid job of your Christian duty. Not everyone could cope with her eccentric ways. It must be a great disappointment to you.'

At twenty-four Adelaide Norris was seasoned in life's disappointments. Against the tide of prejudice she'd grabbed a secondary education with the promise of a Queen's Scholarship, only to have it snatched away when the father she adored died of a collapsed lung. There was no alternative but to seek an immediate appointment to support herself and her ailing mother. In her favour were excellent references. She was a practising member of the Established Church, essential for a post in any church school, and no one need remind her that she possessed that most enduring asset of all, the homely countenance: a face podgy and pitted with childhood scarlet fever, a nose of parsnip proportions and oddly separated teeth. The mirror declared her an ideal choice. She would attract few lustful glances, except perhaps from a passing farrier who might admire her sturdy likeness to a dray horse. Her predecessors, a succession of pretty young teaching assistants, had brought headaches to the managers, barely lasting a year each before being whisked down some aisle in the fashionable suburbs to breed babies. She saw the unanimous relief on their faces at her interview. Adelaide Norris was built to endure and she came cheap. Only her voice, soft and husky, with its refined Lancashire burr and deep resonant contralto tone, belied her outward appearance.

St Anselm's School had been a disappointment to the candidate. It was not her first choice, being too cluttered and gloomy for her taste, but it was close to the centre of the town where there were night classes, social activities, a good public library, omnibuses to Manchester, and frequent concerts and musical evenings. She could still live high and windswept on Plodder Lane where Mother, confused in her private grief, slept away the days. At night that dear thorn in her flesh demanded her time and attention, like a frightened child.

Ada Norris was no shirker. Her duty was to ram into the pupils what was required, to impress the visiting Inspectors with her efficiency, to keep control at all times – even if it meant beating the unruly into submission like disobedient dogs.

There were few opportunities for her pupils to rise above the red-brick streets and wing their way into some profession. Mill or foundry, service or a shop, the choice was sparse enough. All the speechifying about education was a sham. The leavers had merely to pass a simple test, 'the dunce's pass', and only defectives failed! Even the lads who could neither read nor write, who'd spent their schooldays digging the master's garden, somehow made the grade on Inspection Day!

Today she would need three heads on her shoulders to see that her mother did not wander, and make sure her pupils stayed awake until lunchtime. The third head must somehow get her back to town in the evening for a special meeting of the National Society for the Promotion of Science. Tonight the famous Suffragist from Manchester, Lydia Becker, was going to address the floor. This was a meeting not to be missed, even if it meant she had to lock Mother in the cottage and tie her to a chair! Adelaide was depending on Miss Becker's fearsome reputation to inspire and motivate her own wavering resolve. Even plain women could make themselves visible; she still had a voice and a vocation, if only before the rows of dozing children. There was more to any woman than mere outward appearance.

Sophie tried to stay attentive but knew that somewhere between the end of Plover Street and Berisford's Mill her childhood had been lost forever, just three days after her twelfth birthday.

She was roused with Cissie at five o'clock by the tap-tap on the window of the knocker-up man's tall pole as he trudged on his rounds down the street. They rolled and shoved each other out of bed, leaving Ethel snug and warm. Sophie was pushed downstairs to dress by the dismal, smoking fire. A mug of last night's stewed tea was pushed into her hand before she was propelled out of the door in clogs and shawl, to join the others clacking their way up the street.

Sophie stood before the chimney stack, staring blearily at a pile of once red Accrington brick encircled with a cream border on which was etched the date 1860 . . . the year of its erection, as she pushed and shoved her way through the yard gate into the cobbled square and climbed a dark stairwell up to a vast machine hall, a silent strange and hostile place, smelling of oil and cotton fibre. On the dot of six o'clock, the hooter blasted and the engines creaked and cranked, shafts moving up and down, pistons gathering momentum, faster and faster as steam on full throttle yanked the looms back to life. Her first full working day had begun.

At first Cissie and her mates just nodded silently, moving like automata, checking machines, pacing back and forth. Sophie trailed behind, trying to make sense of it all. A piece of rough folded cotton was stuck on the front of her skirt, a 'lap apron' to protect her clothing from the grease.

Cissie wore a belt from which dangled all the hooks and tools of her trade. Never had Sophie's sister seemed so grown up before. As the machines clattered, stunning her eardrums with their cacophony, the terrified child stood as if rooted to the flagstones, shocked and helpless. But Cissie, seeing her distress, soon had her running hither and thither, supplying her needs, giving orders like a 'missus'.

At eight o'clock another hooter blasted the shut down for breakfast. There was no time to run home, just to sit amongst the bales or on the stairs with a mug of tea, purchased from a woman who brought hot water to the millgate. Sophie was busting for the privy but one look at the lav and she ran out feeling sick at the state of its filth. It was stuffed full of smelly newspaper, a slop stone thoroughly blocked with tea leaves. She could also smell mice and would rather wet her drawers than pee in that foul place. Tears dripped down her cheeks. How could Cissie endure this, day after day? Laughing and joking with her cronies; mee-mawing in a silent mouth language, understood despite the roar of machines? Sophie was glad to get back on the job after the half-hour ended, just to forget her bursting bladder, but there was summat up with Cissie's loom.

'Fetch the tackler . . . quick, Phia! Tell Chewbacca me monkey's tail is loose!' She was pushed in the direction of the stairs to an office of sorts further down the vast hall, not knowing who this Chewbacca might be.

'Is the tackler here?' she mouthed, and was pointed towards a machine where a gruff old man with a tea-stained moustache stood gazing on to the cogs with disdain while its young operative bowed her head in tears.

'What've thee bin doin' to it? Feeding it oil or treacle, yer daft ha'porth? What a bloody mess! This'll need a right sortin' out. Just teach you a lesson, lass. It'll slow down thee wages, will this!' He pointed to the slate on the wall where the number of woven pieces completed by each loom was there for all to see. He caught Sophie's button eyes fixed on him, her hand waving excitedly. 'Well, what do you want, Madam Mophead?'

'Are you the Chewbacca, mister?'

'Mr Sharples to you, young hussy. Don't be so cheeky or I'll clip your earhole. Chewbacca indeed! Who sent you?'

'Me . . . me . . . sister Cissie. She's me missus,' stammered the girl, overcome by the stench of his body odour.

'And who might she be when she's at home?' the man spat out.

'Cicely Seddon, down there, far end. Can you come quick – it's her monkey tail or summat!'

'Come quick . . . come quick? Can't you see there's a queue waiting for the tackler, so wait your bloody turn and no more sauce, little piecener!'

Sophie stepped back, abashed at her telling off. Here was another one just like her dad, a tinpot god in his own little kingdom. The engineer was cock of this midden; a king pin to be buttered up any which way. The loom had to keep turning out the pieces of cloth or Cissie would not get a decent wage at the end of the week. Sophie was cottoning on fast and slithered back to mouth to her all that had happened. Her sister stamped her clogs in frustration.

'Here!' She ferreted in her purse pocket. 'Let yourself out the gate – quiet, mind – and run to Mullarkey's corner shop off Lever Street. Get two . . .' she paused '. . . get three Eccles cakes. The best, see to it . . . lots of flake and puff. Bring them back sharpish. Hurry up, our Phia!'

She raced down the stairs, dodging the porter, and out into the bright morning, glad to fill her lungs with fresh air. The drizzle was light and cooling as she scampered across the busy street towards the yeasty aroma of the bakery, her mouth watering at the sight of the golden puffs filled with currants and spice, still warm on the tray. Mission accomplished, she dawdled back into the steamy mill, up the flights of stone steps, back to Cissie and the loom. The tackler was standing there, all smiles at the sight of the bag. 'Just a fiddly little thing. Nowt of a job when you know how. Thank you very much.' He grabbed the buns from Sophie. 'Nice to know I'm appreciated.' He shoved one straight into his mouth, the crumbs cascading over his whiskers.

'Well, I never!' Sophie sniggered. 'He gobbled three cakes in three bites.'

'Be thankful he'll come for just a few cakes. There's one or two next door won't budge unless you give them a private pennyworth of persuasion.'

Sophie looked blank. 'Pennyworth of what?'

'They want to feel your tits and rub you up . . . you know about that sort of thing by now, don't you?' Cissie blushed. 'Just be thankful this old sod is one of them Wesleyan preachers or else you'd have to watch yer bum.'

At lunchtime Sophie raced down the back street to pound the bucket in the privy, wipe her hands and grab a doorstep chunk of bread and scrape, passing Lizzy Walsh from number six pushing a barrowful of babies to the mill to be fed and nuzzled at their mothers' leaking breasts. By afternoon schooltime, the tiredness seeped into her bones. There was so much to be learned if she was to survive in the mill. She knew that there were worse jobs, though: tenting in the cardroom, feeding loose lap blankets of fibre into rotating spiky machines, minding the carding frames among all the loose fluff. Piecers to mule spinners had to slither under machines, knotting up broken ends while the shuttles were still moving.

She remembered the expedition with Grace, and blushed. What a childish and futile exercise it seemed now! There were still four more days to Saturday when the routine would change and the young girls cleaned out the debris from the looms, scrubbing on their hands and knees. Cissie would show her how to take off the worst grease stains in the steamy waters of the Mill Lodge pond. Everything would be swept up and put away. Only then would she be free to escape to the playing fields, race over to Grace's garden wall and tell her at long last her dreadful secret.

The Vicar of St Anselm's peered out into his garden with satisfaction. Three girls in white embroidered afternoon dresses were attempting a lively game of French cricket.

'Look, Maude, I'm so glad Grace has brought some school friends home for tea. Who's the one with all the sandy hair?' He pointed to a sharp-faced child, wielding the bat like a sabre.

'That is Lavinia Shaw. I do believe she is Lord Dunscar's niece or some minor relative – quite a handful by all accounts, and unusual looks for a girl too. Her parents live abroad . . . some scandal, I gather,' Maude Calvert whispered. 'When you move from this dreadful parish, Rowland, Grace will be able to entertain her friends in more comfort. Though, I must say, I had to force her to invite anyone. She can go so silent these days. I do hope we did the right thing in forbidding the Seddon girl. She's gone right off her food, outgrowing her strength. Look! Quite a stoop to her shoulders!'

'You fuss too much, Maude. Grace will develop in her own time. She's a studious child and all that reading hunches her up too much. I think you must get her a firm corset. Just look at her, sitting in the branch of that tree, reading a book as if there's no one else there. Typical!'

'Grace dear, come and give me a hand with the tea!' her aunt called through the dining-room window. The girl looked up, scowled and descended. She tiptoed past the game in progress and sauntered in through the door. 'Do make an effort, child. We went to a lot of trouble to find you some suitable friends.'

'You needn't have bothered. They are so silly and noisy! All they want to talk about is dancing and clothes. They're not interested in flowers and bird watching or Nature at all!' Grace barely glanced in their direction.

'Lavinia Shaw seems a good type of girl, a spirited sort of person.'

'Vinnie's the worst of the lot – always teasing me in class. She's such a show off, says she's going to be an actress or a painter.'

'Heavens! What does Lord Dunscar say about that?'

'I don't think he cares. He never comes to the concerts. She only lives at the gatehouse with the housekeeper's family. Dora and Hetty put up with her moods but I don't. She puts on such airs and graces. How long do they have to stay?'

'They've only just arrived! For goodness' sake, buck up and be a good hostess or they'll never invite you back.'

'I don't care.'

'Oh, Grace. I wish you were more like your poor mama.'

'Well, I'm not. I'd rather play with Sophie Seddon.'

'Don't start that again, child.' Aunt Calvert raised her eyes to heaven with a sigh.

Lavinia Shaw was bored. The summer afternoon was dragging on and it was no fun being cooped up in a measly back garden off a sooty street. She had come out of curiosity, feeling sorry for awkward Grace Thompson who might always be top of the class but was a hoot at lacrosse, hopeless with any bat and ball. The tall thin brainbox was not in the slightest bit grateful for her visit and would never dance attendance at her court. In fact, the dreadful creature had ignored her all afternoon, as if she did not exist! Now she was stuck with dizzy Dora and her simpering sister Hetty, playing silly ball games. The outing had been arranged behind her back as usual, to get her out from under the housekeeper's feet. There were guests in Dunscar Hall and she was banned from roaming around the gardens, as if she were a servant's child.

Why, since her parents disappeared abroad, had she so little say in her own life? They had abandoned her to various relatives, parcelled her from pillar to post, writing occasional postcards with pretty stamps, sending presents and promises – with only the vaguest mentions of her ever joining them on their jaunts around the world. It had not been her idea to live at the gatehouse of Dunscar Hall, shoved in a dreadful girls' school, expected to socialise in a shabby milltown. In her last letter to Mama she had pleaded to be rescued from the soot and grime and third-rate companions! She was expecting a reply any day now and then she would be on that train so fast, never to return.

There had once been a better life but memories were fading of tall windows and silk-embroidered curtains, of servants in uniforms, winding staircases and gilt-embellished furniture. Sometimes she thought she was dreaming this present existence, marking time until the return of the glittering days. There were occasional treats dispensed by Lord Dunscar's housekeeper: visits to the Theatre Royal or the Art Gallery. Lavinia loved to recite poems in the school concerts where she sated her hunger for attention under the spotlight, dressed up in make believe.

Nobody was giving her so much as a glance now. How she hated being ignored! She peered at the precious watch pinned to her pintucked bodice, the swell of her tiny breasts pushing out the gold and setting it glinting in the sunshine. She was ravenous. Would the tea be worth waiting for? Food was her only consolation, especially sugary confections and creamy cakes. 'Let's go home, I'm bored,' she commanded her cohorts.

'Cheer up, Vinnie! Don't be uncharitable. They've put on a splendid tea,' whispered Dora discreetly in her ear. 'Come on inside!'

Lavinia lingered in the afternoon sun, preening herself in the mirror of the miniature garden pond, teasing her corkscrew ringlets, pulling faces at her own reflection, posing as if for a portrait painter. Suddenly she was aware of movement behind her and spied a face poking through the greenery: a small face with keen dark eyes watching her silently, drinking in her pretty frock with its blue silk sash tied in a bow around her hips. The face was framed in a white down of cotton fluff and spattered with greasy blotches.

'What are you doing here?' Vinnie spun round in surprise and annoyance.

'I'm calling for me friend, Grace, to come out and play,' said the stranger.

Lavinia put her hands on her hips and shouted: 'There's a mill girl says she's come to play, Grace!' Vinnie Shaw mimicked Sophie's accent, shouting down the garden for a reply from the house. There was no immediate answer. She looked the intruder up and down with a sniff. 'Go away! Grace doesn't want to play with you, and *we* certainly don't. Shove off and don't bother us!' she said with relish, and the face promptly disappeared at her bidding.

★   ★   ★

Lavinia joined the guests at the tea table and sat down gracefully, spreading a linen napkin across her voile dress. 'I've just seen the funniest creature lurking in the under-growth at the bottom of the garden. She said she'd come to play with her friend. The cheek of her, I ask you! Who would want to play with one of those scruffy millhands?' She wolfed down a sandwich, not taking her eyes from the tablecloth. 'So I told her to allez off. You do keep funny customs, Grace, in your neck of the woods.'

'Oh, Lavinia, you *are* mean. I wish you hadn't sent her away. Sophie is my friend.' Grace shot up from the table, raced down to the hidden exit and pushed through the undergrowth to the path beyond. She scoured the playing field but there was not a soul in sight. Reluctantly she returned to her silent guests and uttered not another word.

Sophie raced out of the park blindly, the rebuff ringing in her ears. '*We* don't want you to play . . .' Unable to speak, choking back the tears, she burst into the back yard where her father was knocking nails into the sole of a boot.

'Now what are you sulking about? You've got that face on yer again, like a wet Wakes week! Stop sulking and be useful to yer gran. Still frettin' for yer school-learnin'?' snapped her father. She shook her head and wandered out again into the back street, kicking the cobbles, sparking her clogs, defiantly wearing out the iron rims.

No wonder the other half-timers did not seem to mind

their work. They didn't know about the other world beyond Plover Street. Why did she feel so resentful? '*We* don't want you to play with us' kept ringing in her ears like a tune. Was it something to do with meeting the girls in Grace Thompson's other world?

Grace did not have to earn a living or do chores even. Grace could lie in her bed on a Saturday morning. Grace Thompson could ride a pony and learn the pianoforte, and now she had fancy friends to play in her garden. Friends who knew Latin. It wasn't fair! Sophie seethed at the injustice of life which had placed her at the bottom of the pile.

That girl in the white dress with the shiny locks and snooty manner had spoiled it all. Now she knew for certain there were two worlds: one for the likes of Plover Street and the clog brigade, and the other for golden girls who danced in pumps of patent leather. She was obviously not good enough for the other world, and if that was how Grace Thompson felt about her, then so be it. From now on she would stick to her own kind.

Sophie stormed back through the yard, tore upstairs to her tin treasure box under the bed and yanked out the Prayer Book, shaking it upside down. The pressed rosebud dropped on to the floorboards. She picked it up carefully, felt the dry crinkly petals, crushed them to dust with her fingers and strewed the ashes of her friendship with Grace on to the floor.

Grace counted the front doors carefully: number five, six, seven, eight, pausing at number nine with beating heart to examine the chalky white doorstep and the Cardinal-polished tiled surround. Children playing in the street stopped their skipping and lined up behind the foreigner in her black velour High School hat and smart fitted overcoat. Cotton window valances twitched as nosy neighbours inspected someone daring to use a for-best-only front door. Its iron knocker was polished like jet. She took a deep breath and rat-tatted twice, waiting on the step. The door was flung open by an old woman who stood foursquare, arms folded across her floury bosom, while a child twined herself under her pinny, peeking out shyly.

'Well?' said Bun Gran.

'I've come to see Sophie. I'm Grace . . . Grace Thompson.'

'Oh, aye. I knows who thee is, milady, but our Phia's not at home. She's in t'mill.'

'Not in Berisford's?'

'Where else do lasses from Plover Street go but as half-timers? Unless their pa is Parson, of course.'

'When will she be back?' interrupted Grace.

'Dunno, expect she'll be out laiking with her pals. She's plenty of chums in the mill nowadays.'

'I see,' said Grace, shuffling from one foot to the other.

'Don't you scuff my clean step. It's just been donkey stoned.' The girl jumped back politely.

'Can I leave a message?' The old woman made no comment and did not budge an inch. 'Please tell her I'm sorry about Saturday. It was all a misunderstanding . . .'

'Is that when she got her cards and you sent her packing!'

'I don't understand what you mean. It was all a mistake . . .'

'Oh, I don't think so, milady. There's been bother ever since she clapped eyes on you and your sort. Now she'd turn milk, she's that sour. So leave her be and let her get on with weaving her own piece. Do I make myself clear?'

Grace nodded, pink with embarrassment, as a queue of small children came to gawp at the scene. As she turned to leave she paused one last time to plead her case. The thunderous look on Millie Walker's face withered her courage. 'Do tell her I was asking after her, please?' was all she could whisper as she sped up the street with tears stinging her lashes.

'I might,' snapped Bun Gran as she slammed the door, 'and then again, I might not!'

Lavinia crammed her clothes carelessly into the leather valise. She was so excited she could hardly breathe. The letter had come at last, arranging for her to meet Mama at Euston Station. She was coming to collect Lavinia and they would be travelling down to the South of France, no doubt to begin their new life together. She swanned around the school saying gracious farewells to those she deemed worthy of her attention. How sorry she was for these pitiable schoolgirls, for Dora Blinkhorn and Grace Thompson, forced to spend their hols in this dump of a town.

Each night she ticked off the date in her journal. One

day closer to Mama! Soon there would be no more sooty moors and foggy streets, no more cold wet mornings and damp walks.

In her mind's eye she smelt the lemon and lavender of the Mediterranean hillsides, danced through scenes from her postcard collection; all those hasty scribbled notes from Cannes, Nice, Grasse, with their elegant boulevards and villas tinted aquamarine and peach, topped by red pantiled roofs and palm trees waving in the breeze, welcoming her arrival. She saw herself dressed in cool lace and cotton, taking French lessons and art instruction, attending dancing classes and circulating amongst the children of the beautiful couples who played cards and gambled on the Riviera coast.

It was all too wonderful to contemplate as she peered out of the railway carriage on that wet morning while Miss Harper, her escort and travelling companion, snored in the corner. She squashed her nose close to the window and drew patterns in the steam, counting the hours and the stations en route to her new life.

Vinnie waited in the draughty station hall at Euston, sitting on her valise, trying not to gape at each of the women who drifted past her just in case she missed Mama. The truth was it had been so long since she had seen her mother she could hardly remember her face. Only the scent of eau de Cologne brought her briefly to mind. The daguerrotype photograph in its silver frame was packed safely away in her case.

Miss Harper had gone to enquire if there was any

message for them but Vinnie knew it was only a matter of time before Mama would be whisking her away to Waterloo on their journey South.

She trundled her baggage slowly to the entrance hall, to where the carriage and hansom cabs deposited travellers with ceremony, where porters gathered luggage, dogs, perambulators, and servants waited deferentially behind their fur-clad employers.

This was her first grown-up journey and now her stomach had opened into a ravenous cavern of hunger. She opened her peggy purse to re-read the postcard, just in case the instructions had somehow been misunderstood. Suddenly she felt small and insignificant in her crumpled sailor suit and felt Panama. What if Mama was ill or injured? Miss Harper was anxious to catch her own connection.

'Darling! Darling, over here . . . Lavinia, *ma p'tite!*' a voice screeched from a cab. She saw a parasol being frantically waved.

'Mama, where've you been? I thought you'd forgotten me?'

'Of course not, silly child. You've grown so and become so gangly . . . but at least those Northern hills have improved your skin. You've got quite a bloom. Hasn't she, Ernst? This is my poor neglected daughter, Lavinia. Come and say hello to your new papa, child.'

Vinnie was introduced to a man with a face as round and shiny as the moon, who peered at her through the cab's window and grinned. His cigar smoke stung her eyes.

'Climb aboard, Lavinia, we've not got all day.' She sat

opposite the couple, full of questions. Who was this man? Why was he here? Where was Papa? Who was this strange woman who reeked of such a strong perfume it was making her choke? This was not the Mama of the silver frame, surely? This woman was quite old with lines around her mouth, wearing a pale brown lacy concoction, all frills and furbelows, overfussy. The housekeeper at the hall would call her fast-looking. Lavinia was tired and hungry and ached for a cool glass of milk for her throat was oddly dry and tight.

'Isn't it kind of Ernst to arrange our honeymoon trip to coincide with your holiday? We'll have a lovely few days with you and show you all the city sights, then see you back on your train. Ernst and I have plans to travel through Switzerland en route for home . . . Why are you crying, child? Aren't you pleased your poor mama has found happiness and is beginning a new life? Don't worry, when I'm more settled you can come for a really long visit. Now that will be nice, won't it? Don't sulk, dear. If the wind catches that expression, you'll be stuck with a fishface.

'And don't look so serious. Remember, a Shaw knows how to have a good time. Like butterflies, we flit from flower to flower, sunning ourselves on good times. You go back North and do well in your lessons and in no time it'll be your turn. Some young man will whisk you away and I'll be coming back to arrange your trousseau!'

Vinnie sat in the carriage, introductions over, tears trickling down her face – tears of rage and puzzlement.

Who is this woman? How could she do this to me? Send

me back when I don't belong up there. She paused to blow her nose. I don't belong anywhere: not with them, or Papa wherever he is, or the housekeeper. I hate them all! This was not how it was meant to be.

Everyone else had best friends, everyone else had party friends and confidantes, sisters and mothers. I'm never going to visit her and that toad-faced Ernst. What do you have to do to belong somewhere? Perhaps my face is the wrong shape. It won't make my fortune, but then even plain Grace makes friends. What am I doing wrong? Perhaps there is a set of instructions on how to get it right. If that's the case, I'll ask Lord Dunscar's housekeeper when I get back. She's bound to know.

Votes for Women
1901-4

Chapter Four

The three students sat on the back row like a set of jugs. Grace, the tallest by a head in a dark blue jumper with a sailor collar, watched with interest the young speaker setting up his magic lantern, noting his broad shoulders, sturdy calves and casual manner. Dora Blinkhorn leaned backwards, tightly corseted into her cream woollen two-piece suit, stealing glances at her diamond engagement ring as it flashed in the candlelight, day-dreaming of her beloved Surgeon Wagstaff, ministering to the sick in the Infirmary.

Vinnie Shaw swirled a green velvet cloak around her skirt with a theatrical flourish, newly henna-ed curls glinting in the soft glow. The Pre-Raphaelite look was very much the rage in her arty circle at Manchester College: all those titian tones and flowing garments, long tresses gathered into net snoods. The uncorseted freedom of the female form was considered very daring. Some shocked looks on her arrival from the soberly dressed matrons on the front rows had already made this boring outing worthwhile.

The Arts and Crafts Movement, with its emphasis on bold designs and hand-crafted furniture, the marvellous canvases of Burne-Jones and Millais, had captured her imagination. How she hoped that her resemblance to Rossetti's notorious model Lizzy Siddal might be noticed! So far no one had asked her to pose for the portrait class, but it could only be a matter of time.

On her last visit to Grasse, where her delinquent parent had at last made a home for herself, she'd spent fine mornings capturing the spectacular colours of the Provençal hillsides, the lavender fields and cherry orchards, with fruit hanging like rubies against the cobalt sky. She'd dashed off enough bold water-colours and pastels to make a portfolio. Enough to pass muster before the critical eye of the Principal of Manchester College of Art who had once studied alongside William Morris in his youth.

Sitting in the Orangery of Dunscar Hall, listening to a boring planthunter show slides of his tour of Outer Mongolia or some such Godforsaken region, was not her idea of fun but she had promised her old school friends to swell the numbers of the local Botanical Society. The Orangery was packed and now they were stuck on the back row. Still, it was always useful to curry favour with old Lord Dunscar who dismissed Lavinia's artistic efforts as mere dabbling.

It was strange how despite their differences the students still stuck together. Such an unlikely trio! Dizzy Dora whose head was stuffed full of romance, wedding plans and babies. Grace who attended lectures and studied Botany at Owen's College, part of Manchester's own Victoria University, and seemed to spend her life drawing and dissecting petals and fronds, stamens and sepals. Clever but boring! The poor girl was drinking in every word of the lecture as Mr Sturges rattled away like a runaway train, positively straining to watch his performance.

Vinnie nudged her, whispering, 'Wouldn't mind being a cutting in his nursery! Look at those hairy hands. Rough, but oh so tender! He's quite a specimen himself, don't you think?'

'Shush!' Grace smiled dreamily at the handsome man in his tweed plus fours and shirt sleeves rolled up like a gardener's. His square, strong face sported a sandy moustache over a full mouth. His beard was sun-streaked and his hair, plastered down with macassar oil, struggled to stay horizontal. Grace was most taken with his weather-beaten arms, gesticulating wildly as his enthusiasm mounted. Vinnie nudged her again.

'Stop it, Lavinia. Don't be so fast! You've hardly met him.'

'Well, anyone can see *you* think he's worth a second glance!'

'Don't be coarse!'

'Don't be a prude! You should see some of the models we draw in Life Class, but they wouldn't hold a candle to our speaker for shape or form. He can view my etchings any time!'

'Do shut up, Vinnie!' Grace thought Mr John Sturges striking but sensitive. She liked the way he stuttered as he tried to convey the mystery and magic of his explorations by packhorse into hidden valleys in search of new specimens. Trust Vinnie to care only for surface details. Grace preferred to search for depth! She turned to check on Dora who was looking at her ring again.

After the lecture had finished, to hearty applause, they drifted through the crowd gathered to inspect the plant-hunter's specimens and photographs. Questions came thick and fast and Grace admired a wrought-iron miniature greenhouse, as small as a suitcase, with a handle on top. John Sturges smiled at her interest.

'Where I go, she goes!' He patted the Wardian case affectionately. 'God bless Nathaniel Bagshot Ward and his invention! With this small propagating case I can transport and transplant my babies, rooted and alive, not dried and desiccated, from ship to soil!' His laughter rang out.

'I bet we've got some weird plants hidden in these hill-sides, Grace. Perhaps we ought to ask Mr Sturges to come and identify some of them for us? Then Grace here can draw them all.' Vinnie tossed her hair nonchalantly and looked the man over. Grace blushed at her boldness, noting the man's puzzled expression, his green-flecked eyes twinkling in response, holding her own shy gaze just a second longer than necessary, enough to make her drop her stare. She noticed the broken veins on his cheeks.

'Are you both Botany students then?'

'She is,' Vinnie jumped in. 'Always was the brainbox. Not that she needs to study. Our Gracey is quite the little heiress, aren't you?'

Oh, Lavinia, that's not fair, thought Grace, but the words stuck in her throat like pebbles. Why was she talking like this to a stranger? John Sturges turned to face the red-haired vixen in the moss green velvet cloak, dazzled for a second by the coquettish challenge of eyes half-closed in a saucy stare. Grace turned away, uncomfortable at the tension between them, but something made her re-enter the arena.

'I think it would be an excellent idea for us all to show you the local moorland flora. You might think there is nothing much to millstone grit but heathers and soot. Actually we grow some interesting varieties, well worth a planthunter's inspection.

'I can show you a rare bush of Labrador tea heather, and we have our own bilberry bumble bee with its extra-long tongue, and of course we sport a few small white orchids too. The Western Pennines are beautiful in their own special way, but I suppose . . .' She paused, embarrassed at her outburst.

'You do right, Miss . . . er . . . to love your landscape. I'm a limestone man myself, not so sure on acid soil.'

The expedition was organised and they set out on Saturday afternoon to walk up from Dunscar Hall, the half-timbered Tudor mansion which sat snug under the fellside facing South, overlooking a forest of chimneys down in the Lancashire plain. The garden terraces sloped gently towards open fields and northwards rose up to wild moorland pasture, with windswept tracks across the rocky outcrops. Grace knew each pathway to the hidden becks which gurgled out of the hillsides, and the banks of heather and bilberry not yet in flower. She brought them to the Labrador tea bush; a thickset evergreen bush with rusty-coloured down on its twigs and little clusters of creamy white flowers just about to flower. John Sturges examined the bush with interest while Ada Norris and Vinnie admired the view.

'You certainly know your territory, Miss Thompson.'

'I've been coming up here for years.' Grace was blushing.

'It's the only thing she does know,' Vinnie laughed to Ada. 'Bit of a dull dolly, aren't you?' No one else laughed. 'Only teasing!'

'Mr Sturges, I don't know why she's being so beastly. Just pipe down, Vinnie, if you can't say anything constructive. We've come to see the plants not your performance.'

'Hell's bells! Who trod on your corns? God, you can be so stuffy!' Vinnie flounced ahead in a sulk.

'Behold the artistic temperament.' Grace smiled sweetly to the onlookers. Ada Norris stood back, agog at the spat between the two young women, aware that the battle for John Sturges was beginning. The first round was definitely a draw and the second bout brought a strategic withdrawal and a change of tactics.

Vinnie never could resist a challenge. Smarting from Grace's rebuff, she decided that young Mr Sturges would liven up her vacation no end. It was time to practise the art of seduction, and if she played her hand carefully she might get to see the world, visit exotic faraway places at his expense. He was handsome enough with his swaggering gait and rough confident air, and she could smell his interest. Poor old Grace was no competition.

To Grace Thompson the planthunter was the very first man to set her pulse racing. She saw him as her lifetime's commitment; herself as his helpmeet and companion, ideally suited to share the work of preparing his herbarium and cataloguing his collection. They would be so compatible, so well suited. Every time she caught his eye, he smiled warmly and treated her in such a gently courteous manner. With Vinnie, she noted, he argued and teased as he touched her elbow jokingly, and she sparked like flint at his remarks. There was something in the way they played about which annoyed and distracted Grace but she quashed her reservations and tried to join in their game.

All through the summer the Botanical Society buzzed with rumours of romance in their ranks, and secret bets were laid as to which student would carry off the prize. The Reverend Thompson and his widowed sister were sufficiently alarmed to invite the young man to tea. The Vicar wanted to quiz him about the China Inland Mission and the outreach of Christianity within the ancient

Chinese civilisation. Grace's missionary fervour had long since subsided but she could not resist imagining herself by his side, Bible in hand, dishing out tracts to grateful peasants in their villages.

Lord Dunscar, patron of St Stephen's where Grace's father was now incumbent, was proud of his collection of Far Eastern exotics, his shrub beds and rose gardens. He also supported the traffic of Veitch Company Nurserymen and the gentlemen planthunters who tramped the Himalayas, Tibet and China in search of new species to popularise in Europe.

John Sturges was one of the new breed of countrymen, bred on tough Northern slopes with that daredevil streak of stubbornness needed to battle through all weathers and terrain, extracting new lovelies for old men to admire in their glasshouse conservatories. He extended his stay at the Hall to advise the gardening staff on the layout of new terraces for the herbaceous perennials. Besides which, anyone could see that all the obvious attention he was attracting was a delightful distraction.

Vinnie skipped lectures to lodge herself once more at the gatehouse and hover around the gardens with her sketch-book, catching glimpses of the planthunter measuring out the borders and examining his handiwork, shirt off in the heat of the July sun, his body tanned dark brown. She observed his discussions with her godfather, Lord Dunscar, in the Nectarine House which backed on to the kitchen garden wall. She was determined to accost him alone.

Stuff the conventions followed by boring women to secure boring lives! The thrill of the chase was fun and such a hoot! Mr Sturges was definitely sniffing the scent she'd laid down, puzzled and flattered by her obvious interest. Men just could not resist being flattered. He had never encountered her forward sort before, forever dangling herself before him, just out of reach.

Grace stalked him furtively, making excuses to roam the footpaths unchaperoned, just on the offchance of an encounter. She saw their romance blossoming like the first season's growth of tender root cutting in rich protective compost, hidden from the biting frost of Vinnie Shaw's glare. She felt like Emily Brontë as she roved over the moors to Wuthering Heights, all passion and prose; a wild creature of the fellside, wrapped in a tartan shawl, her hair for once loosened to fall wantonly down her back.

Her efforts were rewarded a week before Mr Sturges's departure when she caught a glimpse of his silhouette against the setting sun, dark against the flame-coloured sky as he stood surveying the distant smoke of the valley below. There was total silence; no mournful wail of curlew, no bleating sheep or rattle of distant wagon over rail to disturb this moment. It was as if the moor held its breath, eavesdropping on their encounter. Grace went quietly to his side to share the vista. 'This must be so different from your faraway world, Mr Sturges.'

'You should see China for yourself, Miss Thompson, but it is a strange, harsh world to foreign visitors, especially women.'

'Why ever not? Look down there . . . Lancashire at your feet with mills full of women who sweat and trudge like mules at machines. Surely missionary women cope with the climate and terrain?'

'And die like flies with their children of disease and famine, or worse still at the hands of feuding warlords. It's no place for you.'

'Is that so?' Grace felt indignation rising like acid bile and turned to go. A hand seized her own in the dark, pulling her back, turning her to face him. His rough chilled hand cupped her chin gently. He grinned and stared into her eyes.

'Do you know there are poppies on the Tibetan hill-sides with petals as blue as your eyes?'

'Really?' Grace quivered in triumph, feeling a flush of excitement.

'And there are roses as pale as your cheeks. I will bring you one back someday and name it after you . . . *Rosa graciae* . . . if you like.'

She closed her eyes, feeling his tobacco breath on her cheek. How would it feel to be kissed by a man with a beard? As if reading her desire, he lifted her chin, bringing her mouth to his dry lips in a chaste kiss. Grace felt her corsetbones pinging against her ribs.

'You will write to me when I've sailed? I have quite taken to Lancashire blooms.' John Sturges still held her hand.

'Of course, Mr Sturges. I would be honoured. And if there is any drawing, or any way I might be of assistance . . . I'll trace every step of the journey on my atlas.' Grace sighed with anticipation. Hope and roses; a moment of promise for the future. Hope and roses would do for now. Once there had been bread and roses. A brief memory of her first friend, Sophie Seddon, brushed across her mind, tingeing the moment with sadness as she broke free from her reverie, wrapping her shawl closer round her against the chill breeze as they strolled slowly down to the valley of twinkling lights.

Grace lay awake all night planning a wedding trousseau, a gown of blue silk edged with coffee lace. How fortunate she had caught him alone and off guard. He had shown such a tender response to her boldness. Hope and roses would keep them together. Two years were not too long to wait. Besides which there was her study – all the more important now she was to be his assistant for life! But the day of his departure for London came all too soon. Grace made sure that she would be part of the farewell group to see him on to the train at Trinity Street Station. She held back her farewell to last, relieved that Vinnie was nowhere in sight to spoil this private moment.

'Don't wait . . . I hate blubbing on station platforms.

Let me see those poppies shining, not clouded with tears. So skedaddle, young Miss Grace!'

She sniffed meekly and turned to walk up the flight of stairs to the booking hall. On the top step she lingered and decided to turn back for one last glimpse. She was no coward and stepped resolutely down again. Her intended was hanging out of the carriage, his tweed cap waving like a signal. On the bottom step she saw the guard with his green flag waving off the train as it chuffed up a head of steam, beginning to chug slowly away. From behind a pillar holding up the glass roof darted a figure in a green velvet cloak, lugging a carpetbag. She flung it ahead of her into Mr Sturges's carriage. Grace Thompson stood stock still as she watched Vinnie Shaw fling herself into the planthunter's waiting arms.

Grace ran to the edge of the fell, cursing into the wind as it whirled away all her dreams. The rusting cotton grass rippled in waves but she was oblivious to her surroundings. No more hope and roses, only a yawning, aching void opening up before her. What a silly little fool! He pandered to my fantasies, humouring a silly naive maiden, she realised. I was the smoke screen for the *real* attraction. There were prettier roses to pick from another garden. I hope they scratch him!

Grace sobbed with shame and rage. If this was what romance was all about then she wanted none of it. Never again would any man make a fool of her. Nothing would be the same. No snowdrops or larksong would ever warm her heart again. How could Vinnie steal what was hers? Dizzy Dora would marry her surgeon. Vinnie Shaw would make of John Sturges what she would, but Grace Thompson must bury forever her hopes of marriage!

News of the elopement was a nine-day wonder in the village. 'Pagans! I thought old Sturges a regular fellow but he'll have his hands full with that stupid gal . . . Young hussy, just like her parents, rum 'uns the lot of them. Her pa did a bunk with my niece and dumped the offspring on me like a spare pheasant. To be brought up a lady indeed! No breeding. No stamina. A rootless cutting if ever I saw one, is young Lavinia. She'll soon wilt in the sun, mark my words! Plenty of spark, the sort who lights the touch paper then scarpers. Still, that's families for you . . . no gratitude!' Lord Dunscar spat out his piece to the Vicar after Matins.

The letter when it came caught Grace unawares; a long rambling missive covered in stamps and seals, full of information and observations, as if nothing untoward had happened. John Sturges had been so impressed by her interest he was going to send her pressed flowers. A chatty letter to a dear friend. How dare he insult her intelligence! Not a word about his paramour, no doubt basking in some hill station, sipping green tea with the missionary wives. Grace threw the letter on to the fire in disgust. After that there was silence, followed by eulogies and obituaries in the gardening periodicals, alongside news of the blue mountain poppy, *Meconopsis quadruplinervia*.

'Silly young blighter's gorn and caught himself a fever

and snuffed it. No stamina. I bet that young filly wore him out!' said Lord Dunscar as he pinched his snuff and inhaled. 'Still, his latest collection is on its way home, thank God!'

Vinnie Shaw stared up at the plaster moulding on the ceiling which was flaking and peeling. This rented room was depressing. No cheap floral wallpaper could hide its shabbiness. 'Well, that's that then!' She yanked herself out of bed and stretched out her arms, almost touching each wall. 'Serves you right, old girl, to hitch your wagon to a handsome body who goes and dies on you, silly sod. No boats to Shanghai, no silk route expeditions, no ivory, no jade. The holiday's over. So back to plain clothes and porridge for you.'

She sighed as she pulled on her one respectable outfit: a black skirt, grey pintucked blouse and purple tweed overcoat, suitably sombre for her to pass herself off as a widow in mourning.

She looked again at the empty pillow, remembering Johnny's eager face as they'd coupled with an intensity that made her feel hot just to remember it. What a hoot! Sneaking off to London, all that fumbling and laughing and stickiness. Wonderful stuff! Virginity was definitely overrated. Now she could join the Fast Club, and the girls who drank, smoked, and did amazing things with their lovers. The students who discussed erotic art for the sole purpose of experimentation. Then she remembered that all her bridges were burned, her allowance cut off, and she must find paid employment quickly or else . . .

Vinnie dawdled along the Manchester pavements in the dusty sunshine, browsing, killing time before an appointment at Kendal Milne's Emporium. She would take anything to pay the rent. Pride would not let her return to Dunscar Hall with her tail between her legs, to all the gloating faces and Grace Thompson's wounded benevolence. Oh, no!

In her portfolio were some designs for window dressings which might impress, but she had a sickening feeling that her lack of a decent reference would scupper any chance of a position.

It was her fault she'd failed the examinations, and all because of a silly fling. I must have been mad to jeopardise my attendance, she thought. How was I to know I couldn't just elope with him, that some kind soul would make it their business to inform the College of my absence? Vinnie was sure she could lay that piece of treachery at Grace Thompson's door. The jealous bitch! Her course work had been examined and she was carpeted by the beak, like a naughty schoolgirl.

'Art College is not for any fickle madam, to pick and choose when and where she will attend lectures. We have many students more talented than you are, Miss Shaw, clamouring to cross these portals for a chance to learn. Young people with principles and standards in their private lives who will make better use of a place than you appear to have done. It is libertines like you who give female students a bad name! You are dismissed.'

Vinnie flounced out in a rage, hiding her humiliation; a rage which had cooled as the streets grew harder and the pavements colder. Soon came the chill realisation of her predicament.

Now she turned into King Street and paused to peer through the window of a shop she had not noticed before, Emerson & Co. The windows were crammed with artistic furnishings and fabrics, handpainted milking stools and cushions, pottery and earthenware containers, oriental carpets and rugs, swatches of silks and unglazed cotton prints in the familiar hues and designs of the Arts and Crafts Movement. The steam from her breath misted the glass as she strained to see inside. Then she saw tucked into the corner a finely drawn notice in bold calligraphic lettering: 'Part-time Assistant Required. Apply within'. Vinnie opened the door gingerly and the bell signalled her arrival to a girl in a bright smock who sat bent over a drawing on the counter, peering through her glasses. A fellow student Vinnie recognised immediately.

'What are you doing here, Sylvia Pankhurst?'

'Good Heavens! Lavinia Shaw . . . my first customer!'

'Sorry. I'm here about the notice in the window.'

'Even better.' Sylvia Pankhurst smiled with relief at the prospect of recruiting a shop assistant. 'Mother's out at a meeting and Christabel is at the University but if it were up to me you could swap places with me right now.'

'What are you doing?' asked Vinnie, poring over the water-colours scattered across the wooden surface of the counter.

'Catching up on my portfolio. I sketched these in Venice and Italy. What do you think?'

Vinnie nodded, impressed by the strong colourful figures, the vibrant scenes and quality of the brushwork. Sylvia Pankhurst was not only star pupil of her year but had won the coveted travel award. No wonder the Principal called me second-rate! thought Vinnie.

'I just had to come home and help Mother with her business, bless her! She rents me the studio upstairs but I never seem to get up there, what with our meetings and Christabel always promising to do her share but never having time.' Sylvia shook her head with a sigh.

'I do love your stuff in here. William Morris is a kind of pash of mine. You'll have to excuse my enthusiasm.'

'Oh, no! My dear papa used to say to us: "Life is nothing without enthusiasms." Miss Shaw . . .'

'Call me Vinnie, please.'

'. . . you're the answer to a prayer, someone who actually cares about the goods we sell, who knows about the Arts and Crafts philosophy and appreciates good design. We'll have to see Mama. If we can catch her! She is busy lobbying for a petition to get women the Vote.'

Vinnie knew about the Pankhurst girls and their formidable mother who were all ardent Socialists. She had seen Sylvia and her sisters Christabel and Adela handing out leaflets around the Colleges. She'd usually sought to avoid them in the past. Now it was time to strike out for herself. 'If you want to get on with some work upstairs, I'll hold the fort until Mafeking is relieved again.'

Sylvia nodded and showed her how to find the price tags and enter any purchases in the cash book. She was the plainest of the sisters, fuller in the face, with soft droopy eyes and a sad expression which was nevertheless appealing. 'Thanks, Vinnie. If you get any queries, just shout to me. We don't have many customers. I think we are too far off the beaten track or something. When we close, you must come back to Nelson Street and meet the crowd. Mother will want to interview you. Don't worry, I'll put in a good word. I heard about your bother with the Prin. You can carry on your painting here and help us in our campaign. Who knows? I might have found us another recruit.'

Vinnie smiled weakly. She was in no position to argue.

'What a palaver over two shrubs and a rose bush, Ada!' yelled old Mrs Norris, clutching her white widow's mutch cap tied firmly under her chin as she sat in her bath chair among the school children. ' 'Tis a right idle wind, one as goes through yer, not round yer. It's freezin' me boots off. How long've them kiddies to stand around like pit props, our Ada?'

'Shush, Mother! I told you before, these aren't any old shrubs but specials from the Sturges collection, given in honour of the old Queen's passing by Lord Dunscar, carried here across the globe from the slopes of Mongolia. Remember, children, how we traced their journey on the map in the classroom? A rose, a handkerchief tree and a winter-flowering Viburnum – from China to our own amenity park,' said the Headmistress of St Stephen and All Martyrs in her best instructional voice to the rows of shivering pupils lining the paths, waving hand-coloured flags and waiting for the official planting party to get on with the show.

The March breeze whipped down from the Western Pennines, raising bowler hats and blowing full skirts and bustles into balloon shapes. The senior gardener from the Dunscar Estate stood awkwardly by with his spade while the Rector of the Parish, the Reverend Rowland Thompson, tried to control the dancing pages of his Prayer Book, to no avail. 'Heavenly Father, we offer this *Viburnum sturgesii*, this *Davidia involucrata* and especially the *Rosa graciae* to Thy safekeeping, in sure and certain knowledge of Thy tender providence. May these symbols of Thy creation and bounty, offered as token memorials to our dear departed Victoria Regina, honour also the memory of those brave men of Empire who risked life and limb, fire and flood, to grace the gardens of England with Thy beneficence.'

'This Parson's a windbag, isn't he? Spit it out, mister, tea will be gerrin' cold,' croaked the voice from the bath chair. The children smothered their giggles as they jostled for a view.

The assembled worthies stood silently over the holes in the ground, the gardener hovering respectfully as Lord Dunscar placed a shrub into the prepared soil and proceeded to heel it in. The spade was then handed to a woman in a black and grey dogtooth-checked overcoat who carefully manoeuvred the spindly rose bush into place and leaned on the spade. Grace Thompson's face was pinched, drained of any colour by the black veiling of her hat. The droning of her father's blessing was swallowed by the bitter wind. She took no comfort from the bright March morning, herald of an early spring. Spring was treacherous in these parts, often promising what it could not deliver to the wet Lancashire uplands: in this case a warm balmy summer and the safe return of John Sturges to Dunscar Hall.

'Don't cry, my dear. Not everyone has a rose named after them,' said her father. 'Bit of an honour even if that Sturges chappie was a bounder. You are not robust. You have your mother's constitution. A planthunter would never have made a family man. Lucky escape there, old girl! There'll be others. Your time will come.'

My time has gone, thought Grace as she turned her face into the wind to drive back the tears.

The school children filed past the plaque reverently. As Ada Norris pushed the bath chair along the gravel, her mother leaned over and poked her bony fingers at the twigs, shouting, 'Grow, yer buggers, grow!'

The following Sunday the headmistress hovered in the church porch. 'What you need, Grace, is a Cause!' said Ada, nudging her elbow after Matins. 'You're looking peaky again, and far too thin. I've some good books for you to get your teeth into, by Josephine Butler and Annie Besant, and I need your help with my own project. As a representative of the Women's Liberal Association, I want to co-opt you on to our new Committee.'

'Oh, not your Votes for Women again!' came the sharp reply.

'Don't mock. We need you to join us in the Women's Co-operative Guild to spread the Gospel of Emancipation from Farnworth to Darcy Lever, Breightmet to Horwich. Over the border into darkest Yorkshire if needs must! We'll make a missionary of you yet!'

Chapter Five

'I wish he'd stop gawpin' at me,' whispered Sophie Seddon as she sat in the Weavers' Union Meeting at the Spinners' Hall. 'Am I showing next week's washing?' Annie Pilling, who worked with her at Berisford's Mill, mouthed back the answer mill fashion.

'That's Bert Knowles, rep from the Bee Hive Mill.' Both turned and stared back boldly. Flushing with embarrassment, the man looked away.

Sophie saw him most Sundays on the back row of the Labour Church Hall. At first he had attended only when there were visiting politicians, big guns like Bruce Glaiser, Robert Blatchford, and the famous Socialist MP, Keir Hardie. She'd noticed the young man, as she sang in the choir with a full view of the congregation, work his way slowly from the rear to the side of the chapel where the regulars gathered, and had felt his dark eyes burning in her direction. He was one of the *Clarion* men, not just a Sunday cyclist but one of those dedicated to distributing pamphlets and holding Socialist open-air gatherings on village greens and in pub courtyards all over Lancashire.

What a sight for sore eyes they were, riding out in all weathers in short trousers, pennants flying from their bicycle frames! Shy as Mr Knowles certainly was, he had a good pair of legs from all that muscle work.

When the meeting closed and everyone rose from the benches, Sophie watched the man push his way in their direction. The effort to place himself close to her chattering group, she observed, had sapped all his reserves of confidence. He hung back reticently on the fringes of the discussion, listening intently, drawing closer until he felt himself included in the heated debate. He kept his eyes to the floor, agonising over whether to give the sparky, dark-haired young woman another meaningful stare. It was Sophie who decided to put him out of his misery by introducing herself and Annie as casually as she could manage.

'I've seen you at the Labour Church, haven't I?' she smiled sweetly. 'I sit in the choir pews and I don't miss much!'

At close range, his dark eyes were like huge jet buttons, fringed by curling black lashes wasted on a bloke. A moustache shaded a generous mouth. He was neatly turned out for a working man and had bothered to put on a stud-collared shirt and tie which she found touching and impressive. 'I'm Sophie Seddon and this is my chum, Annie Pilling, from Berisford's Mill.' She paused, putting a hand nonchalantly on her hip.

'Albert . . . Bert Knowles from the Bee Hive.' He nodded then fell silent.

'See you're a *Clarion* man,' Sophie laboured. 'How long have you had a bike?' Once given this safe topic he quickly got into gear, falling over himself to inform her of all the mechanics of his Raleigh Safety machine with its brazed sockets and steel frame; it was his pride and joy, worshipped as lovingly as any sweetheart. To her amazement, he then added boldly:

'We sometimes take a *Clarion* van out with us – horse-drawn effort with stove and camping beds. When there's an Election campaign and such like. It's a grand job, is that. The women come with us, make tea and stay over in lodgings. They give us a hand at the open-air rallies, draw in the fellas. In the country they don't hold with "Clarionettes" on bikes, but it's a great day out. I think you might enjoy it. I do.'

'Would I now?' she flashed back, giving him her most saucy stare.

'Well, I meant . . .' he stuttered, staring at the floor for inspiration.

'You're dead right. We would, wouldn't we, Annie?' Sophie encouraged. 'Let us know when there's another do and we'll see if we can sort it out. I take it you meant both of us?' she challenged. For a second a hint of disappointment flitted across his face. 'The more the merrier.' He tried to sound casual.

'Righty ho! We'll look out for you at the Sunday

meeting then,' she retorted, and left the group to grab some tea before the long trek home.

From such a tentative beginning came first a friendship, then a courtship and eventual partnership. From regular outings with the *Clarion* caravan, to walking out in Queen's Park, then a quiet June wedding in the local chapel on the Saturday of Wakes week. They borrowed the van for a tour of the Yorkshire Dales, snuggling under damp blankets on the wettest of holiday weekends, and the resulting souvenir of their honeymoon was baby Phyllis Millicent Knowles in the spring of 1901.

Wilf Seddon had long since found himself a widow woman from the tannery at Rose Hill and migrated to her terraced cottage by the LMS railway line; a sooty side street with not a hill or rose in sight. Sophie was glad to see the back of his messy habits, wishing Florrie Soames well with his bouts of drunkenness. Cissie was wed, and Jack, Walt and Ethel too, but Bun Gran still ruled the roost in Plover Street. Sophie was the last to go. Hung on to the bitter end! It seemed natural for Bert and Sophie to share the double bed there with Phyllis in a wooden crib borrowed from the Mullarkeys who kept the corner shop. Bridie Mullarkey, being a good Catholic, produced a child a year until even she ran out of steam. Now she was delighted that her crib was baby warm again.

Bun Gran shuffled around the parlour in pain. A bad fall had jiggered her hip and stiffened her joints. 'I've woven my piece . . . I'm fit for nowt but the knacker's yard, our Phia! You'll want to be gettin' shut of me, now yer wed!'

'Don't talk daft. You've still got all yer marbles. Nowt wrong with you that a bit of a rest up won't cure. Besides, who'll mind our Phyllis?'

'I'm past mindin' babies. Me time is up.'

'Well, I'm not leavin' my loom so you'll just have to cope,' said Sophie, knowing this command was just the tonic for Gran's pride. 'Our Phyllis is going to have a decent education and proper boots. Neither comes cheap so I'll be back at work as soon as me legs'll carry me. We need two wage packets to take us down Blackpool Prom, and I need some more books!'

Books were her one luxury, her sustenance and her sanity. She bothered them incessantly at the lending library with her continual requests, and browsed regularly through the second-hand bookstalls in the covered market. 'Missus Head in t'Book' was her nickname at the mill where she was always to be found stuck in some discreet corner at break, sitting on the stone steps, curled around a weighty tome, her shirt open for Phyllis to forage while she nourished her mind. At home she ironed with a book propped against the dresser, her eyes squinting in the gaslight.

'You'll wear your brain out, lass,' warned Gran. 'What's the point of dosing yerself with things that are not for our sort?' Sophie pretended not to hear.

Everything that mattered went on inside her head, in its landscape of pathways and rough tracks leading to the lush meadows where she grazed for knowledge. She was never able to decide what to study first: science, politics or classical history. The options were legion. Not that she knew any Latin or Greek, that was to be one of her tasks in evening classes at some later date. Sometimes she felt the urge to learn a foreign language for one day she intended to travel abroad.

Thank God for the WEA, the excellent Workers' Education courses, the public library lectures and the gift of asking awkward questions; even though the one question, always uppermost in her mind never got a satisfactory answer. 'Why was it a woman's lot to feed, clothe, cook, clean, budget, mind the childer and work a full shift?' How could she bridge the gap between all these tasks and the Socialist theory bandied about at the Labour Rallies which gave everyone, in theory, equal rights and opportunities.

Why did this theory never manifest itself in practical help with the chores, or the giving of time for a working woman to study and better herself? But, oh no! Bert and his cronies were blind to the fact that the frequent committee meetings held conveniently for them on a Sunday teatime in their parlour, and with high tea prominent on the agenda, kept Gran from her bed. Meetings required a pile of bread, buns and fancies to be baked. Meetings required meals to rise up through their table as if by magic. Not one man ever offered any assistance to clear away the debris.

Her own brothers, Walter and Jack, were just as thoughtless – until the week she took Gran and Phyllis and their wives for a break to visit sister Ethel's home in Padiham. Funny how, left to fend for themselves for three days, the men had moaned but managed to survive on fish suppers. For a while after their return, Bert had commented on how quiet the place was without women's banter, the nearest he came to admitting they were missed. But they soon fell back into letting the women do it all!

Sophie hadn't the energy to insist on her rights. It was quicker to do it all herself. Phyllis was a quiet baby and made few demands. She hoped that there would be only one child. Not for her the constant tyranny of childbearing, where the best you could hope for was that your bloke didn't trouble you over much.

At least Socialism was hot on birth control – again in theory. Sophie smiled. There was no shortage of discreet pamphlets on suppliers who delivered rubber johnnies in plain packages. They sat under Bert's side of the bed, with backups on the wardrobe shelf. Their lovemaking was regular, nothing to get fussed over after all the horror tales she had endured from other wives at the mill. But how could you put your trust in a flimsy sheath? With only one child they could manage well so long as Bun Gran helped out; two would be too much for the old woman. Sophie watched for her monthlies, relieved when they came on cue. Safe for another nine months! Sometimes her life seemed one continuous chore.

It was Bridie Mullarkey who mentioned women's night at the Co-operative Society. The meetings were held each Wednesday night at the Co-op Hall. For Bridie, it was a night out away from the corner shop. By rights she should have had no truck with the Co-op Movement and its 'divi' coupons for regular savers, but Bridie could afford to be generous. She had enough feckless last-minute shoppers knocking them up for a bit of sugar or an ounce of tea . . . plenty of trade to go round. She was ready for a change of scene. Frank, her husband, was looking out for the lease of a fish and chip restaurant in the town centre. There was a future in take away fish suppers with table trade. 'Take your chances when they come,' she confided to her friend in a soft Irish brogue as she encouraged the young wife to get out of the house for a good cup of tea and the chance to hear an excellent speaker.

So easy to say, so hard to achieve! thought Sophie. It took a frantic juggling of preparations, settling down a for-once fractious toddler and equally grumpy household to the idea that she was not deserting them for life.

The hall was comfortably full of chattering, well-upholstered women in their best hats. At the front, on the raised platform, sat the speaker: a petite mouse-faced woman dressed in a long tweed jacket and skirt, with stiff collar and tie. The draping of her garments suggested she was one of the new-fangled brigade who'd abandoned corsets in favour of a more natural line. Miss Esther Roper from Manchester was introduced by the Chairwoman as the representative of the Northern Union of Women's Suffrage Societies. Her mission was to raise a large petition in favour of Votes for Women from all the constituencies in Lancashire and the North of England. This diminutive woman rose to deliver an impassioned plea for recognition of the right of half the population to some say in the government of their country. 'For fifty years motions have been laid before Parliament, only to be ignored!'

'What a stink!' someone heckled.

'We are now in the twentieth century. It's about time we women took matters into our own hands . . . dear friends, whatever your political persuasion or your religious allegiance, whatever your position in life, forget your differences and be united in the coming fight. Our crusade will end this discreditable situation once and for all. Pledge your support so that your daughters may live as equals with men in the world.'

The clapping, polite at first, rose to a crescendo of cheers. Petition sheets were duly passed along the rows. Several hesitated. 'My mister won't like me to sign owt behind his back . . . 's not right,' said the woman to Sophie's left, folding her arms in defiance.

'How is he goin' to know if you don't tell him, missus?' she retorted, leaping to her feet. 'Come on! Do it for yer childer. It's about time we stood up to them. We're good enough to bear their babies and do a day's graft. We can be hung from the gallows. It's about time we looked after ourselves a bit more.'

'Well said, young woman!' a voice vaguely familiar to her echoed behind.

'Ladies, I think we have a natural speaker in our midst.'

Sophie turned towards the smiling woman whose prematurely lined features were still unmistakable. 'Crikey Moses! Miss . . . Miss Norris from St Anselm's School! It must be you?'

Adelaide Norris peered more closely. 'Do I recognise you? St Anselm's was many years ago. I see so many ex-pupils, forgive me.' She peered over her metal-rimmed spectacles for a closer inspection.

'It's Phia Seddon as was. Mrs Knowles now. Fancy seeing you here. It must be twelve or more years!'

The teacher held out her hand. 'Of course, Phia Seddon, our first prize-winner. How can I forget? You must meet Miss Roper and the others on the Committee. Mrs Wagstaff will want to use your talents, I'm sure. Little Phia Seddon! Well, I never. And how's Ethel?'

The petition had passed by unnoticed. Sophie followed her old school teacher down to the platform and duly signed her name in full there: Sophia Seddon Knowles. She liked to keep her given name, even though it was still from a man. She was introduced around the Committee, and Dora Wagstaff, the Chairwoman, welcomed her warmly.

'You were brave enough to speak up at your first meeting. I do hope you will come again? We like to encourage our members to be active, voice their opinions. We can all have opinions, you know, whatever our station in life. Our Guild is run as efficiently as any male organisation. Esther is staying on a few days to organise sending the petition around the local mills. We have a meeting next Saturday afternoon to get more signatures from the mill-workers. Would you know anyone who might help us?' asked the lady in the smart blue hat trimmed with a rainbow-coloured silk bandeau as she gathered her papers from the table.

'I work at Berisford's Cotton Mill. I can ask there.'

'Do you now?' Dora Wagstaff leaned forward. 'Would you be willing to call in on Saturday to our sub-committee meeting? I think you are just the type we need.' She smiled sweetly.

'I'm not sure . . . I have a child to see to.'

'Bring her along, my dear. I have a nurse for my brood. One more will make no difference. Do come and help us . . . Greenmount House, Park Crescent, after three o'clock. Do you know where that is? Near the Infirmary. My husband's sign is on the wall. Ask for Dr Wagstaff's residence. Do come, Mrs Knowles. We need all our ladies involved, don't we, Ada?' She turned to the older woman but Ada was now at the back of the hall, talking to a late-comer who rushed forward.

'Sorry I'm late, ladies. Father had one of his meetings so I waited to see him settled for the evening.' She paused, looking at Sophie intently.

Ada, following behind, smiled. 'This is our latest recruit, Grace. Would you believe, an old pupil of mine. Mrs Knowles from . . . ?'

'Plover Street,' Sophie replied coolly, recognising the bluebell eyes. 'Good evening, Miss Thompson.'

'How do you do, Mrs Knowles? Do I know you?'

'My goodness! S-Sophie . . . Sophie Seddon, of course, and quite grown up.' Ada stood back, nonplussed by her young friend's flustered response. 'Fancy, after all these years. And married too. Where do you live now?'

'Plover Street, I've just told you,' came the curt reply.

'Ah, yes, and your family? St Anselm's still going strong?' Grace was struggling for a point of contact.

'Don't bother, miss. The Labour Church's more my place now.' The woman in the shabby jacket and shawl stood before her defiantly.

'Yes, well, I hear they have famous speakers there. I've been meaning to hear them myself but I still live with Father near Dunscar.'

'Well, is he?' Sophie's curiosity was getting the better of her shock at this unexpected encounter.

'Not really. He has these shaking spasms. Not a lot can be done but we'll have a nurse if he gets worse.'

Of course, thought Sophie, your sort usually does. She nodded disinterestedly, turning to Ada Norris who, after another awkward pause, jumped to the rescue. 'You missed a good speaker, Grace. Didn't she?' turning to Sophie. 'My mother gets me so vexed. Ten times I told her where I was going tonight, but still she kept on asking until I was almost late. She's worse than one of my infants in the baby class, gets so confused. Such a pity!'

'I must be lucky wi' my Gran Walker. Still twelvepence in the shilling. How do you put up with it?' said Sophie, feeling this was a subject she gladly knew nothing about.

'I just have to remind myself that the Fanny Norris I once knew has been permanently replaced by this shuffling stranger. I'm not putting her away in one of those work-house wards,' replied the teacher. How she wished she had Grace's income, to be able to employ a guardian! No one else knew about all the changing of bedlinen and the constant stench of stale urine, the indescribable messes in Mother's clothing waiting each afternoon when she returned from school.

'I just remind myself that this was the woman who stitched her fingers to the bone to keep me out of the mill, who taught me all I know about embroidery and sewing, who once kept the house so spotless you could eat off the floor. I try to hold on to that when it all gets too much, but I'd go mad if I stayed in all the time. Sometimes I feel like giving her the cane when she plays me up. That's when I walk out of the door and lock her in!' Ada patted her chest with relief at speaking out about her worst fear.

'I think you do a marvellous job under the circumstances. Don't you, Mrs Knowles?' said Grace from what seemed a great height.

Sophie was still so shocked to be talking both to her old teacher and her childhood friend, she was only able to nod in agreement, sneaking a quick sidelong glance at Grace. She was certainly no beauty. Gone was the delicate patina of her childhood bloom, replaced by a sharp jutting chin and cavernous hollows in her cheeks. The once golden hair had faded into a dull sand, crimped and scraped into a severe coil, nestling into the nape of her neck. The once luminous eyes had faded to an ice blue, frosted by the pallor of her skin. Only her mouth, its full lips still cracking occasionally into a wide disarming smile, belied the gauntness of her public face. Standing beside her, Sophie felt a shabby dwarf, like a peg by a clothes prop. Grace was tall and elegant in a deep mauve suit with a crisp white blouse beneath over which dangled a rope of cream pearls. She also wore a delicate cameo brooch on her lapel. Sophie's homespun best was a navy serge skirt with donkey brown jacket, cut down from one of Bridie's cast offs. It was young Phyllis who had the best outfits to wear.

How could this be the same Grace who had once shared all her secrets in Plover Street? A flashback to the days of skipping and handstands in the back ginnel brought a brief flicker of a smile to Sophie's face. It sort of balanced things out between them, remembering how hopeless Grace had been with a bat and ball. Sophie backed towards the exit.

'You will come to the meeting, Mrs Knowles?' shouted Ada Norris.

'I'll think about it,' was all she was prepared to reply.

They want you to play with them. The creatures from the other side of town where houses are large and staffed with servants, where automobiles are parked in the stables. They think you might be useful to their Cause.

All week she struggled with her curiosity and conflict. Long-forgotten feelings plucked at and discomfited her. She even dreamed that she was hiding in the Vicarage garden and a voice screeched at her, 'Go away! We don't want you . . .' She woke with a start. '

Why not, Sophia Knowles? Have your Socialist principles taught you nothing all these years? Don't be a cowardy custard. A working woman is no idle parasite but a force to be reckoned with, equal to anybody.

On the following Saturday, struggling to calm her increasing nervousness, she surprised herself by her boldness as she half-carried a starched and smocked Phyllis across the town to the gracious detached brick houses which fringed Queens Park. Only at the gated entrance of Mrs Wagstaff's did she falter for a second. The stubborn thought that she was as good as Grace Thompson any day urged her on to tug at the bell pull with thudding heart.

The door was opened by a maid in a flounced pinafore who kept her waiting in the tiled vestibule, convinced she was at the wrong entrance. But Dora Wagstaff welcomed her warmly and Phyllis was soon whisked away to the nursery, to be swiftly enchanted by all the toys there, especially a dapple grey rocking horse and pretty doll's house. She was far too absorbed to miss her mother for an hour or so. Phyllis was good that way. She would go to anyone if she sensed that they were kind and warm, too young to be embarrassed by this contrast to her normal surroundings.

Sophie joined the meeting in a drawing room which was the size of numbers nine and ten Plover Street put together. It was a room full of portraits and landscapes in gilded frames. On the polished floor lay soft rugs in pastel shades with tasselled fringes. The large bay window was draped with brocade curtains, looped and swagged lavishly, toning with the fine furnishings scattered around the room. From where she was placed she spied cases of books; glass-fronted cabinets stuffed with leather-bound copies of Shakespeare, Milton, Carlisle, Tennyson, Wordsworth. It was like sitting in the public library. Paradise!

By the window a grand piano, covered carelessly with a fringed silk-embroidered shawl, was littered with photographs in ornate silver frames. Sophie's eyes drank in the sight. For a moment she was struck dumb by the grandeur of her surroundings, but there was a casual careless clutter to it all: petals dropped from the vase of lilies, papers were scattered and a few children's toys shoved hastily out of sight. A family frequented this room, a warm welcoming family, which transformed the atmosphere from threatening to comforting.

The assembly seemed genuinely pleased at the announcement of her arrival and reintroduced themselves to her as Miss Norris, Miss Roper and Miss Thompson, the latter nodding and making room for her on the sofa. Afternoon tea was wheeled in on a trolley. It was served in rose-patterned porcelain cups with gold-edged fluted rims. A silver cake stand was tiered with scones, fruit cake and fancies. There were warm scones and real butter curls, featherlight sponge cakes and the thinnest slivers of white bread Sophie had ever encountered. She worked her way up the tiers cautiously, trying not to make crumbs.

Soon they were all busily working, planning timetables and venues for further meetings. Dora Wagstaff handed Grace a notebook. 'Will you keep the minutes?'

'How do I do that?' said Grace.

'You write down everything that is discussed and read it back to us next time,' Sophie chipped in confidently. 'Well, that's what they do at the Weavers' Union Meeting.'

'See, I knew you'd be an asset to us,' said Ada to her protégée.

The first item on the agenda was the formation of a local branch of the National Women's Suffrage Society. Esther Roper steered them towards deciding on a founding event.

'How can you fire up the townswomen without grabbing their attention at a central meeting point?'

Dora was anxious not to offend anyone and suggested they find a neutral place to meet regularly, preferably in a venue which would bypass any political bias towards either Liberal or Socialist opinions.

'I know a good place right by the Town Hall Square – Mrs Mullarkey's fish restaurant. They have a room upstairs for funeral teas and meetings, nice and quiet. She comes to the Guild so you could ask her. If that's what you want?' Sophie offered hesitantly.

Ada sat back with satisfaction. 'It's going to work, I can feel it in my bones. From Guild to Government, from parlour to Parliament. We'll show them that women can organise themselves efficiently. We'll muster together mill workers and shop girls, teachers and wives of prominent townsmen. All with one voice to make change happen!' Looking at the startled faces in the room, the shuffling papers and hesitation of the group at her outburst, her confidence faltered for a second. 'Of course, it will take time.'

The first formal meeting of the Suffrage Society was a modest affair. Invitations were sent to all the political parties, ladies' societies and local Co-operative Guilds in

the district. Only a few faithfuls from the Guild bothered
to attend.

'It's that Christabel Pankhurst and her mob! Those hot
heads are spoiling it all,' was the general opinion of the
militant activities of the new breakaway organisation,
the Women's Social and Political Union, creation of the
Pankhurst women that year, whose followers were known
as 'Panks'. They were the rowdies who were beginning to
make a nuisance of themselves at political meetings:
unfurling banners, getting themselves arrested, and gener-
ally giving the Suffrage movement a bad name in the press.

'The Pankhurst women have a lot to answer for,' Grace
commented on their own poor attendance. 'Such self-
publicists. How are we ever going to be taken seriously?'

'I'm not so sure,' offered Ada cautiously. 'They've
certainly put Votes for Women in the limelight, just like a
revivalist crusade.'

'That's my point, Ada. Mrs Pankhurst is detracting from
the wider issue of furthering the rights of all women. It's
not just the Vote, that's only a beginning. What about
equal pay for the same work in mills and factories, or
welfare rights and health instruction for mothers with
babies, as well as educational opportunities? Anyway, many
men still don't have the Vote. We need to change the law
by legal means, not by civil disobedience or even violence.'

'I had a letter from Lavinia Shaw the other day. She was
a school friend of ours,' Dora added to Sophie.

'Some friend!' muttered Grace under her breath.

'Well, she's got herself involved in some drama or other

with the "Panks". She says they're very brave women and wonderful fun. Not that she's been in any trouble, of course. Trust old Vinnie!'

'Now I'm really worried, if *she's* let loose in that crowd,' Grace retorted.

'Don't be uncharitable. Lavinia had a lot to put up with, being so neglected as a child. It's good to know she's found a worthy cause,' Dora argued.

Sophie, who was passing tea down the table, felt the tension ripple through the room and butted in: 'They call me and Annie "Them bleedin' Pankies" often enough when we cart round the petition sheets. I've heard what them lot get up to in Manchester. They live in another world to the one me and Annie Pilling have to tout our petition in. I tell you, it's like trying to raise bread wi' no yeast, going from door to door, lugging a girt wad of papers.

'First you get the overseers and managers who love to scoff at us efforts, shouting the odds. "Keep yon bloody women's stuff out of hours, missus. It's all piss and wind. What do women need a vote for with not a brain among them?" Then there's our mates the spinners, weavers and tenters moaning: "Don't keep mitherin' on, our Phia, we've enough on our plate." Like a lump of soggy dough, but nothing to what I get at home! Up jumps Bert with a spoke for my wheel. "Adult Suffrage, Sophie lass, that's the real cause. Why keep bletherin' about women's rights? Mind on, if you've got time on yer hands . . . there's plenty of work to be done down the Labour Club."'

Her audience sat entranced at her newfound oratory. 'And there's more! It gets worse. You should hear my gran. As tough as yesterday's scones is Bun Gran. "Them sort is just a load of women with no corsets, weird hairdos and fancy ideas. Heads in the cloud. Never done a hand's turn in their life . . ."' Sophie stopped abruptly in full flow, censoring her version, omitting the: 'Why do you want to take up with Gracey Thompson again? She'll drop you like a load of horse muck soon as you've done your bit for 'em, just like she did last time. Old maids, the lot of them. You stay at home and mind your bairn, never mind all this galli-vantin'. It'll all end in tears. Won't do you a scrap o' good.'

'You must write us an article for the news sheet about your efforts,' put in Ada with enthusiasm. 'I know you can write.'

Sophie shook her head. 'It takes me all my time to get to do this job, never mind write about it, Miss Norris.'

'Call me Ada, please.'

Sophie smiled politely. They had no idea how hard it was, standing in the mill yard, stopping each woman in turn, her feet frozen to the cobblestones, stomping her clogs and hugging herself with a shawl wrapped around her head while Annie Pilling whined in despair: 'We must be daft in th' head. What's this petition ever going to do for us?' Some days there were a few who signed out of respect for their Union representative; out of respect for the way Phia Knowles would stand up to the tacklers and their bullying tactics; out of respect for the way she turned out with their grievances to the Spinners' Hall and stood up to be ignored, overruled and insulted by the men who ruled the roost on the main Committee. Some days complaints were made about her petition. She smiled.

'It makes yer think though. If it's this hard to get up one legal petition to Parliament, then I have to hand it to them militant Pankywomen – they must be tough old birds!' Everyone laughed, especially Grace.

After Gran's warning about her childhood friend, Sophie tried to keep a safe distance between Grace and herself over the following months, despite their mutual interest in Suffrage work. Sophie preferred to stay closer to her old teacher, Ada Norris, whom she'd always admired. With Ada she felt safe and comfortable, on solid ground.

Chapter Six

Three weeks later at the end of the harsh winter when a freezing cold smog rolled over the damp valley bottoms and coal fires choked back smoke into the grate, filling rooms with floating soot smuts, the women held a meeting in Mullarkey's Hygienic Fishery. They sat huddled in the function room with the evening preparations going on downstairs; the pails of chipped potatoes peeled and soaking, trays of battered fish piled up waiting for the late rush after the last house at the Theatre Royal.

The Committee traced their plans across the green gingham cloths, breathing in the fumes of burning fat and vinegar, speaking above a background of chattering customers in the shop and dining room below. It was hard to concentrate on the details of their next money-raising event, a soiree to be held in the Co-operative Hall, when feet were icy and alien smells enticed. Suddenly a young lad was ushered into the room, cap in hand. One look at his face had Ada on her feet, knocking over chairs in her confusion and concern. 'Freddie . . . what's up? It's Mother, isn't it? What's she done now?'

The boy was still breathless. 'Mam sent us down with a cart to fetch you. She went in to check on yer ma as she allus does. The door were locked but the window was open wide. She's got out of it somehow,' said the boy, shuffling his feet. 'Sorry, Miss Norris.'

'I'm coming right away, Fred. It's so dark and cold . . . No one saw her on the road?'

'No, miss, and we checked through the house. Not a sign. I went slow enough but it's that misty.' Ada fastened her thick overcoat, Sophie beside her.

'I'm coming with you.'

'Me too,' added Grace. 'We'll get a cab. It's quicker.' Ada made no protest as they set out into the foggy night, droplets of mist sticking to their hair and the ends of their noses, damp and chill as the cab chugged up on to the moor road at a snail's pace. Ada was beside herself, rocking nervously back and forth in her seat.

'It's all my fault. I shouldn't have left her. She was very excitable tonight, too restless for me to leave really. I told her I would not be long, that Mabel would call, and I did so need to get away from her and see some life of my own . . .'

Mabel Atkinson was waiting for them by the school house, lantern in hand. 'I've sent Bill and Jo with the Birtwistles to search round the school and the back ginnels. We've sent for Constable Firth too. I hope you don't mind? I've no idea how long she's been gone, with not even a shawl on 'er head or owt.'

'Don't worry, Mabel. I'm sure she's not gone far,' Ada reassured her unconvincingly. Her mother sometimes had incredible energy when she got a notion fixed in her head. Once she'd walked over five miles into town to follow her daughter to a meeting.

Sophie and Grace took turns to wander around the village with the growing number of volunteers from the neighbourhood, around the church and through the graveyard, near the hollow where the bleach and dyeworks chimneys steamed menacingly through the gloom. 'You don't think she's gone to the works?' they whispered. 'At this time of night the late shift is still going. Someone would see her and take her inside. Ada, would yer mam go to the dyeworks?'

'Well, Father worked there a long time ago. Surely not? But she is so confused . . .'

They gathered at the entrance to the works but the porter had seen no one and the wrought-iron gates were firmly closed. Jo and Bill Atkinson escorted Ada back to the cottage.

At the door Jo turned to Grace, whispering, 'There's the Lodge pond behind, a nasty place where one or two workers have ended it all, but it's well back off the road. Happen it's best we go and check.'

Grim-faced, holding the lantern, they all stuck firmly together. Grace knew the footpath well. The mist was denser close to the water as steam rose eerily from the processing sheds. It was pointless to call out for sound was muffled, distorted by the clinging vapour. There was no sign of the old woman near the pond but they circled it twice to be sure. Then they all trundled disconsolately back to Ada in the cottage and stood around uncomfortably, waiting for the worst. The women sat up all night making endless cups of tea, thick treacly liquid; the fire was banked up but spluttered defiantly, as if there was no life in it.

'It's not looking good, is it?' said Ada, pacing the floor.

'Go and lie down with a hot stone bottle,' Grace cajoled the teacher. 'We will wake you if there's any news.'

Ada rose compliantly and retired up the wooden stairs. Her two friends coaxed the reluctant fire into a blaze.

'Thanks for sending a message to Plover Street, Grace. They would have been worried for me,' yawned Sophie.

'Thanks for being here with Ada, and I'm glad of your company too. At least I don't have far to go to the Vicarage.' She paused. 'I did try to see you before we left St Anselm's. It wasn't I who sent you away, it was all a misunderstanding. I didn't realise you were working in the mill.'

'I never told you, like you never told me you were leaving.' Sophie gazed into the flames.

'One minute we were the best of chums and then we seemed to go our different ways,' Grace said pensively.

'That's life for you, full of junctions and separate tracks. Funny how ours keep crossing.'

'You haven't changed a bit, Sophie Seddon. Still full of spark.'

'Well, you have, Miss Thompson, quite a bit,' came the honest reply.

'Whatever happened to our Bread and Roses Society? Please call me Grace again. Do you remember Dragon Castle and those awful breeches? Aunt Calvert fainting at our disguise?' They smiled in the flickering gaslight. 'Now you are married with little Phyllis. Why call her that, by the way?'

'We just liked the sound of it.'

'Such a romantic name – all nymphs, shepherds and madrigals. Did we have it on our list of favourite names, the names we collected from the gravestones?' Sophie looked up with surprise.

'So you never forgot, then?'

'How could I forget? I'm sorry it ended so badly.'

'You haven't wed then?' Sophie whispered hesitantly.

'Oh, I had a chance but he died,' said Grace, and gave a censored version of the John Sturges affair. 'What's your husband like then?'

'Bert? Kindly, quiet, good with Phyllis. I can't complain, there are many worse husbands in the world.'

'Just the one child?'

'Well, that was the plan but to be honest, I'm not too sure.' Sophie confessed to feeling off colour recently in an all too familiar, highly unwelcome way. 'I think I've been caught again.'

'What does Bert think?'

'I daren't tell him yet. He'll not be suited. I'll have to choose my moment. Thanks, Grace.'

'For what?'

'It's nice to feel comfortable with you again. Telling secrets and all. Like old times.'

'Barley.' Grace held her fingers and thumbs in the air as a signal of truce.

'Barley Blobs,' came the familiar reply.

They dozed until first light when Ada clattered downstairs to prepare for school. It was nine o'clock when she was summoned from prayers to be told by the Constable what she'd already feared. Her mother had been found not in the Lodge pond but curled under the hedgerow as if asleep. The doctor explained that, overcome by the chill of the night, she had drifted peacefully away.

The women stayed with Ada as she trembled with shock and disbelief. The body was brought back to the cottage where Sophie was able to warm and straighten the limbs into a dignified shape as Bun Gran had taught her, sponging it tenderly, pressing the contents of the stomach out and tying up the chin, closing the eyelids with pennies, brushing the downy hair, plaiting the wisps neatly around her night cap. It was the least she could do for her friends, for that was what they were to her now. Grace ordered a cab to return her to Plover Street. Sophie lost a day's pay but neither Bert nor Gran held that against her under the circumstances.

Ada busied herself with arrangements for the simple funeral. Once the numbing shock disappeared she filled each moment with meetings, Guild activities, school-work . . . anything to get her out of the house where the silence was disturbed only by her own footsteps echoing in the passageway. Every day she halted at the door, waiting to hear: 'Is that you, our Adelaide?' Sometimes it was hard to turn the key in the latch and face the emptiness. Ada had often prescribed 'doing' for others as an antidote against self-pity. Now it was her turn to swallow grief's bitter medicine. She persuaded herself that what the Suffrage Society needed was a marching banner to proclaim their message on the streets; a banner in the official Suffrage colours of green for hope, red for sacrifice and white for truth and purity.

Following a design compiled by the group, she stitched, appliquéd and embroidered in silk thread the most delicate tracery of lettering on to a white cloth, labouring late into the night on evenings when she missed the familiar clicking of teeth by the hearth, the empty chatter, the restless twirling of those thumbs in an aproned lap. Spreading the pieces carefully across the floor, she hand-stitched the banner with all the love, respect and loss she was now enduring. The funny thing was, sometimes she could swear she felt her mother smiling her approval, just out of reach, a shadow behind Ada's shoulder.

Lavinia Shaw felt the calico banner next to her ribs, hot against her thumping heart. The school hall in Cheetham Hill was packed for the hustings, men in cloth caps and mufflers sitting like rows of overgrown schoolboys, squashed on to wooden benches. At the front was a makeshift platform, covered in old carpet, and a row of aspidistras, with three empty chairs waiting for the speakers. At each entrance to the school hall stood burly policemen, vetting each arrival. Already a crowd was standing at the back of the room, shuffling restlessly.

Vinnie was glad she had linked arms with young Harry Pankhurst, Sylvia's brother, as they'd passed nonchalantly through the door. She wrapped the shawl more tightly over her hair to disguise the garish henna-ed strands, hugged the banner closer under her jacket.

The audience was whispering, awed by the smell of chalk dust and memories of long-forgotten classrooms. The Gothic windows high up on the dark green walls, the treacle coloured book cupboards and dog-eared maps of the Empire were the only distractions. There was a smell of stale tobacco and strong men's armpits mixed. On the side wall, a coke boiler spluttered its fumes and heat into their midst.

A Manchester Board School was not the most inspiring venue for this raw recruit to prove her mettle in and fly the Suffragette flag. Vinnie turned nervously to see if any of the other women from their group were managing to squeeze in unrecognised. Down the gang-way between the rows trooped a procession of worthies in black suits, flanking the young Mr Winston Churchill, already balding and plump-faced, looking determinedly ahead towards the dais and the lectern.

After a brief introduction, the young Member of

Parliament rose to deliver his election address but Sylvia Pankhurst suddenly leaped to her feet, piping up: 'Will the Liberal Government give women the vote?' The room stirred and heads turned. At this signal Vinnie shot up and raised above her head the calico banner with its black lettering: 'Votes for Women!'

A policeman raced over and tried to yank it out of her grip but she was determined not to let go. From another corner up came another small banner: 'Votes for Women!' It was Annie Kenney's turn now, a local girl whose pretty, delicate features belied a battle-axe spirit. She was set upon and quickly escorted out of the door.

'Will the gentleman answer our question?' Vinnie yelled as Harry stood by her side, hanging on grimly to the piece of cloth, sweat pouring from her face.

'Give the ladies a chance, please!' Harry added, and another of their male supporters tried to orchestrate some heckling at the back.

'Come on, Mr Churchill, what have you to say?'

This provoked an uproar of jeers and raucous laughter. The politician, red-faced, raised his hands for silence but the din continued. Stewards were pushing and shoving between the benches, trying to eject each protester, separating the women from their male henchmen. Vinnie felt herself propelled across a row of bony knees and lost her shawl. The steward took delight in grasping her coiled locks, pulling so hard she was forced to follow. Bowed by pain, she was struck by several hobnailed boots but the riot continued.

'Silence! If there is silence, we will let Miss Pankhurst address the Chair.'

Sylvia pushed herself through the crowd and mounted the platform but her words were drowned out by hecklers who pelted pamphlets at her and refused to listen to her soft, hesitant voice. Churchill seized the opportunity to shove her backwards on to a chair. 'Enough of this nonsense. Nothing would induce me to vote for giving women the franchise. I'm not going to be henpecked!'

Sylvia was seized by two stewards and locked in a small ante-room; little more than a janitor's cupboard. From the pavement Vinnie and the other Panks could hear her screaming: 'Let me out!' There was no time to protest, only to race round the side of the building to the open window through which Sylvia was trying to scramble. A policeman tried to bar their way but Harry and his friends darted to the side of him to rescue Sylvia, leaving Vinnie to face his wrath.

She stood alone, feeling foolish, scared and defiant, all at the same time. In her ears were the screams of her friend. Just for a second her instinct was to run like hellfire. Then a well-spring from deep within her, of anger, excitement and defiance, gushed over. A strange exhilarating force rooted her feet to the ground as the policeman grabbed her arm roughly. She kicked out blindly, feeling no pain, only a fierce spitting fury at this treatment. 'Don't you dare touch me! I've done nothing wrong. All we want is the right to be treated fairly, to have our say, be seen as equals.'

Much to her surprise, the crowd around her closed in

to defend the lone woman crying for the release of her friend. A dishevelled Miss Pankhurst soon joined Vinnie and clung on to her fiercely. Shaken but defiant, they found a wooden crate to mount and shouted their slogans on to the waiting notepads of local news reporters.

'Deeds not words! Tonight you have seen why only deeds will gain us the Vote. These small protests, like seeds in the wind, will grow into tomorrow's golden harvest. Wait and see!' Sylvia shouted, and Vinnie echoed each phrase. When the crowds dispersed and they stood shivering on the pavement, Sylvia took Vinnie's arm and examined her bruises.

'Good show, Vinnie, you've earned your spurs tonight. Stout hearts and stalwart deeds! I knew you would be with us. I hope you will be coming with us all to London when we rouse the city to our Cause? There'll be plenty of work for all of us if we're to set up headquarters there. What do you say?'

With torn blouse and blue-black bruising, Vinnie winced for a second then a surge of pure elation shot through her. They want me to be one of them, she thought, smiling to herself in triumph. 'Try and stop me!' was her reply.

Deeds Not Words
1904-9

Chapter Seven

'Shoulders to the wheel, girls, and pu-ush!' ordered Sophie as her friends struggled to shift the cartwheels of the *Clarion* caravan from a dusty pothole in the country lane.

'Whose bright idea was this then, to get us all camping like gypsies out on the moor?' protested Grace to Ada, who was gasping for breath, while Annie Pilling and her friend Jessie Cowan put their full weight into the task. Sophie and young Phyllis guided the sweating horse, pulling its halter.

'You're enjoying every minute of it. Come on, lassies, put your backs in it. Shall I give you a hand?'

'Don't you dare! Not in your condition. You've been on yer feet since dawn, it's about time you took it easy. Hop in the back and lie down,' ordered her old school teacher sternly as she brushed the mud from her own skirt.

'Not likely! We can see Pendle Hill. Look, Phylly,

Pendle's on t'move again! Now you see it, now you don't. It's a magic hill, is Pendle, a witchy place. Each time you turn it's in a different place.'

'Is it playing hide-and-seek with us?' replied Phyllis warily as she skipped on ahead, her long black curls bobbing down her back. 'Are we nearly there? Can I play in the dolly house?'

'In a minute, when we stop to eat.' Sophie smiled as she wiped the sweat from her own brow, hoping her idea of taking a Wakes week holiday together while the mills and local schools were closed would be a success. The aim was to borrow the *Clarion* caravan and travel slowly up to Pendle Hill and East Lancashire, raising the Suffrage banner around the scattered villages, adding fresh names to their petitions. Although heavily pregnant, she was determined to enjoy one last jaunt with her friends and Phyllis, now a curious five years old blessed with Bert's dark looks. He had waved them off reluctantly.

'You shouldn't be gaddin' off, the size you are. Bun Gran would have a fit if she knew!'

'Well, what she don't know can't harm her. She's safe off out of it, staying with our Jack and his wife. So don't you let on!' He shook his head, knowing once his wife got a daft scheme in her head, nothing would shake it out.

The group assembled at Trinity Street Station and took a train to Burnley and the omnibus to Padiham where the caravan was waiting for them to ride out into the Pendle countryside for this holiday jaunt. If the weather held they would journey as far as Nelson and Colne to meet up with fellow Suffrage Societies in the district for a summer rally. There were preparations afoot for a local by-election.

The single women volunteered to camp in the van whilst Sophie and the child lodged wherever they found sympathisers. Grace thought it a crazy notion but came just the same to escape her duties at the Vicarage. Aunt Maude Calvert would turn in her grave if she could see her sporting a divided skirt above her ankles! For Ada there was the joy of caring for young Phyllis, an inquisitive, lively-minded child, and the comfort of feeling the July sun and some release from her own sorrows of the past year.

For Sophie this was a last chance of freedom before her pending confinement with all its rigmarole; the pails of soiled washing and leaking breasts.

'I don't know how you managed to pull this off, Sophie. Bert Knowles must be a saint to let you gad about like a single woman. What's your secret and I'll pass it on to Dora Wagstaff? Do you know, that poor woman has to drop everything when the doctor's off duty. She scurries around like a frightened rabbit to make sure he's not disturbed. That's why we have so many meetings at Bridie Mullarkey's place.'

'Dunno, Grace. Me and Bert made a pact when we wed. He does what he has to for the Labour Club and takes his turn with Phylly so that I get some time for the Suffrage, all fair and square. He's had to put his money where his mouth is this week and manage on his own. Won't do him any harm!' laughed Sophie as they walked along the lane, trying to avoid the horse droppings and cow pats. 'By gum, these lanes don't half pong!'

'You have to admire what Dora achieves though,' said Ada. 'She squirrels away bits of her precious time without Dr Wagstaff even guessing. I think Liberal men approve in theory but Dora never dares put him to the test!'

'I've sorted me life out into two piles of washing: one load is Plover Street, all workaday plains, fit only for boilings, and t'other is fancy starched stuff wi' you lot! Just have to keep 'em separate and they'll come out fine. Menfolk is best kept with the boilings!' laughed Sophie.

Perhaps the single state had compensations all of its own, thought Grace, peering out on to the fellsides. It was fun to joggle along the tracks and camp in the wooden van under the stars. On the first night she lay awake, startled by an owl screeching in a nearby clump of trees, listening to the patter of rain on the roof, feeling snug but uncomfortable on the hard mattress shelf, comforted by the breathing of the other women who'd put modesty aside to share the cramped space.

Sophie was right: Pendle was definitely on the move again. One minute it was a distant backdrop, purple-topped, mysterious. With a change of light it loomed large like a giant beast, curving as if it were a living, moving creature with a will of its own.

They parked the horse-drawn caravan, which Phyllis called 'the dolly house', by a village of stone houses at the foot of the fellside, unfurled their banner and posters, laid out a tableful of pamphlets and tracts with yet another monstrous petition. They waited for the curious to browse while they made themselves a luncheon of flat griddled oatcakes and tasty Lancashire cheese, some apples and slices of clarty fruit cake. In a stone jar under the van home-made lemon and barley water lay cooling. Phyllis put the nosebag of oats tenderly on to the tired horse, helped by Ada. Local children darted around them suspiciously, trying to read their posters, examining this strange company of women with curiosity.

Phyllis skipped off to play tag with them but they ignored her then pelted her with chippings until she cried. There were few women out of doors and those who dared to glance at their literature refused to be drawn into debate. Annie and Jessie found a shop keeper willing to sell them groceries though he peered nervously at their van.

'Thowt you was gyppoes back from Appleby horse fair. You won't get any truck here. Men don't hold with women out of their houseplace unless they's out on't fields. Aye, you picked a poor day for yer hustings, most of them is bilber' picking up on the tops. Good crop of berries this year. If you want to talk to th' womenfolk, that'll be where you'll find 'em all.'

Annie reported back to the others who were resting after lunch. They decided to gather containers and tether the horse to a grassy hedge. Dragging a fractious Phyllis, who wanted to play on the swings and slide on the village green, the women set off in the heat of the afternoon for the higher heathery slopes of the fellside to join the berry pickers. It was a long slow climb.

Sophie, against all advice, refused to stay behind and walked at her own pace, often sitting down to survey the Ribble Valley below, now hazy with dusty sunlight, and view the grey peaks of the Yorkshire Dales shimmering in the distance. Pendle did not feel like a witchy place at all this afternoon. With backs arched over the thick dwarf bushes, the village women were searching between the dark green tufts, sifting between the fresh green growth of next year's shoots, deep into the shrub for the blue beads of the bilberry fruit; the freshest, like tiny pearls, blushed with purple oozing juice. Only for a few weeks in July did the heather hills yield this tasty crop.

Cramming mouths with sweet berries, their fingers stained the purple of bruises, the holiday makers forgot their mission and picked with the concentration of devo-tees. The villagers barely acknowledged their presence as they filled their large baskets in a shared task. Berries were a cash crop: a bonus to be sold at market, jammed or bottled; used as a dyestuff for woollen yarn; a welcome chance to earn pin money. The work was tedious as the berries eluded their sticky fingers.

The natives knew which part of the fell to crop first, where the juiciest ones nestled secretly, and each family guarded its patch from this bunch of johnny-come-latelys. Generations had traipsed up the fell in search of the purple treasure, for the bilber' was queen of pie fillings and it took hours of dedication to fill a family pie dish. Ada and Sophie knew how to eke out their previous gleanings with apples. How delicate was the operation of plucking the pearl from the stalk – one careless gesture and the berry fell deep into the bowels of the bush. Grace found the operation exasperating and filled only the bottom of a pan before she wandered off to engage the village women in conversation, Phyllis was content to swat the myriad of flies as they skimmed over the bushes, whilst Sophie picked on as if her life depended on it. In a few more days the berries would be shrivelled, black and tasteless.

The sun rose over the hill and dropped westwards. Tired, hungry but satisfied by their gleaming harvest, they sauntered down the track towards the village below and a well-earned rest. The holiday stretched ahead of them like a magical sea and this was a good start. Soon the berries would be stewed in the pot and covered with cream for a delicious pudding. What a treat in store!

'You look done in,' said Grace as she took Sophie's arm, noticing the sweat on her brow trickling like tears.

'Overdone it a bit with all that bending. You know me, I don't know when to give over.' It was then that Phyllis stumbled with her precious pan and scattered the berries across the grass on to waiting cow pats. Sophie bent quickly to comfort the howling child, feeling a rush of hot stickiness beneath her. She raised her skirts, cursing, to see where the crushed fruit had stained. But it was not bilberry juice. It was blood.

*   *   *

One minute there was life kicking in her belly then here was only death, torn from her protesting body and wrapped tenderly in newspaper. A boy child, born too early. All that mess and pain but no joy from her hard labour, just a dull aching stupor of disbelief as she lay in the caravan while the local surgeon, dragged from his villa by Grace with the promise of a fat fee, wiped his bloody hands and stemmed the haemorrhage as best he could, shaking his head disapprovingly at the shambles before him. They had lain her on a filthy farm cart and joggled her back to the van. The labour was unstoppable. There was never any hope of life. It was too quick, too violent in its coming.

Grace never left her side, whilst Ada tried to soothe the frightened child. The others stood around feeling helpless, their holiday plans in tatters. Sophie rested a day and then was taken by cab to the station halt and brought back home, shivering with nausea. Once safely in bed she lapsed into a delirious fever. Grace nursed her with a heavy heart.

'She'll pull round,' whispered Bert, but Bun Gran shook her head with foreboding. 'That's the way her mam went west. We'll have to pray her body stands the knocking back.'

Grace peered around the little front bedroom, so sparsely furnished; just a bed with rough wooden bedends, worn floorboards and a pegged rug made from old clothes, a cupboard and a wooden fruit crate crammed with books. This was Sophie's private domain and Grace felt like an interloper here. Bert hovered anxiously like a lost child awaiting instructions.

Childbed fever was common enough and a greatly feared complication; a frequent killer in poor homes. I'll be blowed if I'll let Sophie die for the want of good nursing, thought Grace as she crept downstairs for a welcome cup of tea in the back kitchen. They sat solemnly by the fire and she seized the moment, sensing it was time to take control. 'I think we should call for the doctor.'

'He's bin out once already,' said Bert.

'Not your local man but one who specialises in this sort of thing, someone from the Fever Hospital. I know it will cost but Sophie is my friend, it is the least I can do for her. She's like family to me and I will be proud to take care of any arrangements, if you will allow me? Besides, Mrs Wagstaff is another of her friends and her husband is a surgeon who may be able to help us. I don't like the look of things. Please, please let me help?'

Bert and Bun Gran were both too shocked to protest.

In the Fever Ward Sophie was exposed to all the latest methods of special care. The bed was raised steeply and her womb packed with lint soaked in iodine. She was dosed with salts, and quinine with brandy, to reduce her temperature. Once isolated from other possible sources of infection, kept cool and clean, all that could be done was achieved. Only her own tough constitution, that stocky, well-fleshed frame, could pull her through the ravages of fever and dehydration.

Images of Phyllis danced before her eyes; she saw Bun Gran knocking bread dough back and forth on the scrubbed table, the bread ballooning into a huge mushroom which popped as it collapsed. In her head a little voice whispered: 'Stay alive, keep hanging on.'

After the dreams came pain, like a hurricane lifting the roof. There was no time to duck under the sheet, to curl into the foetal position, hold her breath for it to pass; no time to ride the Big Dipper over the spasms, to embrace the fear, to push back the barricades to beyond pain. Sometimes it was exquisite in its intensity; other times dull, a bone-grinding variety. This pain was particular, peculiar to the moment. Like an arrow off target, the medication missed the mark. This was no longer the birthpangs of life thrusting out the new but the harbinger of death cutting the cords; another haemorrhage; spilling over the sheets, birthing only fear, guilt and sorrow. Then the searing pain subsided enough for her to ring the bell on the bedside table.

'How long will this go on?' Sophie whispered, lifting a fragile hand from the coverlet.

'Another bad night, love? Come, let me straighten you up. We'll soon have you sorted, Mrs Knowles.' The nurse sponged her face gently, moistening her dry lips, and checked her stomach.

'Just keep up yer fighting spirit,' pleaded Bert. 'Don't go and leave us. Think of Phyllis and all them friends of yours, waving their banners!' Sophie gave him a weak smile and steeled herself to beat the pain, the sweats, the furnace raging in her stomach.

It was to take two months of care and nursing to beat the odds and win this battle for life; two months of discomfort, swollen breasts, headaches and fatigue which would undermine her reserves of strength for years to come. Once her stubborn spirit won that first round, it sank heavily into the lethargy of dullness and sadness.

Only then did she weep for the child so easily conceived and so carelessly dispossessed, blaming herself for her wilful stupidity in risking such a journey by caravan. Only an idiot would hike up Pendle Hill six months gone on a hot afternoon. She rued the day she'd laid eyes on the cursed spot.

'If I'd stayed at my loom, none of this would have happened, Grace. I've seen weavers drop their bairns almost where they stood and be back at the loom next day. It's all my fault!' Grace shook her head but was ignored. 'Well, at least I have Phyllis, for there'll be no others. They say me insides is all mangled up.'

When she returned home, limp and listless, even in the face of Phyllis's noisy chatter about her day, Sophie could barely climb up the stairs. But everyone was so pleased to see her back and fussed over her constantly.

Grace filled every room with vases of flowers. They looked out of place, especially in the cluttered backroom.

In the strict routine of hospital, life was ordered and strangely full. Now there was no work at the mill for someone else stood at Sophie's loom. Now there was time enough to ruminate, time to brood. Grace's generosity to them began to irritate Sophie for she could not return the favours. Bun Gran sang the praises of all her Guild friends whose prompt intervention had saved her life. She sat by the fire, lost in her own world, wearing out Gran's patience with her continual questions.

'Why did me mam die and me come through? If she'd had the treatment in a sterile hospital, not a working man's home, would she still be alive today? We'd all have had a better life then, I reckon.'

'Stop yer frettin', Phia. Perhaps the Good Lord in His wisdom saw fit to spare you for a purpose? God makes the back for the burden,' Gran argued. This suggestion wormed itself into Sophie's soul. Perhaps there was a strange justice which balances what life doles out? 'Just be thankful you've been given another chance to watch Phyllis grow. You'll have to pay back all that's owin', tit for tat, Phia. You've had a knock back, now it's time to start proving yourself again. Think on.'

Three events speeded up the process. First came an unexpected trip to Blackpool, late in the autumn, when the whole family and Grace took the train to the coast.

'First one to spot Blackpool Tower buys the ice creams!' laughed Bert to Phyllis as she peered out of the sooty carriage rattling across the Lancashire plain.

'Is that it, Auntie Grace?' asked the excited child, jumping up and down. 'My boots are hurting, Mam . . .' as she pointed to her feet.

'I told you to get her clogs, not fancy leathers a size too big, our Phia!' Bun Gran shook her head.

'And I told you, no child of mine would have hand-me-downs. She'll only come round once so she'll have the best we can afford. That right, Bert? You'll grow into them, so no more complaining.' Bert buried himself deeper in the *Clarion News*.

They rode down the promenade in an open carriage and deposited Gran in a pavilion while Bert rolled up his trousers and piggy-backed Phyllis to the shoreline.

'Let's go up the tower, to the very top!' Grace challenged.

'Not up there?' croaked Sophie, peering to the pinnacle of the iron-framed tower, looming above them menacingly.

'Why not? It'll be fun and you can wave to Phyllis.' Grace steered her reluctantly in the direction of the steam lift which carried them jerkily to a platform of wrought iron railings and wood. 'Look down there, Sophie, I can see Phylly with her bucket.' Grace pointed to a dot as small as a black ant. Sophie steeled herself to look down.

'I feel dizzy. I think I'm goin' to faint.' She grabbed the railings and promptly buckled at the knees.

'Don't you dare, madam! I'm not carrying you down. Isn't this marvellous? We are Queens of all we survey!' Their skirts flapped in the offshore breeze. The golden sands stretched for miles out to the west and the north; to the east were the redbrick outlines of the town. Beneath them holiday makers scuttled on their way, unaware of the scrutiny of a pair of observant pigeons, perched safely within a cage of iron bars. 'Get a lungful of air, Sophie. It'll see you through to next spring!'

'I feel sick, just looking down.'

'I'm not surprised, after a bowl of shrimps and two sticks of rock! You're worse than Phylly with your sweet tooth,' mocked Grace.

'I haven't enjoyed meself as much since we took a charabanc to Rivington Pike and rolled our tackler down the hill. We'd better get back, I suppose.'

'There's no rush today. We must give the shops the once over,' Grace insisted.

In one of the quieter arcades behind the tower the second surprise was sprung. Grace pointed excitedly towards a tea gown in a shop window; a loose-fitting, rusty rose velveteen with a low waist, pleated into soft folds at the front and draping down to the ankle in the latest 'hobble' fashion. Grace nudged her. 'Just you.'

'Don't be daft,' laughed Sophie, looking casually at the price tag.

'Go on . . . try it on!'

'What would I need a dress like that for?'

'To cheer you up. It's just your colour too. Those autumn bonfire lights suit your dark hair. I think you deserve a dress after all you've been through. Just in case . . .'

'In case of what?'

'Well, who knows? Every woman should have a proper frock, something for that special occasion.'

'I'm a mill worker, not . . . not a mill owner!'

'So what! Sophia Seddon Knowles, it's my treat, a birthday present, if you like. Just to give you a lift. I want to buy it for you now.'

Sophie's pride was bristling but just for a second she wavered. 'It wouldn't fit me.' Grace seized the moment and pushed her through the door. 'Let's see then.'

The garment hung gently over Sophie's shrunken hips, sliding perfectly into loose pleats. The colour enhanced her deep chestnut hair, warming the pallor of her gaunt features. She swayed in front of the mirror. Who was this slender elfin creature transformed by a tea gown?

'No, Grace. Sophie Knowles doesn't accept charity.'

'Why not?'

'I have my pride. And besides, I owe you so much already!'

'Rubbish! I insist. I'll buy it anyway, and never wear it!'

'You wouldn't?'

'Watch me!' The dress was parcelled in tissue paper and folded into a box. Sophie would not carry the evidence of this extravagance.

'Bert will have a fit when he sees it.'

'Since when has Bert had owt to do with your fancy washing? Remember what you told us? Menfolk is plain boilings. This is definitely fancy. Remember our Bread and Roses Society!' Grace teased. 'He can see it when the time is right.'

They conspired like giggling schoolgirls all the way

back to the beach. Just the thought of wearing such a dress filled Sophie with excitement. Imagining the silky texture of the soft pile between her fingers, she wanted to tear open the parcel and dance along the prom, declaring: 'I've got a dress and it's all mine, not a hand-me-down!' She recalled her yearning for silk ribbons in the days of St Anselm's Sunday School.

They lingered on to see the sun setting over the shore. Blackpool was indeed a magical fairyland.

The following week brought the third piece of good news. Sophie's old neighbour, Bridie Mullarkey, called unexpectedly after visiting her daughter Tess who lived further along Plover Street. 'Phia, my dear heart, I was wonderin' if you'd give us a hand in the chippy for a while? Frank's been under the weather. It's his old ticker again.' She tapped her chest. 'Roisin's in Bury and Tess's got a handful with another on the way. Sure, the boys are all hopeless. I need someone I can trust. Frank'll rest up easier if he knows you are standin' in for him.'

'Bridie Mullarkey, to be sure and aren't you the very Angel of Mercy?' Sophie mimicked as she flung her arms around the woman. 'Of course I'll help you out. When can I start? Time's been draggin'. Gran isn't used to me under her feet and our Phyllis starts school. We're snappin' each other to bits!'

The hours in the cafe were regular and the pay packet good enough but best of all was the chance to get out of the house and see some life again. The fish and chip trade was doing well and met the need for workers to fetch home a quick and easy meal for the whole family, but there was so much to learn about the fried chipped potato. Customers were choosy and if the batter was soggy and the fish dry, or the chips over greasy and short in measure, then the punters would soon shift their custom elsewhere.

Bridie's place was a model of cleanliness and efficiency, with white-tiled walls and floors, but the fat frier was a devil to clean, being coal-fired and steamy. At least they had a mechanical potato peeler, but the routine was relentless; filling the peeler, checking the scrubbed potatoes for rot spots, soaking them in buckets, chipping, dipping the chips, squeezing out water. There was a knack even to preparing ahead for the rush times, blending the secret batter mix and finding cold wet fish of the best quality.

The sacred art of fish frying was left to Bridie and her youngest daughter remaining at home, Sadie. They knew when the fish was ready by sight alone and from the way it floated in the fat. The flesh had to be snow white and flaky. There were regular orders to be wrapped in parcels and grabbed for a quick lunch break. Sophie felt sorry for the old folks who managed on bags of scrap ends dunked in salt and vinegar. She often sneaked proper chips into the bag.

In the restaurant the meal was served on plates with bread and butter, not wrapped in newspaper and eaten with fingers, and this required waitress service.

Sophie watched the lonely, lingering over their cups of

tea, passing the afternoon away, gazing out of the window on to the Town Hall Square; so different from the brisk shoppers who demanded instant attention and big portions. Often she walked back to Plover Street to strengthen her thin legs, and though the stench and soot from the factories threatened to choke her, the bustle of the crowded streets raised her spirits.

On Wednesdays they closed for half-day. She worked the tea-time shift and still managed to attend the Guild meetings and other committees. At Christmas Bridie booked seats at the pantomime, *Jack and the Beanstalk* in the Grand Theatre, treating all her staff to the best circle seats at the matinee with a delicious afternoon tea to follow. Sophie wore her dress for the first time.

'You look swish,' said Bun Gran. 'Where did that come from?'

'Oh, just one of Grace's,' she lied, her face flushing to match her gown. How could she own up to possessing a dress which cost more than their weekly wage packets put together? No, that would remain her secret.

Life stretched out before her: safe, predictable, surrounded by family and friends. Sophie knew no reason why it should not remain the same for all the years to come, through Phyllis's youth and Gran's old age. It was time to get down to learning those Latin verbs and sharpening her speechifying. Through the Guild meetings she extended her contact with other Women's Co-operative Societies throughout Lancashire. She even ventured to Manchester to conferences organised by Esther Roper where she presented reports, composed agendas, and raised points of order, often being called on to give votes of thanks.

A natural ability to think on her feet and answer hecklers, to put arguments pithily and humorously, was noted by the organisers. They often referred to her as 'the little dark one who smells of fish and chips'. It was in Manchester in 1909 she heard the first rumours of preparations for another General Election and the noisy drums of Suffragettes on the march.

Chapter Eight

'We've done it! Sylvia, I don't believe it. Look, all the wall hangings are up now. Two days and nights we've been up finishing these stencils. What a band of troopers! I don't know how you are able to keep awake!'

Vinnie Shaw was trying to catch the eye of a distracted Sylvia Pankhurst who, paint brush in hand, was putting the final touches to more Suffrage banners to be hung from the ceiling of the Princes Skating Rink, Knightsbridge, which had been converted into an Exhibition Hall hung with pennants, flags and banners, like a medieval jousting ground.

'Come down off your perch this minute, before you fall down. Go and get a cup of tea. For God's sake, take a breather,' yelled Vinnie in concern as she dusted the flakes of paint from her own skirt.

She paused to admire the overall effect, relieved that all the backbreaking work of their team of artists and hangers on was causing such a stir in the Exhibition Hall on that

May afternoon. Vinnie's team had spent hours, stretched out on the floor of the Fulham studio or perched on ladders up to the ceiling; all spent measuring, copying and tracing, blocking and painting Sylvia's magnificent designs: dramatic ornate panels of latticed arches with stencilled ivy leaves and purple grapes, framing separate quotations and illustrations from the *Psalms*. 'They that sow in tears, shall reap in joy', for instance.

'That's my work, up there.' Vinnie felt like stopping each of the stallholders in turn to point them in the direction of: 'He that goeth forth and wept . . .'

'I broke my back to get that just right for you, Sylvia! So make sure you examine every last vine leaf,' she urged.

Vinnie was so proud to be part of the team, weary though she was. This was an occasion not to be missed. Who said there were no women artists? She was bursting with pride as the Exhibition Hall began to fill up. Women would nod to her or pat her on the back, knowing she was one of the key organisers. It was wonderful to feel so appreciated.

'Vinnie dear, mind my stall for a second, I'm dying for relief!' cried a desperate colleague, with crossed legs and a pained expression. Vinnie was far too excited, as high as a soaring kite, to refuse so stood behind the craft stall, watching the queues of elegant women in their afternoon dresses jostling for a view of the merchandise. Ladies with huge chip hats, brims bumping, feathers dyed in Union colours and waving aloft like knightly favours, jousted with each other to examine her wares.

She peered down in amazement at the assortment of goods before her, all priced and ticketed. Everything for the emancipated household in green, purple and white, their own special colours. From satin tea cosies and dollies to hankies and purses, all embroidered with Suffrage slogans. Hours of painstaking work by dedicated bands of sewers and embroiderers, knitters and lacemakers. Everywhere was the motif of a trumpeting white angel, blowing the word 'Freedom' into the air and the purple stripe that distinguished their movement from the red bands of the other suffragists.

In the centre of the stall, on a velvet cushion, sat replicas of the special silver Holloway brooch, designed by Sylvia, with portcullis and chains to honour those who had got themselves arrested. Vinnie had not yet earned this honour but it was on her list. She watched the crowds stroll past and soaked up the atmosphere of celebration and excitement. This was the stuff to give the troops! This sense of being all one big happy family. This is where I belong, at the heart of all the bustle and excitement, she thought. Vinnie sat back, legs aching with weariness, back throbbing and stomach rumbling. She had been far too busy to feel hunger pangs before. This is where I belong, right here and now, she decided. I wish this afternoon would go on forever.

The stall holder returned refreshed and Vinnie reluctantly left her post. She drifted to the other end of the Exhibition Hall where a group of ex-prisoners displayed a realistic prison cell, complete with woman occupant waiting silently in her dark prison garb. Vinnie found herself shivering at the thought of what one must endure in such a place and vowed to steer clear of martyrdom if she could. Prison was a depressing prospect on such a festive occasion but she must endure it one day if she was to belong properly.

When the prisoner had gathered a crowd she gave them a conducted tour of her tiny cell and painted a bleak picture of life inside it which Vinnie was in no mind to hear. It dampened the mood in this corner but was good for soliciting funds.

Since her first visit to London three years ago, Vinnie had become a member of the entourage of artists and designers who kept the Votes for Women campaign in the public eye. Life in London was full of impromptu meetings, rallies in parks, processions, helping in the office at Clement's Inn on the Strand, or making costumes for tableaux and plays, rehearsals and revues. And there were always dignitaries to entertain or show around campaign headquarters. Vinnie was loving every minute of it.

At weekends she often stayed with Frederick and Emmeline Pethick Lawrence, generous benefactors to the Cause. Stays in their country mansion in Sussex reminded her of that far away life of her childhood, before her fall from grace. There were dinners and soirées with interesting guests and titled supporters, nightly jaunts to clubs in the Mall. Occasionally there would be expeditions to throw stones, write chalk messages or daub slogans in paint. London was now ablaze with Suffragette fervour.

Christabel Pankhurst and her mother were gracious hostesses too; so charming, and so well-connected in Society. Sylvia's friends were more Bohemian, artistic and very Socialist in their principles. Her liaison with Keir Hardie was discreet; Vinnie was one of the few who really knew the score. She noticed that Sylvia distanced herself from the other sisters at times, and worried that this might be blocking Vinnie's own progress at court.

Annie Kenney, the millworker from Oldham, was the real key to success with Christabel. Since that first escapade in Manchester, in 1905 when Annie had showed such fierce loyalty to the Pankhurst family, going to prison with Christabel for the Cause that she was cruelly nicknamed 'Christabel's blotting paper', and would keep any other courtiers at bay if she felt they were growing too demanding. Vinnie was not making much headway in the movement. Sometimes she wondered if she had made the right alliance but quickly dismissed the thought. Today had been far too exciting and exhausting for her to end it worrying about politics.

Suffragettes were now the toast of the town, especially since breaking away from the mainstream Suffrage Societies and the Socialist Party. They were stirring up the government with their constant demands for a hearing. Vinnie loved to watch the blubber-faced politicians, eyes bulging with venom, spitting and spluttering as women hurled eggs and flour and unfurled their banners at election meetings. She was part of the gang who stalked Winnie

Churchill at every meeting. 'Hell hath no fury . . .' She smiled to herself.

She paused at a stall selling political games: 'How to Get out of Jail'; 'Pankasqith – the table game which plots a path from parlour to Parliament past fifty obstacles'. Then there was 'Panko', the card game, boxes of jigsaws, pretty stationery and postcards. She must buy something to remind herself of this wonderful day. Dear Sylvia's influence was everywhere. Such a stroke of genius to create merchandise for women which made the articles talking points for their propaganda. She smiled to herself. I'll buy one of these games and send it to Lord Dunscar for Christmas, she decided. I wonder if he even remembers my name?

She rummaged through the garment stall where there was even tricolour underwear for sale. How many husbands, laundry women, lady's maids, would wonder why the lady of the house was suddenly sprouting striped drawers and camisoles? No opportunity was to be missed. Vinnie bought herself a purple satin petticoat appliquéd with bands of green and white ribbon.

There were piles of the *Votes for Women* magazines stacked high, printed by their own Women's Press, with advertisers clamouring to sell safety belts and muff chains, Christmas cards and fancy goods, in their Shopping Directory. She flicked through the latest edition with amusement. Every London store, from Derry & Toms to Fortnum & Mason, was advertising tea gowns and teapots, teaspoons, and even their own special brands of Suffrage tea.

Then Vinnie spied the crush at the craft stall and rolled up her sleeves to relieve the besieged stallholder who was running out of paper bags and loose change.

From her vantage point behind the table she caught a glimpse of the Pankhurst family and their entourage touring the stalls: the mother, Emmeline, tall and elegant in a white gown trimmed with a regal purple appliquéd border of leaves and flowers which swept the ground as she moved from stall to stall; Christabel looking like a bride in purest white silk tussore; and Adela, the youngest of the sisters, parading behind in a broderie anglaise leg-o'-mutton-sleeved blouse and matching overskirt. So simple, so impressive. Poor Sylvia, who was still supervising the displays, had forgotten to remove her splattered smock and looked slightly dishevelled amongst her family. Suddenly the Pankhursts surrounded Vinnie's stall.

'Wonderful! Well done, Lavinia. Aren't you the clever one? I hope you haven't strained poor Sylvia's eyes too much, with all that stencilling . . . Congratulations, there must have been so much to do!' Christabel cast a concerned eye over her sister in the distance.

'She will have to rest up after all this. We don't want her headaches coming back do we, Mama?' Christabel was so close that Vinnie could almost feel the coolness of her porcelain complexion which was always a joy to behold. No wonder she radiated such confidence, such a glow of conviction in those steely eyes as they fixed upon Lavinia.

'I'm glad we've caught you on your own. Annie and I have been thinking that we need to rally our support up

North. If there's another Election we need to pin down those Members of Parliament who will back a Franchise Bill, give them our support and root out any false promises, don't you think? We want to make things hot for Winnie Churchill when he returns to secure his seat. You're a Lancashire lass from Manchester, I hear?'

'Not really . . .' Vinnie tried to stem the flow.

'Well, near enough for our purposes. You could spearhead a campaign there, stir things up for a while. The usual stuff . . . perhaps poach any waverers from the Suffrage Society, shake up their troops. Liaise where you can with them, but we need something big to happen up there.'

'But I'm out of touch now. It's been years since . . .'

'Nonsense, you'll be wonderful! Annie will give you plenty of back up. She speaks the lingo, don't you?' Annie Kenney blushed and nodded obediently.

'But . . .'

'No buts, Lavinia Shaw. Deeds not words! Remember our motto.' The voice trailed away as her party glided off towards the next stall. Vinnie felt her shoulders sagging, her calves aching and the beginnings of a headache.

The train chugged slowly out of Victoria Station in Manchester. Vinnie discarded her *Votes for Women* magazine and gazed with a sigh out on to the dismal back streets, the soot and the grime of the Salford scenery. Why me? Why did they have to pick on me, just when it was all going so well, just when I was beginning to belong? How will I survive? How can I go back there again? Trust me to do my job too well, get myself noticed as Sylvia's aide-de-camp! There was always tension between those sisters and their mother, each one vying for her attention. Now I'm being shunted out of the way to make a place for one of Christabel's henchmen.

Vinnie felt abandoned, expelled from the sunlight to smelly lodgings and smoking factories, living reluctantly among Socialist women who all seemed so earnest and so drably worthy. Women who resented all the fuss about the strict dress code, uniform and fancy accessories of the WSPU.

'A tin badge and a sash'll do us fine. We can't afford fripperies – not like them hoydens down South with their allowances and fancy incomes. They don't have to earn a living in the real world. You'll have to fend for yourself, young woman. We shall be questioning your expenses if they get out of hand.'

It had been hard in the last few weeks to summon up any enthusiasm for meetings and raiding parties, for checking on backsliders and those recently out of jail. Now that the hunger strikes were taking their toll, the released prisoners were often sick and demoralised. It was Vinnie's duty to find them a respite billet in the country and keep tabs on their welfare. How could she shine in such a dull setting? It was so boring . . . boring! How she craved the excitement of being back in the thick of operations, but that meant getting herself back to Clement's Inn.

Vinnie knew the score. She must do as she was told for now. Christabel Pankhurst ran the show. One step out of line and she'd be frozen out of favour with one icy stare from the Snow Queen's eye. 'La Belle Dame Sans Merci', that was Christabel. There was never a second chance for the disobedient. Oh, no! Total loyalty or else. So she'd have to stick it out and go where she was paid to: Liverpool, Preston, Burnley, wherever.

The Cause was her family, and families made demands. Since poor Harry Pankhurst's sudden death in the spring, pitching all of them into the depths of gloom, the devotees at court were constantly changing; some idealists, some martyrs, some hardened feminists. Vinnie knew she was none of these. Nor was she a vapid hanger on or mere socialite, playing at being a Suffragette. No, she wanted her place in the sun, to prove herself in some way. Here was a chance to take part in the making of history, of that she was certain. She was also making some useful social contacts, and who knew where that might lead in the future? But life was no longer one great party for Vinnie. How she longed to be back in the Exhibition Hall again!

I can't let them down, she mused, and peered out of the window, hoping for some inspiration as the train drew into Trinity Street Station. She saw the roof pillars painted in the LMS colours, and remembered the escapade with John Sturges. Her stomach churned like a butter tub as she alighted. This was the last town on earth in which to raise her standard!

Chapter Nine

Sophie watched the woman sitting by the window of the upstairs tea room, gazing out on to the Town Hall Square and making notes in a leatherbound notepad. What was she up to? Women did not usually write notes in Mullarkey's Fish Restaurant, not unless they were journalists or poets perhaps, and not even then with such intense concentration. This woman was smoking openly, one after another, with long deep drags, relishing the stares and disapproving tuts of the other customers in the room.

Sophie decided she was definitely not a local or from the provinces at all. Everything about her was out of keeping with her surroundings, from the colours of her purple three-quarter-length jacket to her heather tweed straight skirt. It was far too vibrant, fresh and stylish to be bought locally. Not for her the conventional broad-brimmed bucket hat. She had plonked on her head a sort of tam o'shanter bonnet, plumed with three feathers in white, green and purple; set at right angles in a defiant cockinga-snook sort of way. Her soft frizzled hair was certainly bobbed, and too pink to be natural, draped like curtains over her ears, and caught in a loose tuft in a tortoiseshell buckle. She wore a straight fringe, not a 'band' of tight corkscrew curls, Queen Alexandra fashion. Bun Gran would call her 'fast' or 'quality'; well turned out but definitely 'forward'. The skirt revealed a stretch of firm calves encased in lilac wool stockings and neat buttoned court shoes in grey leather.

'Don't see many like her in here,' said Bridie with curiosity as she wound up a steaming plate of pie and chips from the lift hatch in the wall. Sophie nodded, admiring the casual but effective way each garment toned with the next.

The same woman came in several times alone and a few weeks later was joined by a group of serious-faced ladies who sat pointing eagerly towards the grand entrance steps to the Town Hall itself, whispering and arguing, smoking, and drawing plans on paper. Sophie was bursting to know why the Town Hall was getting all this attention. She hovered indecently close, trying to catch the drift of their whispers, pretending to clear away crockery, dawdling purposely as the group rose to leave, almost shoving her into the table in their rush to catch a train.

The tam-o'-shanter woman sat back and stretched her arms as if in relief as she stared out on to the street again. It was full of omnibuses, tram cars and dray carts, with the odd motor vehicle chugging slowly among the traffic.

Sophie herself stopped to look out of the window, and smiled. 'It's a right grand building, is that!'

The henna-haired woman continued gathering her writing paper and pad, ignoring the comment, but then she paused, eyeing Sophie carefully. 'Not a bad design, same architect as Leeds and Portsmouth actually. A few too many lions and steps for me. Do you live here?'

'Nay! This is Bridie and Frank Mullarkey's establishment, not mine. I wait on. It's better than the mill,' added Sophie on the spur of the moment.

'Yes, I can imagine. Still the mill women seem to be fighting back these days, and the Lancashire ones are a force to be reckoned with. Turning out the finest cottons in the Empire, so they say,' said the stranger politely.

'When I were at Berisford's Mill, near Lever Street, I were the rep for the Spinners' and Weavers' Association. That were a job and a half, speaking out in front of all them men.'

'Really? Did you have anything to do with the Petitions for Suffrage?' The woman moved closer.

'Didn't I just! What a do! Standing on them cobbles, bawlin' me head off for Miss Roper and her cronies!' Sophie laughed.

'You know Esther Roper and her friend, Eva Gore Booth?'

'Only met Miss Roper the twice. She helped us start up a Suffrage Society.'

'Are you still involved or have you joined the Women's

Socialist and Political Union?' The woman pointed to an enamel badge on her lapel.

'Does it matter?'

'Of course it does if you want to see something done about it all! It's time the Northern women stopped faffing around and made themselves useful. Got themselves noticed. Hell! Thirty thousand women bothered to sign a petition – and where did it get us? I'm Miss Shaw, by the way, from the Manchester branch of the WSPU, a full-time worker for the Cause.' Vinnie stretched out her hand.

'Mrs Seddon Knowles. Pleased to meet you. I've noticed you here a few times recently.' On closer inspection, Sophie was struck by Miss Shaw's firm grip and the energy of the woman's quick movements. Her face was animated as she listened, reflecting her every thought. With her firm jaw and slightly protuberant eyes, fair eyebrows and long lashes, the effect was dramatic rather than attractive. Yet Sophie recalled that same guarded expression on a bird of prey, glimpsed in a cage at a travelling show, the hooded eyelids and piercing eyes, a stare both guarded and compelling.

Vinnie dug into her briefcase and pulled out a pamphlet. 'Here's a leaflet listing our activities. We need to meet your lot soon. We're going to need everyone's support in this town. This local lot, are they sound or all sales of work and debates with the Lady Liberals?' The contemptuous edge to her voice was hard to ignore.

'We do our best,' Sophie bristled.

'I see. So it's softly, softly, don't rock our boat?'

'I suppose so.'

'Righty ho. See if you can fix for me to attend your next meeting. I'm sure I can inject a little enthusiasm into them. God Almighty! A General Election coming is just the time to stir up the debate. You know Winnie Churchill's on his way North?' Sophie shook her head. 'Good heavens! Make that meeting soon. No time to lose. Here's my card. London or Manchester or Leeds – who knows where tomorrow will find me? Try and fix it for the end of the month. I need to do another recce.'

'Why?' Sophie could not resist asking.

The woman pressed her fingers to her lips. 'All in good time, Mrs Knowles. At the meeting.' And dashing down the stairs into the street, she almost knocked a tray out of Bridie's hand.

'What a madam! What were you gassin' to her about?'

'Would you believe it? She's one of them Panks from London. Wants to meet our Committee. Did you know Mr Churchill was comin' to town?'

'Now what's he got to do with anything, bejasus!'

Sophie described all she had noticed about the group who'd met Miss Shaw.

Bridie peered at the card. 'To be sure, those lassies looked out o' place. The dining room of The Swan Hotel's more their style than a fish tea.'

'They're up to summat and she wants us to join them. Can you see our lot ganging up with them "Pankies"?' asked Sophie.

Bridie shook her head. 'Not really. Frank won't want

trouble on his doorstep, and neither will Dr Wagstaff's wife nor the Vicar's daughter.'

'But, Bridie, if we really want the Vote, we'll have to make a bit more of a fuss than we have.'

'Yes, but not *here*! In Manchester perhaps, or Parliament, but not here. I think it's too risky. You can't get up to high jinks on your own doorstep. 'Tis against the rules.'

Sophie plonked herself down with a sigh. 'I'm sure it won't come to that but we must tell Grace and organise a meeting.'

She fingered the white card with its purple and green edging. She had taken to the hawk-eyed woman with her fighting talk. It had released her own pent-up excitement, loosened a catch within her. She would stir their complacency with a challenge. 'Fancy her being in with them Pankhursts, Annie Kenney and yon big Flora Drummond!'

'We don't want their cronies on our doorstep, banging their war drums, Phia.'

'I think we already have them!' came the reply.

'This woman has certainly got you all fired up,' laughed Grace Thompson as she heaved the last of the autumn dahlias out of the Vicarage flower bed. 'You walked all this way to tell me about her designs on Mr Churchill in our Town Hall?'

'I just thought you'd be interested. We have to plan our own Election campaign, surely?'

'I thought we'd agreed to debate with all the political

parties and write to each election candidate to see if they support Women's Suffrage?'

'We've done that every time and still they keep stalling us or waffle from their fence. They'll never jump down.'

'Then we'll write to the press and raise questions.'

'Why not attend the hustings and force a debate?'

'Yes, dear, we could, but they would think we were disruptives and not let us in.'

'So?'

'Look, we've been through all this before, Sophie. *We* stand for the due process of the law, not violence or civil disobedience.'

'Aye, but there is another way. We need to air that washing in the breeze.'

'If you say so. I'll speak to Dora and Ada and we'll ask your Miss Shaw to address the monthly meeting in the "any other business" bit. Will that satisfy your impatience?' Grace smiled as if humouring a child. Sophie was watching the Reverend Thompson shuffle through the kitchen door into the sunshine.

'Good day, Reverend!'

'You remember Sophie, Papa?'

'Indeed I do, the other half of that unholy alliance!' He chuckled to himself, remembering. 'Is your father still beating his Socialist drums?'

'As loud as ever, but th'owd hands is getting shaky. Who do you think will win the Election this time?'

'Oh, I never discuss my politics, do I, Grace? I have my views and she has hers. I can never understand all this fuss about women wanting to soil their hands with ballot papers when they are already fully represented by their fathers and husbands. We know what is best for you. You ladies are far too emotional and unpredictable to warrant such decision-making. It would be bad for your health.'

Sophie's jaw dropped six inches.

'Don't believe a word!' Grace intervened. 'The old rascal knows how to provoke us. Look at that twinkle in his eye! Our time is coming, Papa, just you wait and see. There's more to life than the General Election.

'He knows that I've been asked to stand for election on to the Board of Guardians for the Poor House, and we have got permission at last to start a Welfare Clinic in the Co-op Hall, for poor mothers and babies. Now that's what I call progress, without getting bogged down in politics. We can achieve on a small scale. The Vote won't come yet. They'll all turn their backs on us again.

'Don't look like that, Sophie, all doom and gloom. We'll take it all to the meeting and vote on it. At least we operate democratically, which is more than can be said for the Panks. I gather it is "do as we say or heave ho" there. Esther Roper and her friend received the cold shoulder, and Teresa Billington's crowd have gone their separate way from them with the Women's Franchise League. Take my word for it, your Miss Shaw's lot are trouble. Now come on inside and have some tea.'

Grace lit a bonfire of prunings when Sophie left for her long trek back to Plover Street. The sun was setting low behind the hedge, throwing deep shadows across the lawn.

Grace shivered. She had never seen her friend so agitated about an Election before. It was as if suddenly all her energy was focused, like a shaft of fierce heat. Whoever this Manchester woman was, she had made a deep impression. For herself, she would wait and meet this formidable woman face to face, see for herself. Only then would she be able to judge her. But the surname of Shaw troubled her, surely it couldn't possibly be Lavinia?

The October Suffrage meeting was well underway in Mullarkey's upstairs room when the stranger rang the bell and was ushered up the stairs. All eyes turned at her arrival. She apologised and sat down on the seat Sophie had reserved for her, quickly surveying the scene. As she'd thought, the home team was fielding a front line of middle-aged forwards: plain, wholesome, and totally predictable in their crisp white shirts, ropes of pearls and overlong cardigans. To the back sat the clog and shawl brigade.

'Sorry I'm late, train held up,' she lied, knowing her lateness was entirely her own fault. She peered at the trio sitting behind the table at the front, and looked again.

'Thank you. We'll come to your business later,' said a stalwart with gold-rimmed spectacles and cadaverous face. Vinnie stared closer.

'Good God! Is that Dizzy Dora and her henchmen?' she whispered to Sophie.

'Why, yes,' came the reply.

'Hell's bells! I'm for it now,' she gulped. Grace stood up again.

'As I was saying, we are hoping to give the Co-operative Women's Guild some help with buying weighing scales and baby blankets for the new Clinic. It has been suggested by one of our members that we concoct a *Suffrage Cookbook* containing a collection of favourite recipes from the cooks amongst us. It will raise our profile and help boost the kitty. Any comments on this suggestion, ladies?'

'Pardon me,' said the newly arrived, 'this is the local Suffrage Society? I am at the right meeting?' Vinnie got to her feet.

'Yes, of course, Miss Shaw.' Grace stared at her again.

'Yes, it *is* me – Lavinia Shaw, back from the grave. So what have cookery books and Co-op Guild matters to do with a Suffrage Society agenda?'

'Many of the members here tonight belong to both,' answered Grace coolly.

'But surely it's the job of this society to get women the Vote, not sell cookery books or divert valuable time away from urgent matters, Madam Chairman?' Vinnie waved her agenda paper in the air.

'They are all connected, as you will see, Miss Shaw. And it is Miss Chairman. You can have your say later.' Grace sat down slowly, trying not to let her voice tremble.

'How do you know Grace?' Sophie pulled at Lavinia's skirt, hoping she would sit down and relieve the tension in the air.

'It's a long story. I think you'd better ask her yourself and see what she says. Still a sourpuss,' she added, loudly enough for others to turn round in disapproval. Sophie sank back into her own chair with embarrassment. Lavinia smiled around her as she sat down again, content to have caused a stir. The business was duly completed and Grace announced in a muffled voice the name of their visiting speaker, eyes never leaving her glass of water on the table.

'I call upon Miss Lavinia Shaw, formerly of this town, to address the meeting for a few minutes.'

'I don't know about a few minutes! I'll finish when I've said my piece and made the train fare from Manchester worthwhile,' said the woman in the floppy beret, adorned with feathers in Union colours which trailed down her green velvet cloak.

'Ladies, I am here to call you to arms. Yes, to a battle which will be waged here on your very doorstep. In six weeks' time we estimate our adversary, Winston Churchill, will address a meeting in the Town Hall. We have inside information. We of the WSPU seek to engage all our allied sisters in the struggle to secure justice for women as a central issue in the Election debate. As you may know, we, the Union, have withdrawn our support from all candidates, yes, even the Labour ones, unless they give us a promise in writing to press our case to its logical conclusion. It is time for actions, ladies, not cooking or flying kites. Time for the women of this town to rise as one and stand firm behind us when we make our protest. Don't just suffer as Suffragists, get with the real Suffragettes! Let us share this nickname together.'

Vinnie paused to assess the response. The room was silent, stunned, but definitely still listening.

'I know that you Lancashire women have a proud record of achievement when it comes to raising petitions, but that was years ago. Hundreds of thousands of names, on miles of paper. And where has it got us? Now is the time to strike out on the march for freedom, for our children and their daughters too. Let no mother here tonight be ashamed to tell her daughter that she must stay classed with imbeciles, infants and criminals, still not worthy of the Vote, all because she was too timid to get off her own backside and fight!

'Sisters, I know we have our differences but if I convince one of you tonight to give us your full support, then my long journey will have been worthwhile. Are there just a few sisters here who will show what they are made of? Deeds not words! That is our motto. Our way is effective but it is at no small cost. Already there are martyrs to our cause, frail women broken by their starving bodies but not by their deeds.

'Please think about what I say. The time for debate is over. Thank you for letting me speak to you. I will happily answer any questions.'

Grace got straight to her feet. 'We must thank Miss Shaw for her forthright views. As she so rightly points out, they do conflict with the policy of our Suffrage Society. We do not nor ever will call ourselves "Suffragettes". As everyone here well knows, her Union broke away from us on these points three years ago. My understanding of the Pankhurst regime is that it is not one for bothering with elected Committees itself.'

'If I might just query that point?' Vinnie was on her feet.

'You have had your say, thank you.'

'Just a minute, Miss Chairman!' Sophie stood alongside her guest. 'I am very surprised that the usual courtesies are not being offered to our visitor tonight. Surely there are one or two questions to debate?'

Dora Wagstaff looked at Grace and spoke quietly. 'I'm sure, Mrs Knowles, we do not wish to offend the last speaker. It has been many years since we last had Miss Shaw's company. We mustn't hold her up if she has a train to catch, must we, Miss Thompson?'

'Does anyone have a question?' Grace thundered.

'I do,' replied Sophie, astonished at the fire in her belly. 'I would like to ask the speaker just what the Union has in mind for Mr Churchill's visit? Then we can debate whether we should support such a venture or not.'

Vinnie Shaw smiled as she acknowledged where her support lay. 'Thank you, Mrs Knowles. We simply intend to demonstrate along the route from the station. Nothing violent; a peaceful show of strength with placards and banners, the usual stuff. There'll be no trouble.'

Two or three heads nodded approvingly. There was a hubbub of chatter as each turned to her neighbour to discuss the proposal. Grace banged her gavel on the desk.

'Ladies, please. If you have any comments, address the chair.'

Ada Norris rose from her seat.

'I can't see why those members who wish to show their

support for a peaceful demonstration cannot attend the event in their own right as citizens without jeopardising this society.'

Sophie raised her hand. 'I would like to second Miss Norris's proposal. I think it should be left to the individual's conscience. So long as there is no violent action, where's the harm?' The proposal was duly passed on the general nod, Dora and Grace abstaining.

'Well done, you certainly gave Miss Stiff 'n' Starchy something to think about. What a cold fish she's become!' whispered Vinnie as the meeting broke up.

'She's not normally like that. Grace is my oldest friend. You mustn't judge her. She'll come round to our view when you talk to her alone.'

'I must dash, actually. But I couldn't have hoped for more from you. This leaves the field open for us to gather support for other things now.'

'What other things?' asked Sophie.

'The Preston gang have a meeting in a month. Gather who you can from this bunch and we'll see what we can cook up for your recipe book! I shall tell Christabel Pankhurst about you.'

'Never! Do you know her?'

'Of course. I work under her orders at all times. Strong leadership is best when there's a war on!'

Sophie did not know whether to be flattered or flummoxed. Somehow she had been roped into yet another meeting. Grace came forward looking tetchy, her cheekbones flushed with colour.

'Good evening, Lavinia, it's been a long time.'

'Good evening, Grace, I did not expect to see you here.'

'No, I didn't expect you'd choose to return and meet your old school friends but you've made one convert tonight, it appears. Sophie, I would like a word with you. In private.' She yanked her away from the guest into the upstairs kitchen but Vinnie followed behind silently, observing the two of them rattling tea cups on to trays with bowed heads.

'I hope you know what you're letting yourself in for with that woman? Lavinia Shaw starts arguments in an empty room. Can't you see she's a troublemaker? Her sort don't play games, you know. They court danger, embrace prison sentences for the attention their hunger striking brings. Nothing is too mad for them to try, so long as it makes newsprint.'

'Honestly, Grace, I don't know why you're getting so steamed up. Miss Shaw's troops will make things happen, that's all. She's been sent from the top brass.'

'Oh, she'll make things happen all right. She'll set the fuse and light the touch paper then scarper like she did last time.'

'What last time?' Sophie asked, but Grace, catching sight of Vinnie, shook her head.

'Never you mind. It's past history now, but she's not to spoil our hard work.'

'How can she spoil what we are doing? Strikes me, we'll be doing that for us selves. We need a bit of a shake out, we've been getting a mite too cosy.'

'Since when?' snorted Grace. '*I've* not noticed anything.'

'Happen you've seen nowt 'cos you're that busy with the Baby Clinic and gettin' yerself elected on t'Board.'

'So that's what this is all about, is it? I'm not pulling my weight here now?'

'That's not what I said . . .'

'I think it's what you're hinting at,' Grace replied stiffly. Sophie stood her ground, conscious of her audience.

'You're right, Miss Shaw, about one thing. About us losing sight of our aim. The Welfare Clinic is Guild business. The Suffrage Society has other fish to fry.'

'Perhaps I'd better resign?' snapped Grace.

'Oh, get off that high horse of yours. Don't be like that!'

'Like what, pray?'

'Sulking like our Phyllis when she can't have her own way!'

'How dare you say that to me, of all people?'

'See, you're in high dudgeon again. All of a tremor. You're taking this too personally. I'm just telling you how I see things. No need to start the Boer War all over again!'

'I see.' Grace drew herself up to her full height and brushed past her friend with an icy stare, pausing by the silent onlooker. Sophie called after her: 'Don't be vexed with me. I think this demonstration will do us all good.'

'Don't expect me to come. I'll not be party to this woman's little show,' replied Grace with a sniff.

'Do come, please. You'll see. Won't she, Miss Shaw?' pleaded Sophie, looking to the stranger for support.

Grace turned her back on them both and stumbled out into the noisy room, eyes brimful of hot tears, not seeing at all.

'You certainly trod on her corns,' laughed Vinnie, taking Sophie by the arm. 'We don't need her sort to slow us down!'

'The cheek of her, Ada, turning up as if nothing had happened and taking over our meeting as if she was in command.' Snip went the first stem from Grace's rose bush. 'How dare she come touting round for temporary lodgings from us? Well, she won't be sleeping under *my* roof, that's for certain.' Snip went the second, third and fourth as she marched down the row. 'Who does she think she is? I'm not fooled, not for one minute.' Snip, snip went the secateurs as Ada grabbed her wrist.

'I've heard about autumn pruning but you've just hacked that poor rose to pieces.'

'Too bad it isn't Johnny Sturges's precious specimen. It's all his fault. That blessed Lavinia! I always did think her name reminded me of cheap scent! And to cap it all, have you seen the letter in the *Evening News*? Some pompous idiot in my Ward states his objections to me, as mere womankind, standing for election to the Board. Have you seen the list of his snide remarks?' spluttered Grace.

'I think you and I need a strong brew of tea. It's getting nippy out here and my joints are giving me gip.' Ada steered her friend down the path to the kitchen table where the local paper was folded at the Letters column.

'Lord give me strength! Look at this drivel. I shall have to reply at once. How can I ever be elected when people write this about me?' A distracted Grace wafted the paper before Ada's face.

'Calm down. We'll go through his arguments, point by point, construct a dignified reply. You're too het up now to answer anything. Rest inside and we can concentrate on using this piece of bigotry to your advantage, right?'

Ada sipped her tea as Grace read out the letter. Finally Ada commented: 'If someone has gone to the trouble of foul-mouthing you, you can be sure they're worried about your chances of success. We can tear this to pieces politely and you will get some free publicity. What does it say again?' Grace knew it off by heart by now.

' "At the risk of being described as ungallant, I have to ask our electors to make sure that all three male candidates in this Ward are elected Guardians. I hold that the interests of women are not neglected by administrative bodies consisting entirely of men." '

'First point then. Reply that only women can best attend to the interests of females; the girl orphans, meals and provisions for mothers and babies, the needs of elderly incontinent ladies in the workhouse. List them all, go on.'

' "In the male candidates, the ratepayers have Guardians who are lovers of their work and have the leisure, without the domestic ties which embarrass women, to perform the duties required of them." '

'Stop there. You must say something about being a single person of independent means, with few domestic duties and no paid employment. Making you amply suited to the dedication of your leisure to the above task.'

'And anyway, who is it who creates the domestic tasks which embarrass women – the washing of their blessed shirts and the minding of their children? We all know!'

'You can't put that in. It'll get their backs up. Play them at their own game, Grace. What comes next then?'

'You'll never believe this. "It is my considered opinion that women are, as a whole, too indifferent to what happens outside their domestic life, to take a prominent part in public work."'

'Good! Go to town on that one, wipe the floor with him. He's asked for it! Start with the Royal Princesses. Were they indifferent to public work? Is our present Queen Alexandra indifferent, were Florence Nightingale or Elizabeth Fry? List all the pioneers of public service you can think of. What an insult to half the adult population, to presume, because we take our duties in the home seriously, we can have no interests outside! List all the women teachers, nurses, doctors. Give him the full works. Bang each of his arguments down like ducks in a shooting gallery. Then bring in your own big guns.

'What about how women elsewhere have given balance to the Board, add a different perspective to decision-making? Tell them who your sponsors are. Dora's husband carries some clout, and so does Lord Dunscar!'

'Ada Norris, you're a diamond among coal.' Grace dashed into the study to find a pencil to write down all the arguments before they disappeared in the chaos of her overactive mind.

In the following weeks Ada found herself in the middle of a frenzy of preparations for the Election campaign on all sides. It was as if Vinnie Shaw's presence had fractured the group into different parties.

Grace spent all her waking time canvassing in the district for her own election to the Workhouse Board. Dora Wagstaff and her crew were busy organising the new Welfare Clinic, posting up handbills and writing articles in the paper, setting up the rooms for the opening day – only to be thwarted by a pea souper of a fog which choked the streets and prevented any mothers from venturing forth with newborn babies. They were all too distracted to take any interest in the General Election itself. Ada found herself somewhere in the middle of a busy school term with all the excitement of the Christmas preparations to come, carols to learn and a Nativity play to rehearse, plus examinations to adjudicate.

Vinnie stood in the fish shop doorway, peering out into the gloom, her scarf muffling her mouth. Only the faintest golden glimmer of gaslight was visible across the Town Hall Square; the streets were eerily silent and she did not fancy the long trek back to Manchester in such a pea souper. She huddled into her thick coat and prepared to walk.

'You can't go back in this,' said Sophie with concern,

catching her arm. 'Come back to Plover Street and we'll find you a perch to lie on. You'll have to take us as you find us, though.'

A perch it was, like trying to sleep on a bed of slate, with no privacy, crushed against Phyllis who tossed and turned and woke at dawn, demanding the stranger in her bed should read her a story. Vinnie could not wait to get dressed. There was no bathroom, no toilet, and only a smoking fire which spluttered limply. How could women like Sophie bear to live in such shabby surroundings? The old woman downstairs grumbled at the extra mouth to feed and barked orders at everyone like a sergeant major. There was no standing on ceremony in this house. Even her solitary digs in Levenshulme were preferable to this cramped little terrace with its clutter of children, visitors and damp washing. If the foggy November nights continued she would have to look elsewhere for lodgings. She needed privacy and a bit more comfort. The hints she had dropped at each meeting were falling on deaf ears. There had been no offers so it was time to take matters into her own hands and force the issue. There was only one port of call left, one safe place to harbour her over the next month while the campaign meetings were focused around this town.

She rang the bell, waited for the light to go on down the passageway and arranged her face into an approximation of a this-is-me-at-the-end-of-my-tether expression.

'Miss Norris, dear Ada, I hate to do this to you but needs must . . . Can you possibly put me up for a few days? It's vital I stay in touch with you all over the next few weeks. I can pay you some board, if you need it? I'm sure you rattle around in this old school house like a pea in a drum. We single ladies should stick together.' Vinnie plonked down her bags in the hall and walked in as if she owned the place.

'It's freezing out there, not fit to throw a cat out! Where shall I put my stuff? It's been so awful travelling on the train alone. I don't feel safe. I know you wouldn't want to let Sophie down. She tried to accommodate me, but . . . well, you've seen her poor place, not an inch of spare space for a temporary lodger.' Vinnie unpinned her hat and handed it to the woman who stood with gaping mouth as she watched the visitor inspect her house, hang up her clothing and place a large leather valise at the foot of the stairs.

'You can show me where everything is later. Let's make you a cup of tea just to show you how grateful I am.' Vinnie smiled warmly in an attempt to thaw the frozen look of surprise on Ada Norris's face.

It was the most misaligned of faces, as if each half had collided over the bridge of the nose and gone off in a huff in the opposite direction, quite fascinating to observe. Poor woman, thought Vinnie. If I had a face like that I'd never be seen out in daylight. She felt the warm glow of doing this unfortunate a favour in bestowing her presence.

'I'm sure we can come to an amicable arrangement. It will do you good to have my company. We old maids can get so set in our routines. It will be so helpful to the Cause if I don't have to worry about meals when I come in from meetings. No travelling late at night, lots of warm baths, hot buttered toast and crumpets for supper. How cosy we will be together . . .'

Vinnie flopped down with a sigh, draping herself over the sofa like a loose cover and toasted her calf-skin boots on the fender, her eyes raking in all the hand-sewn furnishings and polished mahogany, the gleaming brasses and smell of fresh baking. This was a much better billet.

'Isn't this cosy?' She sank back into the cushions. 'There, I feel at home already.'

'What's for tea?' called a shrill voice as Ada crawled through the door the very next afternoon, laden with marking.

'Haven't you bought anything in?' she yelled back in exasperation. The coal bucket was empty, the fire almost out, the dishes were unwashed and Lady Muck was lolling over mother's favourite chair, shoes kicked off, reading her *Votes for Women* magazine. Vinnie poured out excuses like weak tea.

'I've been dashed off my feet today, and I've got another meeting coming up later, and a letter to write to Sylvia and Christabel.' As if Ada cared with whom she was corresponding! But Vinnie liked to scatter famous names about like loose change. 'When I was in London we used to have tea with Keir Hardie, and do you know? The Duchess of Derwent gave me a diamond brooch to auction – placed it in my very hands. You walk into the Pethick Lawrences' drawing room and you never know who you'll be dining with . . .'

To cap it all she had arranged one of her interminable

preparation meetings for the coming demonstration to be held at the school house, without even a by your leave to Ada who sat there fuming, knowing there were a thousand and one jobs she needed to attend to that evening.

How this woman ruled the roost! One minute charming but cool, then suddenly puffed up with her own importance, all gas and hot air, fanning the flames. Ada wondered, when shove came to push, whether Miss Shaw would crack in the firing. She herself was counting the weeks to December when this guest would hopefully move on, for if their dinner was anything to go by, she would eat Ada out of house and home with her hearty appetite.

Having a lodger was making it awkward to entertain her own friends. Grace would have nothing to do with Lavinia and made it plain to Sophie that this Pank was no longer welcome at any Suffrage meetings. Grace continued to act as if the demonstration was not about to happen, and there was a distinct chill in the air. Sophie went out of her way to be awkward and kept reminding them of the event.

Ada lay awake at night, thinking: Why do I feel so guilty for being slap-bang in the middle? As if it was my fault? Why do I feel so uneasy? Is it because I foresee trouble? I must distance myself from any repercussions. My resignation would be expected if I stepped out of line in any demonstration. Doesn't Miss Shaw understand that my hands are tied? I can't afford to lose my home or my income, just to satisfy her demands.

There was more being planned than a mere demonstration along the roadside, of that she was certain from the whispered hints Vinnie let slip from time to time at their meetings.

'Isn't it exciting? Suffragettes are coming from Oldham, Manchester, Burnley, Blackburn, Preston and Southport. The Preston gang will be drumming up recruits for their own Lancashire welcome to Winston Churchill as well. Edith Rigby . . . you've not met her yet . . . has ordered two Suffragettes to disguise themselves as cleaners and chat up Council officials in order to work out how to climb on to the roof then through the skylight into the auditorium. Panks are too well known in the town to receive any invitation to the meetings. Oh, this is how I like it! Deeds not words, eh, Sophie?'

Sophie would sit there, lapping up all the excitement, eyes bright with admiration. Ada feared for her protégée once that stubborn Seddon streak in her was unleashed.

'It's now or never, Ada. You have to make a stand sometime in yer life for what's right and fair. I may wash dishes for a livin' but I'll give 'em hell if they try to put one over on me again!'

'Do be careful, Sophie, you have a child and a family. What if something goes wrong and you are arrested? Have you thought of the consequences for Bert or Phyllis? If there is trouble on my doorstep, I'll have to leave this school. The managers don't hold with any political activity by women staff.'

'Oh, it won't come to that,' interrupted Vinnie Shaw. 'And if it does, we'll just have to see what mettle you're made of, won't we?' Lavinia was confident that she now had the locals eating out of her fingers and hanging on her every order like faithful retainers. Deep within her, in a dark, hidden place, she revelled in the sense of power it gave her.

Ada watched warily, hoping that with her restraining hand in evidence some of the more madcap schemes could be contained or modified. Once Vinnie was in full flight there would be no stopping her silliness. Ada shuddered to think of it. Why did that wretched woman have to come back at all?

Stone Walls Do Not A Prison Make

1909

Chapter Ten

'Where's our Phia gone now?' whined Bun Gran, wringing her hands. 'Phia!'

Bert Knowles was at his wit's end to know how to calm the fractious old woman who lay on the horsehair sofa bed, her swollen legs resting on a buffet stool.

'What's it now!' snapped Sophie, storming in from the yard with a basketful of soggy washing which she threw over the ceiling rack and draped across the fender rail. 'Someone up there's just turned the tap on and forgotten to turn it off. Couldn't you all see it was bucketing down and bring the stuff in? What's up wi' her?' Sophie wiped her dripping face on a grubby towel, looked at it in disgust and tossed it across the room.

'She can't settle, love. On about a clean night-gown in the drawer and pennies,' Bert whispered. Sophie shrugged.

'It's just her way of saying her time's up and she wants to be fettled proper now her burial money's in the Club and her laying-out stuff ready in the chest.'

'You'll put me away tidy . . . no one else is to do it. You'll sit with me right to the end like I taught you, wait till I've drawn me last, then close the curtains and give me thirty minutes to pass over before you put me on show in the parlour.'

'Give over! It's morbid, is that. I'll see you right when the time comes, but I want you to hang on a while longer. We need you up and doin', not mitherin' and mopin'. Here, help me fold these bits. They'll be damp enough to iron while I'm out at my meeting.'

'Meetin's, meetin's, all you do is meetin's. Bert, show her who wears the trousers in this house. Tell her she might as well take a pillow and sheets to them meetin's, dirty stop out! If I'd the strength, I'd tie yer skirt to the mangle. That'd fix you, lass. You should be at home with yer kiddy and yer man. He's too soft wi' you.'

Bert stood by his wife, shaking his head in frustration. 'Phylly is fine. Me and Soph is partners. I'm not her keeper. She does what she feels is right. Think on, she's a mind of her own, just like you. Born stubborn. Any road, it's my night in tonight so no nonsense, Millie Walker.' He winked and nodded to his wife to make a quick exit.

'I'm not lookin' forward to the meeting tonight. Someone's blabbed to the *Evening News*. Told them to expect hordes of screaming hooligans to storm the Town Hall. Somebody got scared, pointed the finger at the Pankhurst brigades, and scuppered our surprise for Winston Churchill.'

'Then you'd better go early and find out more,' Bert replied. 'Surely none of your friends blabbed?'

'Friends! One by one they've all been dropping out. "So sorry I can't make the demonstration meetings, I have to do the Welfare accounts." "So sorry, I have a lecture tonight." "So sorry, I have to visit the Orphanage." We're down to Annie Pilling, as was, and Ada. Even Bridie Mullarkey's back pedalling. Frank's getting funny about leasing us the room. As for Grace Thompson, we shan't see her for dust now she's got her fancy seat on the Board of Guardians!'

No wonder she was feeling snappy. There was only Vinnie Shaw to rely on these days. Gran's illness had knocked them all back. The doctor explained that her heart was not doing its job and the puffy legs were a bad sign. It was one more worry to stuff in Sophie's basket of cares. There was no denying the old woman was shrinking before her eyes; the woman who had mothered her, leathered her backside for cheeking, who was always there in the house-place, elbow deep in flour or beating hell out of the rugs. The house without her was unimaginable. Bun Gran must go on forever and ever. Amen!

Sophie shivered, wrapping Bert's muffler around her ears on the long trek past the tannery with its stench of dyed hides, then The Spindlemaker's Arms where no doubt her father was propping up the bar. Word had been sent to the family to visit Gran. Any gossip or scandal had them queuing out the yard but not one of the selfish buggers bothered to throw their hat round the door when it was a question of old age and sickness. Only Ethel called, all the way from Padiham with her latest, Doris Annie; arrived one Sunday and tired them out, Doris Annie being of the age when she put sticky fingers all over Gran's ornaments and spilled crumbs everywhere. Funny how I get lumbered with nursing, cleaning, waiting on. Walt and the wife never call. Jack's flitted to Bury so it's just muggins and Cissie to do for her now, Sophie groused to herself.

The rain was pouring down, but then it was always raining – smirring, lashing, shitting, pissing down like stair rods or sheeting down, according to how polite was the company present. So many words to describe the rain, she mused. Tonight it was the fine sort that soaked into the bones and chilled her to the core. If it was like this next week for the protest, there would be few on the streets to watch the show. At last she turned into the Town Hall Square and bumped into Grace, sheltered under a black umbrella. They smiled awkwardly.

'How's Phyllis and your gran?'

'I don't like the look of th'old 'un.'

'Should you be leaving her? This meeting can wait.'

'Bert knows where I am, thank you,' Sophie bristled.

'I didn't mean . . . I hope you don't think . . .' They reached the side entrance to the chip shop and went up the stairs. Vinnie was waiting to welcome them.

'Sophie, dear, you look like a drowned rat. Come and sit by the fireplace. Good evening, Grace.' Vinnie steered them both inside. 'Good turn out for a filthy night! Come to see the fireworks?'

'What fireworks?' said Sophie.

'Wait and see.'

Vinnie sat silently through the agenda with her head bent forward, not moving a muscle, waiting for 'any other business'. Then she sprang up, waving the *Evening News*. 'Whose clever idea was this? I might have guessed there'd be spies in this camp. All the advantage of surprise gone by one cowardly act of spite! An anonymous letter, how pathetic! Is this the best you can do?

' "I wish to inform our worthy citizens that militant Suffragettes are planning an offensive against Mr Churchill and the Liberal Government." Who has the guts to own up and tell us why?'

Grace sat at the head of the table with her head bowed but her fingers tap-tapping in agitation. Everyone glanced around suspiciously. The stubborn silence held. Ada broke its spell. 'I'm sure there's been a mistake. No one here would do such a thing. Have you contacted the paper?'

'We have and the Editor refused to reveal the name of his informant. Said it came from a local person of impeccable reputation.'

Grace rose deliberately, fidgeting with the cuff of her plaid shirt. 'I'm getting the distinct feeling that I am under suspicion here. My Liberal sympathies are well known, as are Mrs Wagstaff's and Miss Norris's for that matter. My opposition to any violent protest is also well known. I will not bore you again with my reservations. I will not deny or admit to any dealings with the press but will only say this: should any serious bother arise from next week's visit,

I will not hesitate to disassociate myself and this Suffrage Society publicly, in the newspaper or wherever, from any criminal behaviour. If this Suffrage Society chooses to uphold militant action, I will resign immediately as Chairman. I'm sure others will also follow suit.'

There was a loud burst of applause. Dora held up her hands, face blush pink. 'Ladies, please. I'm sure it won't come to that. As Minute Secretary may I remind you that I have to put down remarks from any quarter, and it is written in our constitution that we shall expel militant members from our midst. We cannot be associated with criminal violence.'

There was a pin-dropping hush; a fearful pause as if waiting for another cracker to explode. Grace stood up again like a wounded animal. 'Thank you, Madam Secretary, for reminding us that as members we do have the right to vote. May I remind Miss Shaw, whose accusations have sparked off this debate, that she is not, nor ever has been, a member of this society. She is not entitled to speak from the floor. *We* all know which membership card she carries.'

Sophie exploded her own cannon fire. 'Madam Chairman, I protest! You have deflected Miss Shaw's rightful enquiry very skilfully. The question still stands, whether from a member or not. I will take it up with you myself, as a point of principle. Did you inform the *Evening News*?'

'From the way you present the question, it seems you presume I did?'

'Did you? Answer my question, please!' pleaded Sophie, with trembling voice and legs.

'I will not stay here to answer such a question. If my honour is in doubt, I have no alternative but to quit this meeting and tender my resignation. If the Vice Chairman would be so kind as to continue in my place . . .' Grace turned to Ada Norris, gathering her handbag and spectacles. 'I will not be party to this debate, I have better things to attend to.' She pushed back her chair and left the room, followed by Dora and half a dozen from the floor; mostly Guild and Liberal Women representatives.

Sophie watched in horror the effect of her words. Her first instinct was to rush across the room and stop her friend. 'Grace, I'm so sorry. I don't believe it for one minute, please don't go!' Was this how friendships were broken? Like flour, leavened with suspicion and misunderstanding, sifted, kneaded together, festering and swelling into rottenness.

Sophie could not move. Her limbs felt as if turned to lead, her heart was bursting. Vinnie touched her arm gently. 'Well done, that boil needed lancing.' Sophie was not listening. In her mind's eye she still saw that look on Grace's face, a hunted, frozen expression which frightened her. Why did the old words ring in her head: 'When trust departs, love soon follows'? She felt sick to her stomach.

Only Ada stayed calm and closed the meeting quietly, leaving immediately afterwards. The others sat limply with their cups of tea, stunned by the turn of events, drained of emotion. Vinnie seized the moment and talked them all through the change of tactics. 'There's to be a heavy police presence en route to the Square so we'll have to act independently, swiftly and off our own bat. Each group must fend for itself. If arrested, act in a way which gives maximum publicity to the Cause.'

'Arrested?' The word hung in the air like the clash of cymbals. That was the reality, the consequence of their actions: to be arrested, cautioned, sent to court, fined or imprisoned. Sophie sighed to herself. She was past the point of no return. 'What happens to us if we get caught?'

'Don't worry, girls,' rallied Vinnie, sensing the general gloom. 'Enjoy being part of history. I'm sure you'll all be absolutely splendid. It'll be a hoot! Let's show them that women can fight. We'll give Winnie a welcome he'll never forget. We'll make this town sit up and take notice of our Cause!'

Grace paced the bedroom floor, hugging her body, trying to douse the raging bonfire in her gut. Banging her pillow had not helped. How could they do this to her, believe she would betray confidences to the newspaper, especially after her own mauling in the Letters column? Not that any one of them had noticed her own letter of reply or bothered to comment upon her arguments. They were all too busy, caught up in this childish escapade, seeking attention for their Cause, winning Lavinia her corporal's stripes in the Pankhursts' army. She was well suited to that attention-seeking mob!

One look at that damned velvet cloak brought back all the grief and shame of her own youthful fantasy. Lavinia was like a knife, slicing them to pieces, carving out the best bits for herself. Vinnie the victor, heroine of the hour, stealing what was rightfully Grace's!

If only we'd stuck together, stomached her madcap schemes and then ignored them, Grace thought. Surely Sophie can see she's just a fly by night, stylish but of little substance? Does she not recognise her as the one who, long ago, sent her packing from the garden? Would she be so smitten if she knew who this wrecker really was? How could she stand up there and humiliate me before my friends? How can I ever forgive her for that?

A bitter acid rose in her throat, taking away her ability to swallow, eat or sleep. She paced over the carpet like a caged animal. This is not happening to us, all the years of friendship ripped apart by the machinations of a greedy, gaudy cheat! A fearful sense of isolation and jealousy raged within her, drowning out the voice of common sense which could only whisper: 'Let it pass, all things pass over. This is of no consequence.' Her first instinct was to seek revenge; a steel cold plot to scupper their plans further by passing on all the information so easily gleaned from Ada to the police.

Poor old Ada, the bridge builder of the group, who'd tried so hard to make her part of the event. Ada was a true friend and faithful companion. Grace could not betray her trust. Perhaps she might transfer all her affection to this one true friend? But that was no good. Sophie was her oldest friend; her bread and roses friend. Grace thrived on her fire and rough, outspoken, careless spontaneity. And she loved

Phyllis like a daughter. There were so many shared memories. Surely all was not lost?

Then the rage would surface like a tidal wave and crush her with its ferocity. Why should I care? I can manage without anyone close in my life. They all let you down in the end. Mother died on me, John Sturges deceived me, and Vinnie's made a fool of me again. I'm better off on my own. Ada and Dora will always oblige me with their company.

A hurricane of emotions whirled in her head. Perhaps I was too hasty, too easily removed? Lavinia cornered me and like a rat I attacked in defence. No! I'm no rat. Someone else has done the squealing and I will find out who. When Sophie knows the truth of the matter we shall be friends again.

Chapter Eleven

Sophie was up at dawn, coaxing the range into life, scrubbing the deal table top, yanking down the flour bin from the shelf to make a start on the baking. Whatever the evening would bring, the larder cupboard must be filled, just in case. Tucking up a restless Gran with a quilt, rousing Phyllis for tea and bread, sorting Bert's pack-up, all were done to the chorus of Bun Gran's ramblings. A bed was made from two chairs by the fire so she could glean warmth for her chilled bones. It was easier to manage her there in the heart of the house.

'You don't know when yer well off, Phia. He's a good 'un is Bert. You've had it lighter than most of us beasts o' burden. Be thankful he tips over his wage without a murmur. I never knew what my lord 'n' master would cough up and I never asked or I'd get a side winder round th'head for my trouble. Yon Phyllis'll never oil her hands in the mill or go deaf with the din like our Cissie. I knows she's all there with her lemon drops but you've stuffed 'er head full of nonsense. I shan't be here to see where it all leads. Heartache and trouble, that's what's brewin'. I can smell it on you, lass.'

'Oh, don't go on at me again . . .'

'I'll have my say, it's all I've got left. All this gaddin' about wi' folks above yer station. Remember where you come from: plain not fancy bread. *We* keep this country goin'. Them others may brighten place wi' fancy plumes but it's labour force what made them rich. King Cotton, they say. Queen Cotton, say I, with all them women's backs she's broke. So don't forget your place, My Lady Muck, I'm watchin' you.'

'Change your tune or I'm not going to listen!' Sophie bristled with indignation as she pounded the dough roughly and set it to prove by the fire. There was so much to do before she went to work: cleaning up and shopping, tidying away the remains of her wash day, checking, rechecking, just in case. At least if she was away for a few days – she hesitated to name her fear – there would be provisions; cakes in the tin and clean clothes and a pile of mending to keep Gran occupied. No one need complain of neglect.

Later Sophie dressed carefully for warmth and plainness in an old sacking skirt with layers of red flannelette underskirts, her oldest clogs, a thick shirt and burred shawl. Daringly she pinned on her shirt her own tin badge with 'Votes for Women' in Union colours. She patted Phyllis's head, shouted 'Tarrah!' on her way out of the door, and clattered excitedly down the street to call for her friend Annie.

Annie was already in a state, standing by the corner with her arms folded. 'There's thousands down there . . . police, incomers . . . all standin' round gawpin' at each other. We'll never find our crowd in that crush!'

Sophie grabbed Annie's arm and smiled to herself. She knew all the hidden ginnels and snickets, narrow foot-bridges over the canal and railway line, the back alley rat runs which linked and looped the town centre almost to the Town Hall Square itself. They half-ran and half-walked to ease the stitches under their ribs, then sauntered casually into the Square.

It looked as if the King and Queen were due for a visit, such was the fuss that night. Brass-buttoned bobbies stood along the pavement, leaving few gaps for the crush of onlookers to get a view. The town was seething with groups of women carrying placards and banners, sheets bobbing aloft like a regatta of sailing ships: 'Salford Lassies Must Have The Vote' read one; 'From Prison To Citizenship' read another. And: 'Stop The Torture Of Women In Our Prisons Today'.

The atmosphere was jovial at first and the women jostled for the best vantage points, bantering with the constables. 'Fancy needing all you lot for one man to hide from a few women! He *must* be scared.'

'Nah then, we know all your little tricks. If there's trouble, you'll be nabbed on the spot,' came the joking reply.

The two women skirted round the Square, pushing and shoving their way towards Bridie's place, but were barred by a policeman guarding the passageway. 'Move on, lassies. Shop's shut till this palaver's over! If you want a fish supper, try Rimmer's off Bradshawgate.' They pretended to move away but squeezed through another group of strangers, shouting, 'Any of you know Vinnie Shaw?'

The women shook their heads. 'We're from Liverpool. Try over the other side by the Southport group. They've roped off the entrance to the Town Hall.'

Annie, being the tallest, jumped up and down and caught sight of a familiar green velvet cloak bobbing in the distance. She propelled them forward blindly. 'Over here, quick! I've just seen her feathers flying.' They elbowed themselves slowly through the mass who were now chanting slogans to hymn tunes, pressing the bobbies further out into the cobbled square. The men linked arms tightly, holding the line.

Vinnie was in the middle, shouting orders in every direction, waving her arms like the conductor of a band. She caught sight of them both and yelled, 'We thought you'd deserted us! Isn't it bloody marvellous? What a crowd, and most of them ours!'

'We tried to get to Bridie's but got turned back,' mouthed Sophie, relieved to be among friends.

'Frank Mullarkey got cold feet and shut up shop. Won't let Bridie out the door, but she says she'll sneak out later. Come on, it's nearly time. I've got a place saved by the corner where the motorcade will turn into the Square.

Wait till you see what I've got from the fruit market!'
Vinnie lifted a cloth from the top of the basket hidden
under her voluminous cape. The stench was overpowering
from a mass of cracked eggs and rotting fruit. 'We'll give
'em something to remember us by!'

'Is this as far as we can get?' Sophie looked round in
disappointment, hoping against hope that they might catch
glimpses of Ada and Grace. The hall had been netted and
roped and there were policemen on the roof, guarding any
skylights from demonstrators.

'Don't worry if we don't hit him here, we'll get him
later in Preston or Liverpool. What a turn out! Lancashire's
afire from top to bottom.'

Sophie noticed that Vinnie always addressed her remarks
exclusively to herself. She ignored Annie, standing by her
side. It was if, in her intensity, her eyes focused on only one
subject. The rest was a blur to her. 'Has Ada come with
you?' asked Sophie, knowing that Vinnie was still lodging
at the school house.

'What do you think?' she sneered. 'Cried off at the last
minute, some feeble excuse. She's just scared she'll have to
resign from the school if there's trouble. We could do with
her bulk and her face. One look at that would frighten the
enemy!'

Annie nudged Sophie in disgust. 'She's no right to call
our old teacher like that. Miss Norris is one of the best.
She's no oil painting herself. Who does she think she is?'

Vinnie ignored this criticism. 'Those Liberal ladies are
all the same. No spunk when it comes to action. Perhaps

they'll wave their cookery books! They want emancipation in theory but won't get off their backsides to achieve it. Revolutions are never run from armchairs – or committees for that matter!'

'Who said anything about a revolution?' argued Annie.

'You're either in this or against us. Petition stuff is tame. It's the getting there that's the real hoot. Look up there! I think something's happening at last.'

The crowd waited excitedly, impatiently, ripples of information, rumour, anticipation, running through it in waves. Then a cavalcade of black motor vehicles with curving hoods snaked slowly down from the Station Brow. A wave of banners and flags surged forward, engulfing the cars. Women jumped on to the running boards of the limousines, battering the windows, throwing eggs, bombarding the occupants, whilst bobbies lost their helmets trying to pull them away. The screaming, violent onslaught brought out police reinforcements who had been lurking in the backstreets. They beat at the protestors with truncheons, dragging at their coats, pulling them roughly to the ground. The men lower down the route stiffened and closed ranks, grim-faced. The atmosphere was changing, hardening. Local onlookers looked away in disgust and embarrassment.

'You want drownin' for this!' said one man, and spat green phlegm over Vinnie's cloak. 'All these bobbies. What a waste! Go 'ome and mind yer babies. Gerrof, the lot on you!' He was knocked over by a group of young men, tipsy mill hands in peaked caps, whose loyalties were swayed by whoever was providing the best entertainment; lads on a night out with not a political halfpenny between them. Behind them came the troublemakers who picked on the women.

'Here's a right load of rubbish! Go on, give us a turn, you Suffragettes!'

'Let's go now!' whispered Sophie in alarm.

'But we've not seen the procession. Look, there's my uncle covered in egg and flour. Silly old buffer! Serves him right.' Vinnie pointed to a white-haired gentleman leaning out of the window. 'I bet that's the nearest he's ever been to baking ingredients!' Sophie was already on the move.

'We're going. Remember Plan B?'

Vinnie was dragged reluctantly from her stronghold. 'Look, we can join up with that crowd. I can see a woman six foot tall and built like a locomotive engine. That must be The Manchester Mauler. Let's get nearer the Town Hall and catch him coming out of the back entrance. That's his usual trick!'

The surging crowd was now on the move and edged them further away, swaying and yelling like banshees. Vinnie pushed forward against the tidal force. 'You're right. Plan B it is. Just time . . .' She raced down an alley to an ash pit covered with a wooden lid, standing outside a back yard entrance. She delved inside and brought out two buckets of distemper and brushes. 'Here, take these, you two. Daub 'em where you can. On the walls, anywhere. VOTES FOR WOMEN!'

They were now at the back of the Town Hall and the

crowd here was curious and sympathetic, letting them plaster the grey stonework, cheering at each stroke of the brush. Annie and Sophie, urged on by the other women's cheers, splattered every window and doorpost, pavement and step, in a frenzied, futile gesture of contempt. An official marshalled some policemen and they raced over in their direction, egged on by youths yelling: 'Get them Pankies!'

In the shouting and pushing, Sophie dropped her can and, grabbed by Vinnie, was dragged down the back alley again.

'Annie! Where's Annie?'

'Never mind her now. She can take care of herself. Run like hell! They're behind you!' Sophie raced over the cobbles, running until her lungs were bursting, turning anxiously to see the lads giving chase. They rounded another corner and ran through a gateway. 'Down there!' With chest pounding, Sophie tore at the sneck, forcing open the door into a yard with a privy and coal bunker. 'Quick, inside!' Vinnie pulled her into the dark hole and they squeezed themselves into the shadows. Sweating and panting for breath, they froze, listening to the clatter of clogs on cobblestones closing in and rough voices jeering. They were overwhelmed with relief when the sounds faded as the men moved onwards in their futile search.

'I never saw him.'

'Saw who?'

'Mr Churchill. All this planning and falling out. What a fiasco!'

'Not at all. It was a great show. Should make every newspaper in the North of England. He caused a riot. You'll see him tomorrow.'

'Tomorrow?'

'In Preston. We move on there and regroup. Do it all again.'

'But I must go 'ome. I can't just leave,' said the other anxiously, thinking about Phyllis.

'They'll be looking for you now, and you with paint all over your skirt. We can go back with Edith Rigby's crowd. Now she's a suffragette and a half!'

'What about poor Annie?'

'She'll be bound over for good behaviour. A five-shilling fine, that's all,' said Vinnie.

'Five bob! Where will Annie find that?'

'She can refuse to pay and go to prison, the best way to get attention. That's what we must do.'

'But who'll look after her kids? Her hubby works shifts and her mother lives away,' protested Sophie, not thinking of herself.

'They'll cope. One usually does. Neighbours and such. It is her first offence and it was only a splash of paint. Hell's bells! Hardly a crime. Come on, it's safe now.'

'Have you been to prison, Vinnie?'

'Not yet, but it's next on my list.' She giggled as she brushed down her clothes.

'We look like pitbrow lassies.' Sophie felt sick to her stomach. 'I must leave a message at Bridie's.'

'No time for that. It's too dangerous to go back into

the fray. Don't be such a worryguts! Enjoy the fun.'

Squashed down flat in an old cart with the stench of six other sweaty women in her nostrils did not feel like fun to Sophie Knowles. The keen sharpness of the December sky with its glistening hoar frost bit into her bones; the bone-shaking ride over the moors lowered her spirits. Nothing had been as she'd imagined. A mob of hooligans, women as well as men, rampaging like naughty school kids. What had that to do with justice for women? How did that win them respect as equals? Try as she might, she could see no point in their escapade, only feel a sickening fear that poor Annie had been abandoned to her fate, left carrying the can. Now she was miles from home, dependent on strangers, and her spirits sank into her clogs. She felt no pride. If this was militant action, they could stuff it!

In the small hours of the morning she was billeted on a young school teacher and her family. Sadie Orrell lived in a terraced house in Deepdale and was married to a mill tackler. The Preston woman rose from her bed without a murmur and made up a bed on the couch for Sophie. 'If you can give me a hand with the copper boiler in the morning, I can get my washing done. If we get caught tomorrow, I'll be inside this time for two weeks so I need to leave everything for Fred to find.'

It was comforting to know someone else shared the same instinct to leave a tidy ship. Thank God Sophie had left some food in the house. What would they be doing now? Bert would be worried and Gran furious. Did they get her message, left with The Manchester Mauler and her friends, who'd promised to call in at the chippy and pass it on?

'What's prison like, Sadie?'

The teacher sipped her tea with relish, draining her mug.

'There's not much of this . . . we stick together as much as we can. It's worse in the third division. We're treated like common criminals. Get in the first division if you can, conditions are a bit better in there and they let you do things. I expect we'll all go on hunger strike again. Edith Rigby's done it once already this year! It caused such a fuss, but they let you out if you're badly. People on the outside pay your fine and then out you go.'

'Have you been on hunger strike?' Sophie shuddered at the very thought.

'Not yet, but our leader says we must give it a go. You just refuse to eat yer grub and after three days they march you out and stuff liquid down your throat. Still, it's the only way to get a splash in the papers is prison. Forcible feeding, release, and then arrest again. What a game of soldiers!'

All day, as she minded Sadie's young sons, Sophie thought of Phyllis coming home from school and waiting for her return; Phyllis with her long pigtails and Bert's coal black eyes and lashes. Sophie longed to hug her tight. It felt all wrong to be twenty miles away, out of reach. She comforted herself with the thought that Bun Gran would be holding the fort and tried not to think about the other matter: the starvation tactics. At the very thought her limbs started to tremble. What have I let myself in for? How can it be endured? I'm scared, plain terrified, but I mustn't let the others see my fear. How could I look Vinnie in the eye if I chickened out of the final test of courage? If Mrs Pankhurst can do it, and Edith Rigby's done it twice, then I will follow.

Vinnie stayed up all night, talking tactics with Edith Rigby, lodging at her Preston residence in Winckley Square. As she looked around the gracious drawing room, with its elegant draperies and soft furnishings, she sighed with relief to be back on civilised terrain. The woman before her was renowned for her pranks, not above throwing black puddings at visiting politicians. Poor Doctor Charles, what a wife to live with! laughed the magistrates. To Vinnie she was an oasis of unconventionality amongst a desert of bland respectability. It was all going to plan. Next stop Preston jail. Hopefully, then her task would be complete and she would be on the next train South to civilisation. Slumming it with the natives was all very well, but Vinnie must get herself back to court, to Clement's Inn, the centre of her world.

She slept all day and a maid brought a delicious meal to her room which she ate with relish. The evening parade followed the same pattern as the night before but the violence was worse. Drunken gangs of youths chased them at every turn.

Edith insisted that they all carry small rocks and potatoes wrapped with paper slogans like parcels: 'Preston Lassies Must Have the Vote'.

Vinnie had to admit that flinging harmless missiles at windows already boarded up was futile. Mr Churchill was spirited out of the meeting hall discreetly in a guarded van, well out of reach of any trouble. Edith stamped her feet in frustration. She flung her potatoes whilst the bobbies stood by and watched with amusement.

'Nah then, Mrs Rigby. None of yer old tricks. What'll the Doctor say?'

Vinnie was furious at the baiting, and yelled, 'Come on, girls. Time to strike a blow for Women's Emancipation.' She beckoned the crowd along Market Street, fingering a rock in her pocket with her gloved hand.

She paused outside the Bank, waited until she was in full view of the following policemen. 'Votes for Women!' She flung the stone into a pane of glass. The crash brought the men running. She turned to the other women, to Sophie cowering next to Sadie Orrell. 'Throw, Sophie! Give it one!' She pushed a large smooth pebble into her hand roughly. 'For God's sake, wake up and do something!'

For a second, Sophie Knowles froze in panic as the consequences of this action danced before her sights. She was a law-abiding citizen, a mother, and the pride of the Plover Street matrons. How could she get arrested or go to prison? Then she saw the look of contempt on Vinnie Shaw's face.

The hard lines of her mouth twisted upwards into a wicked smile as Sophie's arm catapulted the stone at its target. I've done it now! she thought.

Frank Mullarkey unboarded his shop front with

satisfaction. 'No damage done, Bridie, me dear heart. The police protection's done the trick.'

'How did we manage that then?' asked Bridie as she tidied away the dressings from her makeshift first aid post.

'If I tell you, to be sure you'll only be vexed.'

'I'm listening to yous, Francis Xavier Mullarkey.'

' 'Twas only a little favour for a spot of information I gave them . . .'

'Jasus, Mary and Joseph! 'Twas you who sang like a canary to the *Evening News* about the demonstration! *You* told them, and here's everyone thinkin' 'twas Miss Grace!' Bridie flew at him in a rage. 'If I'd have known that, begorrah, I would have opened up the place as a canteen, not hung a few banners from the flat and doled out cups of tea to the wounded. How can I ever hold me head up after such a shaming?'

Frank stood there laughing at her antics. How he loved her spirit; that fiery Irish spirit, her sense of justice and Catholic contrition. Out it would all come at Confession: all the sinning and blaspheming, the penances dutifully performed; over and done with for another week, like this blessed visit.

'I don't know what all yer fussing is about. Sure I have the Vote meself, isn't that enough for yez?'

Bridie stormed off, fuming. 'I shall have to resign from the Guild if this comes out.'

'And why should anyone but the two of us have to know?' was Frank's reply.

They were just retiring to bed when they heard a thunderous rapping on the downstairs door. Frank pushed open the bedroom window and yelled: 'For the love of God, pack that in! What do you want at this time of night?'

Bert Knowles stood there, cap in hand. 'Is there any word of our Phia? We can't find her,' he shouted up. Bridie pushed Frank aside and peered out in her hair net.

'Oh, the poor dear must be away with them Panks. Poor Annie's spending the night in t'nick. Goes before the court this morning with her cronies.'

'Did you see Phia last night?'

'Sorry, not a sight nor a sound.'

Bert returned home and scribbled a note to Grace Thompson. She arrived promptly the following afternoon.

'I came as soon as I could, Mr Knowles. We've no idea where she is but you can be sure she's not alone. Lavinia Shaw will be right in there, fanning the flames. How's Mrs Walker?'

'Come in and see for yourself, Miss Thompson. Not good. Keeps asking for our Phia.' Grace took one look at Bun Gran's ashen face and rasping breath, and shook her head. 'I think you should call a doctor. I can collect Phyllis from school. Ada Norris and I will be pleased to look after her until your wife returns.'

'Phia doesn't appreciate who her real friends are, Miss Thompson. I don't know what's got into her these days, leaving us without a word.'

Grace paused and almost patted his hand but held back for propriety's sake. The poor man looked exhausted. Such a handsome face, such a sad look in those jet black eyes. She got up quickly and went out into the gathering gloom.

Gran rasped and spluttered all through the night, waking in fits, sitting bolt upright with her arms out, calling to some unseen figure. Bert sent for the family and even Wilf staggered out to pay his last respects. They stood around, asking awkward questions, giving Bert queer looks. 'Don't know how you put up with Phia's nonsense. I never did. If she were here right now, I'd belt her from here to kingdom come.' Wilf Seddon took the pipe out of his mouth as he watched Bun Gran slip away, her breathing faint and finally still. Between them, Cissie and the next-door neighbour laid out the old woman, 'putting her away nicely' as custom demanded. Not as expertly as Sophia would have done, thought Bert sadly as he sat alone by the fire.

Next morning he called at the Police Station where Jim Storer, their local bobby, blushed as he shoved a piece of paper across the counter. 'She's been done for wilful damage to property in Preston town centre, bound over for good behaviour, fined twenty shillings or fourteen days in prison. I'm afraid Mrs Knowles has elected to go to jail in the third division.'

'But she doesn't know about her grandma. What can I do? The funeral's tomorrow.'

'Sorry about Mrs Walker. One of the best, was Millie. If you could pay her fine, perhaps?' Bert shrugged his shoulders as he staggered out into the streets. The first soft flakes of snow whirled in his face.

'What a bloody Christmas pantomime!'

Grace returned later with a sleepy Phyllis who begged Bert to sing her favourite rhyme. 'Sing me Mam's special song, please? When is she coming home?' Bert sat her on his knee, trying to be jolly. Grace saw the tears gleaming in the firelight as he sang:

> 'Rock-a-bye baby, Daddy is near,
> Mother's at meetings; she's never here.
> Out in the street, she's rantin' all day
> Or at some rally, talking away!'

Bert paused choking back his feelings.

'Go on,' said the little voice as Phyllis snuggled against his chest.

> 'She's the king pin at the women's Rights show,
> Teaching poor husbands the way they should go!
> Close thou your eyes, there's dishes to do.
> Rock-a-bye baby: 'tis Pa sings to you.'

'Don't cry! Is my mammy gone to heaven with Gran?' Phyllis looked up with alarm, thinking the worst.

'No! No, she's gone to prison for being a "Suff".'

'Me mam's safe, even if she is locked up. She's a proper Suffragette now. Wait till I tell them at school!'

'No, dear, keep it as a little secret, Phyllis. Think what

197

people might say to your father. He's enough to put up with just now,' said Grace, as she shook her head.

'Up the wooden hill, our Phylly. Up to bed and your Auntie Grace can tuck you in for once.' Bert smiled at the visitor. 'You'll have to excuse the mess. I'm ashamed of the place. Bun Gran would have a fit if she could see her steps so grubby.' He bent towards the fire, stoking it with a poker. 'I'll give her one thing, that wife of mine knows how to time it! That Suffragette mob has a lot to answer for. Turned her silly head. Wait till I get hold of her, I'll show her who's gaffer in this house! Gran was right all along. I've been too soft.'

'I'll see myself up.' Grace rose shyly.

Bert caught hold of her hand for a second. 'How can I ever thank you, Miss Thompson?'

'Grace, please. If I can be of any help . . .'

'Come and cheer us up over Christmas. You and Miss Norris, of course.'

'Of course,' came the reply. 'What will you do now?'

'I think it's about time I wrote a letter to Preston Jail.'

Chapter Twelve

'Link arms and stick together,' whispered Edith Rigby as the prison doors slammed behind them. Sophie inhaled the acrid stench of the cold, grey, forbidding place and shivered, her hand tightening on Vinnie's as if to draw courage from her one true friend who stared ahead coolly.

'Make them work for their wages, girls. Refuse all nourishment. Drink only if you must!' came their leader's call to arms, echoing around the stone walls. At the end of the flagged passageway stood a line of wardresses, barking orders like snarling dogs, herding them like cattle into a changing room with a table piled high with uniforms.

'Strip! Everything! Now!'

'No!' yelled back Edith, pulling them closer as the wardresses advanced to separate them, tugging and wrenching the women apart. For a moment the defiant line held. Then a whistle was blown and reinforcements appeared, overwhelming them by sheer numbers. One by one they were dragged by the hair or the scruff of the neck, pinched or cuffed into sullen separation.

'Get them clothes off!'

Sophie cringed with humiliation and embarrassment at this demand. Edith, a seasoned veteran, merely discarded her clothes and underwear without a blush, as did Vinnie, both standing naked as if waiting to be dressed by servants amidst a pile of lace-edged undergarments in Union colours, thrown like battle flags over the slain heaps of grubby cottons which the mill women nervously slipped off.

All those bare bosoms and bottoms made Sophie colour brightly, aware of the audience of wardresses who watched, silent and unmoved. A coarse calico chemise was flung at her, short scratchy socks and a pair of navvy-sized boots with stiff leather uppers, each boot a different size.

'Can I swop this one?' Sophie enquired.

'Put them on! This is not a fashion parade,' was the reply.

'A cattle market more like,' muttered Sadie, half-smiling with contempt as she pulled on her flannel singlet bodice and sludge green skirt, painted with black arrows, afterwards wrapping an enormous boxed jacket around her petite shape. Sophie had to laugh at the apology for a skirt, a huge sack-like affair with tapes to hold it vaguely in the vicinity of her waist. Over the top came a checked pinafore with a kerchief pinned by the shoulder. The hat was the crowning glory and they all burst into giggles as they tried to squeeze volumes of hair into the prison mob caps which tied under the chin like mutch caps without the frills. The overall effect was so hideous and so pitiful that Sophie pretended it was all some grotesque fancy dress parade. After that it was easy to toss back their heads with pride.

'So what if we are in the third division, we're not criminals! Don't let the buggers get you down,' a message was passed down the line. 'We are political prisoners. And remember: no food, no tea. Refuse from day one. Take water if you must. Sip it only to relieve your parched tongue. Be bloody, brave and resolute. Let them have to give in first.'

Vinnie looked at Sophie.

'The Pankhursts expect! Don't worry, it'll soon be over and you can go home for Christmas and stuff yourself silly!'

Clutching a Bible, hymn book, rules of instruction and a pair of flimsy bed sheets, they lined themselves up like a flock of sheep and marched defiantly to cells deep in the maze of corridors with grilled doors to either side. As they passed down the passages there was the sound of tins banging, foul cursing, screams and cackling, which turned their bold strides into silent shuffles. Sophie found she kept leaving her boot behind as she tripped over her skirt hem. Soon it was her turn to face a cell door. It was unlocked and she was shoved inside. One look confirmed her worst suspicions.

The cell was the size of a small walk-in larder with a shelf bed fitted to the wall. This dark and dingy room was to be her home for fourteen long days. The provisions for her comfort consisted of a piece of hard soap, a towel more like a dish cloth, a water bowl and can, one mug, a skillet, tin plate and wooden spoon, a slop pail and one grey blanket which barely stretched over the mattress. The only indulgence she could find was a cheap printed religious tract, exhorting her to repent of her sins and receive instant salvation.

As the doors were locked behind her, Sophie's knees buckled. A feeling of panic ran through her like fire, stopping her breath until she gasped and sweated with fear. 'I can't stay in here, the walls will crush me!' Her first instinct was to arrange and rearrange the equipment to her satisfaction so that she might put her own stamp on the room. The fear deep inside sent an urgent message to her bowels, demanding release. She looked at the bucket in disgust but nature must be obeyed or else. To perform into a bucket, to live with your own filth, to have nothing but the Bible for company . . . How could she survive a day, never mind two weeks?

But I'll show 'em. She smiled to herself. There's plenty in the Bible about defiance and suffering, strong women and good over evil. That would take her mind off the smell.

So her first constructive act was to ration herself to reading a portion of Old Testament history, then she would tackle the Bible from a woman's point of view. Where better to start than with Adam and Eve, the cause of all this mess? She would read with the eyes of a free-thinking sceptic, learn any good bits by heart as future ammunition. Then she would cast her mind back to her schooldays and poetry chanting there, and see how much of Miss Norris's desk thumping had stuck! Anything to take her mind off the coming ordeal.

Dear Ada, she thought, I am glad she's not in here. She would be sacked, like Sadie Orrell, for being a dissident. Sophie dared not think of Plover Street; any remembrance of it brought on a fierce attack of shaking. She could not afford to be weakened by guilt if she was to begin a hunger strike. It was one thing feeling brave with a group of other rebels within reach to urge you on, but alone in this cage with only herself for company was another matter. It would be so easy to cave in and cheat. Keep busy, distract your jangled nerves, scrub the floor . . . do anything to survive this first day.

The only break in the monotony of confinement was the exercise yard; walking round the brick enclosure with head bent, trying to challenge the communication ban, touching and mouthing while the regular inmates looked on in curiosity and disbelief. This was where the mill girls came in useful with their mee-mawing mimes. Some could interpret a conversation at fifty paces.

The first meal offered was a bowl of lumpen porridge and a thick dry chunk of gritty bread. It looked so tempting she almost felt the slops of cold gruel warming her protesting stomach. Sophie resisted by an act of supreme will. Her whole body craved this vile mess of pottage. The tea had also to be left for it contained nourishment. She sat with her head in her hands as it was taken away; so tired she could have slept on a washing line.

Later came the same meal with lumps of gristly meat and

gravy mixed into the bowl. She imagined they were dog turds and the smell in the cell made it easy to refuse. Her belly was screaming in protest and kept her awake all night. On her tongue was a rancid, acid breath which tainted her teeth, conspiring with the orchestral gurglings in her stomach to keep her mind firmly on this sacrifice.

The next day they assembled in the chapel for a service and managed to sing messages of encouragement to the hymn tunes, like giggling schoolgirls in some Ladies' Seminary. 'How goes it? . . . First day is worst. Sip your water . . . save your energy. The tube man cometh soon to have his wicked way.' Three times daily came the food. Three times daily it was left for collection.

The effects of starvation were beginning to take their toll; headaches and blurred vision, trembling limbs and faintness. Restlessness gave way to a strange elation and a defiance which then sank back into edginess and fear. It was only a matter of time before the forcible feeding would commence. Sophie was terrified and chanted to herself: 'I will be strong for the others. Without loyalty to my friends and comrades, my life would be a stale crust indeed. I will feed on friendships, one by one. They will sustain me.'

She knew the ordeal had begun when she heard Vinnie screaming as the cell door opposite slammed. 'I protest! I refuse to eat your bloody food! Can't you get that in your numb skulls?' Her voice was echoed by cheers and the banging of tin plates on the walls. Sophie did not know what to expect. Forcible feeding was still a new tactic, adopted first in London during the summer of 1909 and now being tried out in provincial prisons. 'Ordeal by Torture', that was how it was described in the pamphlets.

If WSPU colours were green for hope and white for purity of purpose, then purple was the Way of the Cross, the ultimate test of loyalty to the Cause. 'I will not let my friends down.' Sophie found herself praying as footsteps stopped outside her cell. The wardress was carrying a tray on which there was fresh bread, tasty Lancashire cheese and a shining red apple; a welcome sight to starving eyes. Sophie looked away and heard from the open door the sound of singing, faint at first then swelling into a chorus of Ethel Smyth's famous 'Suffragette Anthem'.

'Shout, shout, up with your song!
Cry with the wind for the dawn is breaking.
March, march, swing you along,
Wide blows our banner and hope is waking . . .'

The food was carried before her like an offering as they processed down the passage and the Anthem stirred her courage as she heard the final crescendo.

'Shoulder to shoulder
And friend to friend . . .'

The tray was placed on a table like a sacrifice. Only then did she see all the paraphernalia of this torture chamber. In the centre of the room stood the chair. A bald man with a bushy beard and rimmed spectacles took a perfunctory .

glance over her and pronounced her fit for the coming experience.

'Will you eat?' said one of the wardresses.

'No,' said the acolyte calmly in response, 'I have the right to refuse to eat.'

'Rights? Rights, woman! We are here to do our duty, to enforce our right to see you fed. If you're stupid enough to resist, that is not our concern. Struggle and it will be the worse for you. I promise we will begin again.' This doctor was angered by the extra work force-feeding regulations and procedures were giving his staff. He no longer felt these silly women had the right to be treated as human beings, and believed they deserved their suffering. The coldness of his contempt allowed him to attack the task with a brisk efficiency, untempered by a modicum of sensitivity.

Sophie found herself propelled to the chair, strapped by leather thongs and tilted backwards for their convenience. She struggled as panic swept over her, screwing up her eyes tightly to blot out the terror of being pinned down, the knowledge that four women were assisting the monster in his black frock coat, holding her arms and limbs, forcing them rigid. Her mouth was prised open and a clamp screwed her jaw so wide she thought her mouth would split. They were becoming experts in this art.

Then came the rubber tubing like a snake, probing its way down as she swallowed and gagged against it, jabbing her throat, tearing the roof of her mouth. She tried not to swallow but the force was too powerful to resist. Fear of choking, the instinct to survive too basic. The funnel was already in place and liquid poured down into her stomach with a gurgling rush of coldness. She willed her mind away from the room but the best it could manage was to hover on the ceiling above and watch the horror of this violation with a strange detachment. Part of her wanted to remember every detail, to process how human beings could do this to each other. The other part wanted desperately to block it forever from her memory.

They raised the chair suddenly and the tube was pulled out. With it came a rush of vomit, spurting on to the doctor's frock coat. She saw the veins twitch on his forehead as he fought a desire to strike her. 'Do that once more and I'll start again. I'll stuff your insides like a Christmas turkey! So full, your stomach will burst, madam!'

Sophie was untied and staggered to her feet in a daze, swallowing back the liquid, her eyes watering. Then she was walked to her cell and the door slammed behind her. She flung herself on the mattress and wept, banging her spoon and skillet in fury against the wall. Ashamed of her tears, she began the last act of defiance. Victory must be hers. Slowly she knelt before the slop pail and forced her swollen fingers down her bleeding throat, feeling the jagged edges of torn flesh, down, down, until she forced back all the food they had pumped into her. Only then did she stop to rest.

With each gut-wrenching pain, with the tears, came a fierce determination to win this battle of wills at any cost to herself. Her spirits flamed with the righteousness of their cause. From now on food would hold no power over her.

Twice a day this ritual was to be repeated and twice a day she would resist. With each refusal came a burning stab of pride: I am stronger than them. We have defeated them. Together we are making them uncomfortable, afraid. As I grow weaker so I grow stronger and more defiant. They have no control over my body however they abuse me. I will survive and tell my story.

She felt almost delirious with this sense of control and power. Her cell was becoming a holy shrine and she was the martyr.

On the tenth day of her confinement, the door opened and the Chaplain stood outside awkwardly, unable to look her in the face, ushering her out into the guardroom.

'Your fine has been paid. You are to be released.'

'I don't want my fine paying, I'm not going!' she croaked, scarcely able to stand. Her throat was on fire. She did not want to desert her post or her friends.

'You will leave now, Mrs Knowles. You are released. I think you should go home. There are friends outside with a motor cab.'

She was given back her old clothes which hung limply over her shrunken shape. A side door was flung open and she was bundled out into a strange white world of snow, the winter sunlight blinding her bloodshot eyes. Grace and Ada stood side by side like a committee of black hats.

'What possessed you to pay my fine? I can look after myself!' She half-stumbled as her defiant stance crumbled in the warmth of their obvious welcome and the effects of fresh air.

'My God! Sophie, you look awful. Come and take a seat in the cab. It's "Home, James" for you by the looks of things. Nearly Christmas and there's no one to look after Phyllis now. She needs you at home and so does Bert.' Only when they were all safely on the way homewards did they break the news of Bun Gran's death and burial. Sophie sat dry-eyed, unblinking, uncomprehending, like an automaton on a musical box, making the motions but with no expression on her face.

In the days following her release she spoke to no one of her ordeal, showed no emotion at the loss of her beloved gran, and performed her duties both at Bridie's place and in Plover Street with a sullen distant nonchalance which made Bert and Grace fear for her sanity.

All Bert's anger and bombast melted like warm butter at first sight of her gaunt pallor and the way she would stop mid-sentence, staring into empty space as if in another world. He could see she found it difficult to eat, or swallow for that matter. Worst of all she would not share their lumpen bed but preferred to tuck herself alongside Phyllis in Gran's old room. Only once she was seen in St Anselm's churchyard, paying a brief visit to the family burial mound. Her friend Annie called in unexpectedly and Sophie dashed upstairs in embarrassment, leaving a bewildered Bert trying to make polite conversation.

Christmas was a sad affair; a candle and some holly, a piece of Ada's fruit cake and cheese, a cloth-wrapped pudding from Bridie to boil in the copper and a gift of ham shank from Grace. It could have been a funeral tea but for the efforts of Ada and Grace to make some merriment for Phyllis.

On the Sunday after Christmas they were all invited to the school house for a festive tea. Sophie went under sufferance after Bert insisted that they give Phyllis a chance to go sledging on the moors behind the village. Grace found a toboggan and Ada produced some tin trays.

'Last one up the hill is a girl's blouse!' shouted Bert and Phyllis. 'Come on, old soldier, put yer bum on a tray and skoot.'

Sophie trundled up to the higher ground with a sigh. Dotted across the snowy fells were revellers, sledges and snowball fights. The excited screams of delight muffled the whoosh of blades over ice. I am not part of this, none of it. I am different now. I've crossed that river into another world. She rummaged for its name in her memory. I didn't mean to cross the Rubicon but I have. Nothing can ever be the same.

'Come on, Mam. Give us a shove!' yelled her daughter impatient to be off down the slope with pigtails flying. Grace was already sliding down sedately on her tin tray, giggling as if nothing was happening to their friendship. Sophie pushed the child and, on impulse, jumped upon the back of the toboggan, face into the wind, clutching at the sides. With the speed came fear, satisfaction, certainty and the first smile of 1910. No one was going to stop her now!

★　　★　　★

Vinnie stepped out of Preston Jail to a heroine's welcome. The local women paraded in the forecourt with huge banners: 'Stone Walls Do Not A Prison Make!' and 'Courage and Constancy!' Edith Rigby's emergence always created a stir in the press. They all linked arms, more to hold themselves up and keep limbs from trembling with weakness than from solidarity.

'Come home with me,' was the invitation on everyone's lips, but there was only one place Vinnie Shaw intended to spend Christmas and that was in the safety and comfort of the Pethick Lawrences' lavish hospitality. She accepted the offer of a cab straight to the railway station and sat facing South into the pale wintry sunlight. As she pored over the Suffragette newspaper, an advertisement for 'Militant Fruit Jam with stones intact or the stoneless variety' caught her eye, making her laugh out so loudly that the sedate company in the carriage looked up in alarm. Who was this gaunt woman to disturb their slumbers?

You did it, girl! You've seen enough stones in walls to last you a lifetime! You deserve a rest and a cigarette.

Snug inside her was the cosy thought that she had earned a Holloway brooch, a long rest and some thundering good meals. Her throat was sore but not as inflamed as those who had refused any tea. Suffering for the cause was one thing but martyrdom was another and she was not martyr material. Oh, no! From now on she was going to pull every string, rope or chain to stay put at Clement's Inn. If she had to feign nervous exhaustion for a few months, then so be it. Vinnie Shaw had done her bit!

Once back in London, she was on the receiving end of wonderful Christmas gifts of tea, chocolates and biscuits, all boxed in Union colours, entertained to dainty lunches at the Home Restaurant in the City where even the home-made cakes were iced in the colours, given packets of special toilet soaps – 'Once tried always used!' – and in her stocking was a battery-operated brooch which flashed 'VOTES FOR WOMEN!'

No one queried her right to be back amongst them but Christmas was tainted by the fear of a summons to return to her post. When Sophie's scribbled letter came, Vinnie could have jumped for joy. The last bit of the jigsaw was in place.

Dearest Vinnie

I hope you have made sufficient recovery to enjoy your well-earned rest. After all we have been through, I have decided to pledge myself whole-heartedly to the Pankhurst Cause and the WSPU, especially since I found to my dismay that while we were in prison, our local Suffrage Society actually wrote a letter to the *Evening News* disassociating itself from the events of 9 December. Would you believe, they even offered ten shillings to the Police poor box for *any inconvenience caused*!

I am sick of their smug attitudes and small minds. I am finding the sameness of my humdrum routine vexatious to

my spirit of adventure. Please bear me in mind for any future position.
Your true friend,
Sophia Knowles

Vinnie wrote back by return, offering her paid work as a local representative in the North-west of England. Sophie could be the willing dogsbody now, releasing Vinnie herself for a senior clerical post in London. Let someone else tramp the streets for a change! As usual she was going to look after number one.

A Bitter Harvest
1910

Chapter Thirteen

'Can I have a private word with you, Miss Thompson?' whispered the Workhouse Matron. In her grey uniform she looked cold as charity, starched cap and apron stiff as a board, handling this first visit nervously, ushering Grace into a small office and shutting the door discreetly. 'I am so glad to see another woman elected on to the Board of Guardians at last. I am sorry to burden you so soon but matters are desperate.' She coughed. 'Might I put in a request for undergarments, night-dresses and other female pieces?' She mouthed the words as if they were the foulest of oaths.

Grace looked at her in amazement. 'What do the women wear now?'

'Whatever can be spared, thin chemises . . . it's not decent for them to have no drawers.' She sniffed with embarrassment. 'I did not like to ask before on account of the Committee's being mostly gentlemen and Miss

Chadderton might deem the whole matter indelicate,' said the Matron, looking at the floor.

'Surely they must know it's inhumane and indecent for women to be so poorly clad? Does this apply to children and young girls too?'

The woman pointed across the rough grass to a large brick house where boys with shaven heads and girls with cropped bobbed hair held hands like blinded soldiers, walking one in front of the other.

Orphan children were so easily recognised by their dreary uniform. Fed and watered but no frills, thought Grace sadly; bread but no roses. If only her presence might change their lot a little. This request was worthy of her full attention. The smile on her face did not last for long.

The Union Workhouse stood like a fortress in a field, its crenellated towers rising high above the town as a warning to the thriftless and destitute: Abandon hope all ye who enter here. This was the last retreat for poor, feckless, old and feeble alike; silent shuffling inmates stooped and sagged in clothes ink-marked: 'Given'.

At her first induction meeting to the workings of the Board of Guardians Grace surveyed the assembly with dismay. What a hotch-potch of political backgrounds and persuasions sat before her, and all so prosperous-looking with round bellies on which gold fob watches bobbed across best worsted like lifebuoys over a dark sea; what a conglomeration of interests, from the impoverished aristo-crat with his bloodshot eyes, imperious accent and patronising manner, to Socialist Councillors, the 'we had

it tough' school sitting uncomfortably alongside Tory
gentleman farmers, a Liberal Quaker businessman and a
Methodist minister. The Chairman was none other than
mill owner Jairus Berisford, King Cotton turned charitable
benefactor.

The men sat back on their chairs in uniform
respectability, grey hair slicked back, sporting a variety of
moustaches and whiskers. The only other female present
was elected by another Ward; an elderly woman in a black
silk crêpe cape dotted with jet beads who held a pair of
lorgnettes and sat throughout the proceedings, nodding in
and out of consciousness, until she started awake and smiled
like a ventriloquist's dummy, much to Grace's amusement.

The oak-panelled room was the most opulent in the
building, set apart from the general austerity by a sumptuous carpet upon which stood a huge mahogany table
carved lavishly at each corner. The walls were decorated
with sombre portraits of the great and good of the district;
stern-faced benefactors who presided over the proceedings
with wandering eyes.

The token welcome given to the newly elected
members was perfunctory and without warmth. I'm not
going to dangle here like a puppet, mused Grace, as
comments were passed on the closeness of her particular
election ballot. She peered through her spectacles for any
likely allies, covertly glancing at each member in turn.
Would the little mouse in her black cape squeak out any
support, or perhaps the Parson?

It was hard to grasp that any inmate of the Workhouse

was recognised as human. They were labelled unfortunates, moral defectives, feebles, to be maintained and occupied like caged animals in the zoo.

Grace felt such pity but the sweat was pouring from her neck, her cheeks flushed, as she rose to speak for the first time. 'As you probably gather, I fought my election on the need for more females to join this Board. This will be my special service to the community. I am greatly looking forward to the task ahead and to see another lady present to support me. Already Matron has asked me to put before you the need for extra clothing for the females.'

'What do you mean, extra clothing? Matron knows our budget,' said a Councillor. 'Wanting fancy stuff, is she?'

'Not at all, just the basic intimate garments necessary for feminine decency. Night attire which covers the whole body in cold weather. Plain stuff, not fancy,' Grace argued.

'Well, why didn't she speak to us before then?' was the curt reply.

'Because, Mr Chairman, such matters are not easily addressed before male members. Women have need of special comforts.'

'That may be so, Miss Thompson, but Matron must go through the proper channels,' said Jairus Berisford.

'Yes,' interrupted the Parson, 'that may be so but Miss Thompson too has a point. Females must be made comfortable.'

'Comfortable! They aren't in here for comfort. It's their sinning and feckless ways what's got them in this sorry state, adding extra burdens to our rate payers. Their illegitimates have to be paid for!' spat the Socialist Trades Union rep, jumping up, quickly followed by Grace.

'Are children to be punished for the circumstances of their birth? I'm sure Miss Chadderton here will support me in this matter?' Grace replied, looking earnestly in her direction. The woman smiled blandly.

'I'm sorry, dear, I didn't quite catch that but I'm sure you are right whatever you said, being a parson's daughter.'

Jairus Berisford used this pause to rise to his feet and look at his watch with an avuncular smile. 'It is grand to see such youthful enthusiasm in our midst, Miss Thompson. If I remember rightly, you and I have had the pleasure of acquaintance many years back. Ever the crusader as I remember?' At the twinkle of recognition and remembrance in his eye, Grace blushed, half-smiling, thinking back to the escapade in Dragon Castle.

'I can see we are going to have to mind our P's and Q's with this young lady, show her we've not been idle all these years. I think a sub-committee might be the best way to deal with these matters? Perhaps it can report back to the next monthly meeting.'

In one fell swoop Grace felt herself patronised and sidelined as irrelevant. How clever these men could be at diverting a threat, but she was not going to be so easily dismissed! How naive of her to think that the full Board was anything more than a rubber stamp to the real decision-makers in the sub-committees. If this was where the power lay then Grace realised she must act fast. 'Thank you, Mr Chairman, for your confidence in me and for the suggestion of a small working party. I will be more than happy to serve upon it as representative of female interests on this Board of Guardians.'

She sat down with relief but saw that Mr Berisford was not amused at his outmanoeuvring; his smile tightened. Nothing was said but she sensed he was thinking, Not here five minutes and causing trouble, demanding change. I knew it would come to this with women nosing themselves in where they're not wanted – interfering busybodies!

He paused to gauge the silence and then said, 'Thank you, Miss Thompson, we'll let you know in due course. Now it really is time to get on with business in hand. Who's first before the Board? Ah, yes, a request for outdoor relief and yet another Irish lass in trouble. Will they never learn, these Paddy lasses? Mary O'Flynn. Call her in.'

Matron was called and a young girl in a tight-laced bodice and lumpen full skirt entered, hiding behind the warden. 'Are you Mary O'Flynn?' The frightened white face nodded. 'State your case, please.' Silence, as the lass began to weep and snivel.

'Come on, we've not got all day. Why should we give you Parish Relief?' The girl opened her mouth but only a faint garbled sound came out.

'This is a ridiculous waste of time, holding up the Committee. Spit it out. Are you in trouble?'

Miss O'Flynn nodded.

'Can your parents support you?'

At the mention of parents, Mary O'Flynn collapsed, weeping noisily. Matron pulled her up sharply.

'It's too late for tears, young woman. You should have thought of your poor parents when you let yourself be seduced by promises. Silly girl. Now your parents have shown you the door and your employers are scandalised by your claim that their son assaulted you. Really, one of the best addresses in the town!'

'Mr Berisford, she has no work and no abode . . .'

'I don't think we can offer support after such wanton behaviour. Miss O'Flynn will be better off interred here until the unfortunate offspring can be disposed of suitably.'

'No! I want to work in the mill. I can support myself, I know I can. The nuns will help me at the Convent. Please, your honour, 'twas none of my doing. Do not punish me.' At last the girl was finding her voice as her temper flared in protest.

'Don't you argue with me, young hussy! We will do what we think best for you. You are in no position to dictate terms to us. Was it not you who was apprehended trying to jump into Doffcocker Mill pond? Take her away, Matron, to the female ward for moral defectives. She can stay there while she contemplates her condition.'

Grace watched the proceedings in shocked silence while the girl was dragged out of the room, her wails echoing down the tiled corridor like a banshee's. Grace got to her feet again. 'How can young girls plead their case when we shame them and ask them intimate details in mixed company? Surely it would be more profitable to hear these accounts in private before an all-female panel?' This caused a stir of dissension within the room. The minor aristocrat came to life at this point and argued back.

'I like to hear these gels tell their tales, all those gruesome details to test 'em out. Ask for it and like it, I reckon, don't you know!'

'Miss Thompson has a point again. Females will be more comfortable talking to our ladies and Matron,' said the Parson mildly.

'What's all this again about comfortable? Twice today this notion has reared its ugly head. Let's shoot it down once and for all. "Naught for your comfort" should be our motto or we'll have the whole town wanting to come here for a holiday! Let's have some tea and cakes before we deal with the next lot.' The Labour man sat down and wiped his brow.

Grace stood alone, totally exhausted by the unnatural effort to be sociable and feeling thoroughly demoralised. It was the Reverend Nuttall who rallied to her support, turning his back on the others as he sipped his lukewarm tea in her company.

'I'm sorry that you seem to be doing all the work. You've had a reluctant welcome, as you can see. It warms my heart to hear such genuine interest and concern. I only wish others were as enthusiastic. Don't worry, I'll let you know if they set up a sub-committee. You must be involved and they will have to recognise that.'

It proved not to be so straightforward a process. Months

went by: months of argy-bargying, seemingly banging her head against brick walls, those stubborn men with their blocking procedures and filibusters. All for the sake of a few pairs of drawers! Somehow she was never informed just when the meetings were to be held, letters always arriving too late for her to attend. Her own letters were mislaid or ignored.

She drafted an agenda for improvements in the nutritional content of the Workhouse diet, especially for young children, based on the doctor's experience at the now thriving Welfare Clinic for mothers and babies in the town. She tried in vain to get extra provisions allocated for everyone over the Christmas period. A measly beer ration for the men was abandoned for fear of encouraging intemperance. Every time she stood up there was a corporate sigh of 'whatever next?' in the air. The only success she secured was a promise of a special outing for the children of the cottage homes to the New Year Fair and Menagerie, with free rides, a bar of chocolate and a fish supper at Bridie's place.

It was there, full of contrition and Christmas port, that a blushing Bridie took her aside and told her of Frank's secret betrayal as they stood watching the orphans singing carols. 'Everyone thinkin' 'twas you and all. It's weighed heavy on me heart, sure it has.'

Grace was too tired to fuss over what was long past but asked Bridie to help Mary O'Flynn support her baby by finding her work. Bridie was only too pleased to be able to oblige as penance for Frank's behaviour.

Every request Grace made became a personal battle of will, forcing her natural reticence to take a back seat for the greater good. She dug deep into her reserves of energy to cope with constant rebuttals and denials of her very presence at meetings.

She would return to the Vicarage and slump into a chair, too tired to take up her other interests. Her father looked on with alarm but said nothing. Just when at last she felt she was being accepted, the sad but now familiar case of Mary O'Flynn flared up again: a case so unfair she could no longer stay silent.

After the birth of a healthy son, the Board decided that the baby should be farmed out to a couple who wanted a replacement for a dead child. Grace was horrified. 'We can't just give this child to strangers! The mother is quite capable of looking after her son and I think I have found her a position. She claims to have been the victim of a lustful attack.'

Jairus Berisford stood firm. 'What is the word of an Irish slut against a respected family, against a man of hitherto blameless reputation?' Grace watched the ranks close against her plea. The child was removed and given to the sullen farmer and his wife without a qualm. There was to be no mention of the story of his birthing. He would be given a new identity and every creature comfort, or so she was promised.

Was it so surprising that Mary broke down, frantic at the loss of her baby? In the days following her delivery she was confined to a padded cell then transferred indefinitely to the secure wing of the Lunatic Asylum.

'We can't do this to the girl. I believed every word she said,' pleaded Grace.

'Then she will only cause trouble, so better to prevent any misunderstandings,' came the reply.

'Trouble for whom?' she retorted. 'The man who defiled her? Surely as gentlemen you can appreciate how reprehensible his behaviour was? Why must only she be punished?'

'You are getting too involved, Miss Thompson. Gentlemen, this is just what I feared. Women are not strong enough to deal with such matters. You have emotional tendencies which affect your judgements, Miss Thompson. You do your sex a disservice to get so . . . so worked up over a mere inmate of dubious morals. Her parents will not support her. The infant is far better off away from such a background of degradation, poverty and Papism!' said the Chairman firmly. Around the table heads nodded in agreement.

Grace felt weariness flooding her limbs. Sinking back in her chair, she tried to stem the tears as rage stuck in her throat, hard as a croquet ball. *Why do I cry when I want to tear his arguments to shreds? All that moralising humbug! He is covering up for one of his own cronies. The poor woman never stood a chance once she named her assailant.*

Sophie would have carved them to pieces like a lioness

227

fighting for her cub. Sophie would have made them understand. I must talk to her.

Then she realised that all Board matters were confidential and she could not break her membership oath. Grace felt utterly alone. How she longed to write to the newspaper, to share it all with Ada and Dora or anyone who would care about such injustice. Every time she took a cab to Plover Street, Sophie Knowles was never home. Bert was always so pleased to see her, sitting by the fireside looking lost. Perhaps if she took Phyllis under her wing more it might cheer her leaden spirits? Sophie was completely swallowed up by the Panks, travelling from town to town, away for days on end, out of touch and out of reach just when Grace needed her advice.

The aching and yearning for the days of bread and roses never went away. The loss of them tore at her heart like a rusty blade. No matter how hard she worked at other duties, the pain never went away; like the dull ache of a tired muscle, a leaden weight constantly inside her.

She left brief notes for Sophie to read on her return but there was never a reply. On Sundays she invited Phyllis over for tea and Bert often turned up with the child, tagging on two steps behind in his own silent world as Grace and Phyllis walked or played games together.

Phyllis was so easy to entertain and often brought along her mother's scribbled notes for Grace to read. It was from the child she learned of all her old friend's escapades.

Summer passed into autumn. Everyone was waiting to see if Lord Asquith's famous Conciliation committee, consisting of twenty-five Liberals, seventeen Conservatives, six Irish Nationalists and six Labour MPs, would settle the Suffrage argument once and for all. The Bill, giving women householders and the wives of male householders the vote, was passed by the House of Commons but must wait for its chance in the House of Lords.

The local Suffrage Group still met at Bridie's place, arranging bazaars, American teas and entertainments, sending representatives to regional rallies, but membership had dwindled noticeably since the Churchill visit. Enthusiasm was waning on all fronts and even the militant Panks had offered a truce from their capers.

My life is just one round of meetings, committees and nursing Father, thought Grace. There is no satisfaction in it. A creeping disillusionment stifled any sense of direction in her life like a thick smog. The burden of more and more of the same duties was choking her spirit. There was nothing to look forward to but middle age and infirmity, more partings; an ever-circling spiral of birth and death.

In dreams she soared like a bird, roaming high over the moors or resting on craggy rocks to watch the town below. The future held no promise. Nothing was as it appeared on the surface: her election to the board, a single life or the freedom of modest wealth – nothing eased the aching.

She found strange comfort in her visits to the demented girl in the Asylum wing as she sat remote from the world around her, breasts bound, all hope drained from her. The wards were full of other unfortunate girls, their only crime to have borne a child with no man to support them. Here she felt useful and needed.

To Grace their existence was a living death and she agonised over their fate with a tenacity which bordered on obsession.

'I wish every one of you at this table could live for five minutes as these women do! Then you might understand why they are so listless and without purpose. If you would grant me leave to add some colour to their lives, some useful activity to add variety to their routine – basket weaving or embroidery, sewing classes even – I would be more than willing to contribute myself to this end.'

Slowly, with the help of the Matron and the Parson, pricked by the troublesome woman's incessant demands, it was agreed to set aside a room for such pursuits. Grace spent afternoons reading aloud to the women as they stitched and embroidered 'Union Workhouse' on to handkerchiefs cut down from threadbare sheets and offcuts from Berisford's factory floor.

They came to rely on her regular visits for she brought news of the outside world. Then came the brilliant idea to fund a small garden, walled off for privacy like a courtyard; a garden filled with tubs of flowers and borders, climbing roses and shrubs from Grace's own collection. Just a small corner of softness in a bleak brick world. Why should they not have bread and roses too! Slowly her life became inextricably linked with theirs as they shared with her stories of violence and abuse. She became a warrior on their behalf, trying to get each case reviewed by the Board.

Mary O'Flynn recovered slowly and the fight to gain her release became a cause célèbre within the Union Boardroom; a cause Grace fought largely on her own; a case which further eroded her spirits. There was no unbending among the men. This was one battle too many against the power they wielded by right. It was felt Miss Thompson craved too many indulgences and needed to be held in check. Mary grew despondent and made an attempt to mutilate herself, slashing her arms in a half-hearted cry for attention. This gave the Board the opportunity to commit the woman permanently to the Asylum. Grace's campaign for leniency was discounted as unworkable.

A sense of failure and futility gnawed at her constantly, removing the last vestiges of her appetite. Her clothes hung from her bony frame but she struggled on. It was easy to withdraw from the sociable company of her friends pleading pressure of work, to refuse invitations which would lighten the spirit and ease the pain. There was no one to query each and every withdrawal to her bedroom for hours on end, to write numerous letters on behalf of her 'fallen women'.

In her desperate attempt to rally support for them, she herself became an object of ridicule amongst the Board members who found her persistence indecent. Thus was Grace Thompson dismissed as a crank, an eccentric wealthy old maid with little charm or any appealing features to recommend her. She shielded her true feelings from both Ada Norris and Dora Wagstaff. Grace felt consumed from within, starving herself into submission with a punishing regime of frenzied activity, but the morning she first felt the peculiar bump protruding from her left breast, she was almost relieved. It was the size of a large walnut with broken puckered skin, tender to the touch, set in relief against her shrunken flesh, shining under the surface. She fingered it at first with fascination, then with the sickening certainty that this was no ordinary lump but the curse of the Hendry women, whispered about once in hushed tones by Aunt Calvert after a sherry too many in the drawing room.

Grace peered into the mirror and smiled grimly. After all her futile efforts to subdue her flesh, her own body was wreaking its revenge. Suddenly, like an image in the mirror, she remembered her mama and that terrible smell; remembered as a little girl being ushered by the nursemaid into a sickroom where a waxen yellow face peered from a lace-edged pillow, the sickly stench of death filling the room. The little child had recoiled and run out of the room, crying for her mummy with disgust. Now sweat was pouring down Grace's cheeks like tears. With insight came renewed energy and a sense of release. No one must know of her weakness. This was a challenge not to be ignored and there was so much to be done!

Chapter Fourteen

The man in the bowler hat sidled up to her sideways. 'Doing the business, love? How much for a quickie?' Sophie could never get used to this harassment as she stood selling pamphlets outside Victoria Station. Her usual quick retort stuck in her throat for once. The man would go home to his neat terrace, no doubt to his wife and bairns, thinking he was doing mankind a favour by humiliating another human being as she went about her job. Why was she considered fair game whenever she stood alone on the street?

Working for the WSPU was disheartening enough; a humdrum existence trying to raise funds for the organisation, lonely at times. Even the liveliest of her Manchester colleagues seemed ground down by their mundane efforts to squeeze pennies out of working folk. She was sick of jumble sales. Only last week she'd found herself humping tables in the pouring rain across the playground of a Ragged School so that they could sell pitiable rubbish for coppers.

Then there were the street collections: standing in the rain at the mercy of insults and the 'Go home and mind yer babby' brigade.

Equally depressing was the dash to meet newly released hunger strikers from Walton, Strangeways or Armley Prisons; to make sure there was a crowd to meet them, with the black velvet banners held high to cheer them on. She was quickly learning how to assess the condition of each woman as she staggered, fuelled only by willpower, into the light. Those near collapse were escorted to safe houses to recuperate or in some cases to die; those able to appear at a rally were assembled before the press and onlookers to protest at their barbaric treatment.

Usually she rang a large brass bell and chalked the time and venue of the next political meeting on the city pavements; sometimes they wore sandwich boards or messages pinned to their coats; then the open cart drew alongside the pavement at the appointed hour and a makeshift platform was made for any visiting Suffragette speaker to gather a crowd before the Police would move them on.

Sophie was always on call, squeezing Panks into hidey holes in Town Halls to heckle politicians. Being small was an advantage when she herself curled into an organ loft or a broom cupboard, washroom closet or under seats; holding her breath when random searches were made through the building before a meeting, bluffing her way out of any accidental discovery by pretending to be the cleaner.

Now that the Panks had abandoned their Socialist allies,

refusing to support the local Labour candidates, once-sympathetic people would jostle and heckle, seeing them as traitors. Not that the Suffragettes fared any better with the Liberal candidates who considered them anti-government, evicting them from meetings at every opportunity.

Another blow to Sophie's morale came from an unexpected quarter. The total obedience demanded by the Pankhursts caused derision among serious-thinking women who refused to support an organisation which did not even give its own membership a vote. Sometimes she wondered why she was still supporting them herself. Then sudden memories of the torture chair would invade her mind; it dangled over her, hovered next to her every waking moment, jumped out of empty spaces, bringing back the fear, the pain and the anger. This anger sustained her through all the frog marching, spitting, groping, punches and blows, fuelling her resolve to get even and stay militant.

Yet operating away from her own home town made her protest easier to perform; all the caterwauling and yelling like a fishwife was done out of sight of loved ones. She admired Edith Rigby's ability to shock her Preston neighbours in Winckley Square. What a caution! There she would sit in the middle of her sitting room on a Persian rug, chain smoking cigars, swathed in scarves like a Sultana! Bang on nine o'clock she turfed everyone out into the cold so she could make supper for her hubby, no matter where they had reached on the agenda!

Their campaign was nothing if not thorough: petitioning voters at the election booths, selling books at any fair, fête or concert which would permit them to exhibit, street hawking badges and flags and posters outside city offices and alongside bags of Votes for Women tea, chocolate and home-made marmalade. Anything to bring in cash for the cause.

Yet this wild nomadic existence was taking Sophie far from home. Other reps had nursemaids for their children or families who supported them and compensated for their absence. More and more she was relying on Bert's good nature and a few loyal friends like Ada and Bridie. Her constant demands on their generosity were beginning to grate.

'Don't you think you ought to stay home a bit more? Phyllis is fretting. Where's it this time? How long are you going to be away this time?' Bert's nagging dripped like rain through a leaky roof, drip-dripping away into an iron bucket, first the rattle then the ping, noted but usually ignored as it plip-plopped to the brim. Then came the verbal torrent, pouring over her: 'One of these days, lass, you'll come home and we'll have flitted. Isn't it time we got a look in? I wish you were a proper wife and mother, instead of dashing here and there like a demented chicken!'

They circled cautiously around each other's responses, stabbing into the air, standing stubbornly in their separate corners. 'Don't you think this has gone on for long enough? Every time Miss Thompson calls to see you . . .

you'll have no friends left! They don't agree wi' it any more than I do, Phia.'

'I'm doing what I think is right. I make sacrifices an' all. Any road, our Phyllis can manage with a door key like all the rest in the street,' snapped Sophie as she wafted a duster across the furniture.

'How do you know how she manages? You're never here,' Bert answered back.

'Come off yer high horse! When have either of you gone without clean clothes or a cooked meal? Or haven't you noticed I'm up at dawn, seeing to it all before I go?' stormed his wife.

'I wouldn't know when you got up,' replied her husband as the gloves came off for the fisticuffs proper, each trying to inflict the most hurt, lashing out with verbal ammunition; explosions of bitterness and frustration stock-piled for months for just such a skirmish. 'Ever since you got yersel' jailed up, you've hardly looked in my direction, never mind slept in the same bed!'

'Oh, so that's what this is really about, is it? Not getting your marital dues? That's all you men think about, is getting yer hands up women's skirts. Animals!' Sophie spat.

'Go and boil yer stupid head. You want a good seein' to!' came Bert's reply.

'You and whose army? Stupid? Oh, yes, I must be stupid – made to match you. I'm sick of doing for you and yer Labour shower, sick of scrubbing, washing, and filling yer fat bellies. Sick of all this argy-bargying. You only come round the once and I'm going to do what I please, so stick that in yer pipe and smoke it!'

Sophie lashed his pride with her words, trampling his manhood. She watched him redden, his black eyes narrowing to slits. Now came the moment when Bert was tempted to exert brute force to subdue her will. He leaped forward to clout her but she was too quick and put the table between them, grabbing the bread knife as a weapon. 'Move one step further, Albert bloody Knowles, and you'll see what Suffragettes can do! I've taken enough insults from your kind and I'm not takin' a hiding from you or any other bloody bloke. If that's all you think of me, the sooner I'm out of this place the better. You can just fend for yersel'. I have a job to go to.'

Sophie grabbed her jacket from the back of the wooden chair to flee down Plover Street for a bus.

'I'm leaving him, Ada.' Sophie stood at the door of the school house, soaked to the skin. 'I can't be doin' with his mitherin' any longer so I'm off for a bit to sort meself out.' It all spilled out in a garbled rush.

'Come in, Sophie, I'll put the kettle on. Do sit down.'

'I can't stop. Will you mind our Phyllis for a few days? I'll sort summat out when I get fixed.'

'Where will you go?' asked Ada in alarm.

'To London and Clement's Inn HQ. I'll go where I'm needed. Vinnie'll see me right. I have some travel expenses owin'. I can't stand this town anymore – it's so narrow-minded. I'm sorry, I don't mean you. I'm all of a do. Say goodbye to Grace for me. She keeps callin' but her and me is strangers these days.'

'More's the pity, she could do with her friends. She's been acting so oddly. I'm worried about her. She never goes out. This charity work has worn her out,' sighed Ada.

'She's not the only one worn out! But I haven't time. I want to nip back home and gather a few bits. I'll leave a message for Phylly to catch a bus up after school. She can come in yer class. She'll be no bother.'

'I'm sure she won't be but I wish you'd discussed this with me before. It's all so hasty, Sophie dear, and I've a lot on myself at the moment. But I suppose it will be only for a few days . . . How long will you be away? Have you told Phylly your plans? You can't just walk out on her,' pleaded Ada.

'She understands the Cause must come first.'

'Before your only child? You do surprise me. I would have thought you of all people would question that argument. Sounds like one of Vinnie's little mottoes does that. Easy to say at a meeting but hard to explain at bedtime. Take Phyllis with you if it's that important,' said Ada with concern.

'No, not possible. Vinnie hasn't room for a child. But if I settle I will send for her, don't worry. Thanks, Ada, you're a brick. I must dash.' And Sophie tore off down the cobbled street, her clogs ringing against the cobblestones.

Ada slammed the door. You've been dumped on again! she thought. Why did people always think she would pick up their mess behind them like a skivvy? The spell in prison had turned Sophie from a caring mother into a headstrong wilful child, a whirling dervish of perpetual motion with no thought for anybody but herself. It was too much. It really was. Is it because I'm a plain old maid with no ties, always obliging with a spare room and tea and lashings of sympathy, that muggins gets lumbered? she wondered resentfully.

Such thoughts made her recoil with guilt. What did Mother used to say? 'If you don't put others first, then you won't have been worth the trouble of bringing up.' But what about me? cried her selfish heart. No one gave her a second thought. Poor Phyllis was not to blame for her thoughtless parent. The child was a good companion. How could she be so ungracious? Nevertheless the feeling of being taken for granted needled her. Being upset with Sophie at this imposition on her good nature was a new and bitter feeling.

'Where you goin' with that bag, Mam?' Phyllis sat on the top stair watching her mother throwing clothes into a pile with a distracted air. 'Are you leaving us again? Where's it this time?'

'I'm goin' to London to see Miss Shaw and sort out my life.'

'Am I going too?' Phyllis jumped up with excitement.

'No, love. I have to go on me own.'

For answer Phyllis grabbed the bag and strewed the contents on the floor. 'Yer not goin' . . . I don't want you to!' The child wrapped herself round her mother's waist and clung on tight.

'I'm sorry. I can't manage for both of us yet. Let me get on and I'll take you to Auntie Ada's for a bit of a break. You like her school.'

'No I don't! I want to come with you. I heard you and me dad yelling yer heads off last night. I'm not deaf. You've fallen out and yer leavin' us and then I'll be nobody's child!' sobbed Phyllis into her mother's floury apron pockets.

'Eeh, love, I'm not leaving you behind. I have to go and be useful. This is important work, this getting the Vote for Women. I'm doing it for you and for your future. You'll thank me when yer grown up. How could you think you were nobody's child?'

'Well, you won't take me and Dad has to go to work. Auntie Grace is too busy and Auntie Ada has hundreds of kids to look after. I don't want a stupid vote when I'm grown up! I want me mam at home and speaking to me dad, not on a platform getting pelted with tomatoes and rotten eggs. What if you get hurt? Who'll look after you?'

'I'm not putting you near any danger so I must go alone. Sometimes grown ups have to obey a higher cause and set an example, Phylly, whatever . . . I'll send you lots of post-cards for your collection.' She unwound her daughter's hands from around her waist. 'You're yer mam's great hope. I want you to have a good education and pass your qualifying exam, do well at yer lessons – not like yer poor old mam who only got a dunce's pass. You'll never be stuck in t'mill with no choices.'

'But I don't want a stupid education! I want to come with you now.' Phyllis pulled at her mother's skirt with tears rolling down her cheeks.

'Stop snivelling and I'll give you a whole penny for the sweet shop. You can have kali crystals and a Spanish stick, gobstoppers and a lucky bag. We'll put on our coats and hats and catch the bus to Ada's together. Now how about that for a somebody's child?' whispered Sophie with a heavy heart.

Vinnie Shaw scrumpled the letter and chucked it on to the floor of her bed-sitting room in disgust. Oh, Sophie! How dare you just up sticks and leg it down South on a whim? she thought. You can't leave your post until relieved. I shall have to send a telegram. The timing's all wrong.

How could she explain that the emphasis was now on recruiting Society debutantes and West End women, rather than encouraging the toughies and the clog and shawl brigades. Christabel Pankhurst ruled supreme as their Commander-in-Chief and allowed no dissension among the rank and file.

Sophie was not the type to fit in at HQ. She was too rough-spoken and too Northern; a simple working woman like Annie Kenney, but without the slavish devotion and lapdog spirit which kept Annie firmly by her Commander's side. There were plenty of beefy roughnecks to serve body-guard duty already.

Their nets were cast in a different direction now; a harvest was being reaped among the gilded youth of London Society. Beautiful girls in white robes and sashes, women of breeding, delicate but well-connected, whose ever-increasing defections from the other Suffrage societies swelled their coffers as well as their subscription lists. They garlanded the summer processions with academic gowns worn over miles of white lace; with wide-brimmed millinery trimmed with ostrich feathers and silk flowers. Swathed in yards of tulle netting like vestal virgins they offered oblations to their beloved Queen of the Mob.

The Women's Parliament which met each year was a showcase for the ruling triumvirate, two Emmelines and a Christabel, in which to trumpet their call to arms. Vinnie knew it was not a standing conference to encourage open debate and delegate decision-making but rather a vast Cathedral of worshipping believers. Christabel screamed for a new Jerusalem on earth and they responded with rapturous applause and total obedience. Vinnie smiled to herself cynically, recognising how the charisma of the leader was milking her audiences dry. She had to admit that the woman positively steamed with power and Vinnie enjoyed every minute spent basking in its reflected heat. To sit at top table and hear the real gossip, to be invited into the inner sanctum, was something she did not want to relinquish.

Now stupid Sophie could spoil all her stratagems by deserting her post, leaving a gap in the Northern defences which would soon be noted and expected to be filled. In no way was Vinnie prepared to leave the excitement at the centre of operations for yet another foray into Godforsaken territory. I must humour the woman, make her see the error of her flight South and get her back to Euston Station before her absence raises comment, she thought. Perhaps I can pass off her stay as a brief induction visit to rally the troops in the provinces? Perhaps if I play on her motherly feelings, she will pine for her brat and return of her own accord?

Vinnie tossed and turned in her bed. If she mishandled this impromptu visit, she could kiss her own promotion goodbye. Within her sights was a senior post at HQ which was tailor-made for her experience in the field; a post recently made vacant by a backroom squabble over Annie Kenney. She was to have a new role liaising between the press and the WSPU which would entitle her to good expenses and a transport allowance. There was too much at stake for her to fall at the last fence. Plotting and scheming, Vinnie lay awake all night.

Bog-eyed and furious next morning, she scanned the notice board at Euston Station for the arrival of the Manchester train. How she hated this place! The noises and smells took her straight back to that disastrous holiday when Mama had traipsed them all over London then abandoned her with scarcely a tear on the platform, shoving her into a Ladies Only carriage like some left luggage and swanning off with her new husband without so much as a backward glance. The occasional letter with a money draft was all the mothering she'd ever received since. Not that it bothered her overmuch so long as someone met her bills at the end of the month.

As the crowds streamed out from behind the ticket barrier she caught a glimpse of a shabby little woman with a cluster of bags, standing wide-eyed and weary in an awful grey outfit from under which poked a pair of hobnailed boots. Sophie was standing quite mesmerised by the rush around her, drained of her old fire, as out of place as a bunch of dandelions in a silver and gilt vase.

Just for a second, despite her annoyance, Vinnie experienced a pang of sympathy as she came forward to greet her. 'Well, what a surprise. Let me look at you. Definitely filled out since we last met, eh? Do I spy some grey hairs? But still the old Sophie.' She was trying hard to sound welcoming.

'Oh, Vinnie, am I glad to see thee! I've bin countin' th'hours on the train. Phyllis sends her love and Ada asks to be remembered.'

'And Bert too?' Vinnie probed, needing to assess what was going on.

'Don't know. He can go jump in the Lodge pond for all I care,' said Sophie, but her words had a hollow ring to them. 'I'll do anything, Vin. Just find me some stairs to wash and I'll be content.' Vinnie ignored the request as she ushered her firmly out into the morning.

'First you must have a little holiday. I'll show you all the sights of London and HQ in due course. Look upon this break as a well-earned rest at WSPU expense. You've done sterling work and it's not easy to find replacements, but no more of that for now. Where would you like to begin?' laughed Vinnie as they marched along the pavement.

'Need you ask? Give us a butchers at them Houses o' Parliament, of course. Let's have a recce and see what all the fuss is about.' Sophie smiled with excitement, a sparkle in her eyes for the first time in months.

Vinnie's flat was their first port of call. It was in Trentham Gardens, tucked away in a quiet cul-de-sac. They climbed up flights of echoing stairs to a set of rooms almost on the rooftop, overlooking chimney stacks and attics; not a bit how Sophie had imagined it all to be. It was just one living room, one bedroom, and a tiny washroom carved out of the hallway. Sophie sniffed all the strange scents of unfamiliar territory as she picked her way over the clutter of pamphlets and magazines in the hall.

The sitting room was cheerless, without a fire in the grate. Dust rose in the afternoon sunshine which crept through the attic window and showed up the mess. This room needed a good bottoming, she decided. She would be up all night coughing if she did not find a beater for the rugs and cushions. Her fingers were itching to tidy up. Vinnie was obviously not one for everything in its place and a place for everything. The walls were crowded with oil paintings and sketches, ledges littered with vases and statuettes so bare-bummed they would have made Bert blush.

It was really a rather shabby little room but having an indoor lavvy with a tiled floor was quite a treat. Sophie stood on the mahogany seat to examine the contraption, pulled the chain and heard the cistern flush with satisfaction. Every house should have one of these.

For two weeks Vinnie kept them both so occupied that the visitor had no time to draw breath. They tramped across the parks of London, scrunching the October leaves with their boots like children, hiked along the river banks, peered into museums and galleries, around palaces and monuments, until Sophie's feet, swollen in ill-fitting shoes, gave up in protest.

Vinnie played the charming hostess. She made up an officer's canvas camp bed in the tiny sitting room, waited on Sophie, cooked exotic meals with strange vegetables from Covent Garden Market for she was in a vegetarian phase – the latest craze among the cognoscenti of Clement's Inn. Once a week a pasty-faced woman trekked up the stairs with a huge basket, doled out all the clean linen, freshly starched and pressed, and collected all Vinnie's laundry. Sophie had never seen such extravagance. It was all right for some!

She was glad that she had not dragged Phyllis down with her. This was no place for a child. For all Plover Street was narrow and dark, there were plenty of alleys for kiddies to let off steam. This was too much like a prison cell for an energetic youngster. Thinking about Phylly made her yearn for home. It might not be much but at least it was clean and tidy and you could eat off cutlery which was not stained dull and sometimes not even washed up properly. Hard as it was to admit, Vinnie barely kept the smells down.

They explored the street markets where Sophie grazed for bargains among the bookstalls, but Vinnie avoided HQ.

The pressures of the past year rolled off Sophie's shoulders, bringing a fresh spring to her step. She sent post-cards with her address to Phyllis and Ada and even wrote a note to Grace and a brief letter to Bert, informing him she planned to stay on indefinitely. Vinnie suppressed her own unease.

Autumn sunshine faded into grey mists, bringing the first hints of dampness and frost to the city. They lit a fire in the evenings or queued for seats in the gods at West End shows. Vinnie threw up smoke screens whenever Sophie mentioned her future but the thought hung over them like a damp blanket, suffocating any serious conversation. Sophie was restless. 'Have you thought about a job for me here? I'm dying to see your offices.'

Vinnie took a deep breath and launched in.

'We really need you up North, Soph. It's a bit too busy at the moment, what with the Houses of Parliament about to be re-opened and the possibility that our Conciliation Bill will be chucked out again. Rumours are rife that it's going to be squashed one way or another, then it will be action stations all over the country to protest. The summer truce will be over with a vengeance. All hands to the pump, old girl. Each to his outpost.'

Sophie shook her head.

'I can be useful here then. I've taken enough knockings back. Phylly will be fine with Ada for a bit longer. Bert can stew in his own juice. I want to stay with you where I can be useful. No one bothers with our lot unless there's a big wig to clobber with us banners. I'd like to see who I'm working for and where we stand.'

'You know what we stand for. The Vote is a symbol, a safeguard and an instrument,' said Vinnie, puzzled for a second.

'Oh, aye, but I were thinkin': we shouts "Votes for Women", yet not all the fellas get the Vote. Are we sayin' "Votes for Women" with the same provisions as there are for men now?'

'Come on, you know we aren't an Adult Suffrage Campaign. We focus only on Votes for Women,' replied Vinnie in exasperation.

'But if we win, I still don't get the Vote, do I? I don't qualify, not having any property or owt, do you see what I mean? All this shouting but we never make it very clear to ordinary women where they'll stand, do we?'

'Who's been getting at you? Grace Thompson? I thought we'd seen the last of her sour grapes. She would certainly qualify for the Vote,' said Vinnie, bored with the way this argument was heading.

'Nobody's been gettin' at me. I just figured it out. Fancy never bothering to reckon it up before! Makes you think . . .'

'I suppose so, but when we put a point across it needs to be simple and eye catching,' Vinnie said firmly.

'Even if it's not exactly true?' quizzed Sophie.

'Look here! It's true enough for most of the women here

in the WSPU. When we win the war, time enough then to dictate the terms.'

'But the other societies say they want votes for everyone over twenty-one, regardless of their sex.' Sophie was clinging on like a terrier with a bone. Vinnie was growing bored with the debate.

'Why all this nit picking all of a sudden?'

'I'd hardly call being beaten up and hounded, spat on and unpopular with everyone "nit picking". It gets me down, being chased by snotty-nosed kids and pelted wi' rubbish. Landladies suddenly discover they're full up when you arrive for a kip. They can smell us coming. I've been belted more times than the wives in Plover Street on a Sat'day night when the Wanderers lost at home,' came the reply.

'I think, Sophie Knowles, you are getting homesick. Perhaps it's time for you to go back and sort out your life? You'll not find it easy to support a child and live in the city. Believe me, I can only manage with the help of my old pater and mater who would rather keep me here than have me land on their doorstep! I've told you before, the Pankhursts don't like us to speak out of turn. They prefer things done their way, and they've not put a foot wrong so far.'

'So when do I get the honour of meeting them?'

'The Pankhursts? I don't know, dear,' stalled Vinnie. 'They are very busy people but I'll take you to Clement's Inn tomorrow and you can see the powerhouse for yourself.'

★   ★   ★

The Committee rooms were bustling with a frenzy of activity: women racing round with copy for the news-letters and pamphlets, avoiding piles of paper stacked on the floor. On the walls hung huge maps of the country with flags indicating all the main rallying points. Secretaries typed furiously while others with purple-stained fingers rolled out leaflets on the duplicating machine. Sophie had never been in an office before. There was a constant noise from the machines and people brushing past as if she was invisible.

She was briefly introduced to the office manager, Jessie Kenney, sister of the famous Annie, who scurried by on her way to a meeting. The other women were more of Grace and Vinnie's sort, well-dressed and with plummy accents. 'Lah-di-dah,' Bun Gran would have said; pleasant but cool in their welcome.

Sophie was looked up and down with interest, like a traveller from a foreign country. Now she knew why Vinnie had been putting off the hour! It was that other world again; the over-the-wall world where she didn't fit in, shabby and homespun, awkward and tongue-tied. They seemed to have their own secret language and jokes in a code she couldn't fathom out; the key to this closed society would never be given to a Plover Street resident. Vinnie was one of them in her lavender silk shirt and WSPU tie, her dark green skirt and martial air. They seemed all to be wearing a uniform in the battle colours of the Union. Some wore badges and brooches and service medals pinned to their jackets; marks of distinction that set them apart as crack troops.

What a contrast to her own mob up North! In her mind's eye Sophie could see them still, heaving those trestle tables across church hall floors, holding back the hordes of scruffy bargain hunters, rummaging and rooting through the piles like scavengers in their mud colours. Then there were the night vigils with the collecting tins outside grimy factory gates, or the occasional summons to hear Edith Rigby and the long traipse home. All to keep this show on the road.

Without being told she knew her efforts did not count for much with this bunch of kite flyers. My accent is wrong, my clothes are graceless and tatty, she told herself. I don't like the smell of this place. Vinnie was right all along. Suddenly the penny marble dropped down the bagatelle. What a fool she was, what a spoiled child she had been, humoured and fobbed off by Vinnie as she bided her time, never intending to admit Sophie amongst the hierarchy. They already had their token clog and shawl in Annie Kenney.

Vinnie had her own plans. Plans which would never include Sophie. This was just a visit, and visiting time was over.

That night Sophie tossed and turned in her narrow camp bed, watching a moth flicker round the bedside candle. It fluttered across her cheek, making her jump. She had courted sleep for two hours but it was elusive. Why had she invested so much hope in her flight South when it had obviously been a waste of time, abandoning Phyllis just to pander to her own fancy? Her welcome here had worn distinctly hollow. Vinnie seemed relieved when she'd talked about train timetables and bag-packing earlier that evening. The holiday was over.

She woke with a scream. A large black moth with silken wings was thrashing about on top of her, smothering her. Fighting for breath, she tore at the bed sheets to escape the struggling creature as its wings, on fire, melted into a bloody pool of boiling liquid. Her screaming brought Vinnie to her side with a candle. 'Shush, shush, it's only a nightmare,' said her friend, sitting on the edge of the bed.

'Something is wrong at home, I can feel it. I must go. Someone is ill. Fetch me a cab and I'll get the first train.'

'Calm down. You're overtired. And we did have cheese for supper, remember? You heard from Phyllis yesterday. Nothing is wrong. Settle down again and I'll get you a drink.' Vinnie patted her hand gently.

'Don't leave me . . . I saw this thing falling, falling, and I couldn't stop it . . . I tried to catch it but it was crushing me. Oh, Vinnie, what have I done? I must go home now, just to check . . .'

'Not before tomorrow night. There's to be a rush on Parliament. The truce is over at last. Put your glad rags on, girl, we've been invited to dinner with the gang. Let me get you some cocoa. And no more talk about premonitions. That's an order from your superior,' laughed Vinnie as she dismissed Sophie's fears.

Chapter Fifteen

'Let's have a look at you. Where did you get that dress? It's gorgeous and suits you so. Why haven't you put it on before?' said Vinnie as she fingered the material with amazement. 'I've got just the necklace to set it off.'

She opened her jewellery case and lifted out a silver necklace from which hung an enamelled pendant in the shape of a butterfly with purple and flame-coloured wings tipped with delicate beads.

Sophie had packed Grace's dress on impulse, just in case. It was always called 'Grace's dress', hardly ever worn, kept enveloped in tissue paper and camphor candles. Now, glowing from a hip bath in front of the fire, her dark hair puffed out over a pad, Society fashion, dressed with flair by Vinnie, Sophie felt like a princess going to a ball.

'Grace bought us this . . . Why is it you two never got on?' Sophie paused for some answer, conscious her smart outfit was giving her confidence to tackle this long-time puzzle.

'What has she told you?' Vinnie replied.

'Nowt. But I know she were agin you from the first moment you clapped eyes on each other. Come on, tell me. I know you were at school with her and Dora Wagstaff. Did you fall out?'

'You know how it is with some people. Grace always takes everything too seriously, can't take a joke or a hint. We just got up each other's nose. She's so tight-laced about some things and she was odd even as a girl.'

'No, she weren't. She was just used to being on her own. She never had a mam,' argued Sophie.

'Neither did I, for that matter. At least not one worth having. Grace always had a peculiar way with her. The first time I went to her house, that awful Vicarage somewhere down your end of town, we had to play silly games and I remember standing in this garden when up popped a dirty little creature, some mill hand, asking to play with her.'

'Say that again?' Sophie gulped at Vinnie's words.

'Grace never had any proper sense of her station. All that money and . . .'

'. . . never any airs and graces with it.' Sophie turned on her icily. 'That was me you shooed away like a flea off the table. Grace and I never spoke for years after because of that and I blamed her, but it was all your fault!' She stared at Vinnie with fresh eyes. Yes, of course. That brassy hair, that haughty stare. How could she not have recognised the girl in the woman? The girl from the other world who'd spoiled their Bread and Roses Society?

'Well, it didn't do you any harm, did it? Never too early

to stand on your own two feet. Look how well you've turned out.' Vinnie could sense the tension and giggled nervously.

'Have I now? You were rotten to come between us. Grace saved my life once and it was her influence got me the care that cured me. How could I ever forget that?' And again Sophie felt a cold stab of fear inside her.

'Nonsense! We were all only children. All in the past, no sense harking back.'

'So what did you do to her then, to make her so frosty with you?'

'Oh, just some silly prank when we were students. She thought I took her young man, but he was never interested in her in the first place. She gets so wound up about nothing! Let's change the subject. We've been invited to dine out with the crowd and then retire to the Pethick Lawrences' to await further orders.'

Vinnie brushed down her own blue velvet gown. Sophie could not help noticing that the pile was worn shiny at the back. Suddenly Vinnie's sparkling company was turning flat and distinctly sour.

'What's going to happen?' she asked, studying herself in the mirror. Her necklace glowed in the lamplight but her chestnut eyes were dull.

'I'm not sure yet. It's not safe to plan too far ahead just in case of spies. You know we're watched all the time. That's why we'll be going off to dinner in our best togs, to put 'em off the scent.'

Vinnie was ready to leave the flat in the usual tip but

Sophie could not resist an instinct to clear away clothes and tidy surfaces, shoving her own unopened post into her pocket. The uneasy feeling inside her persisted, whispering: 'Write to Grace and apologise. Write and tell her why you ran away. She will understand.'

They took a cab towards the West End and Sophie shivered in a flimsy jacket borrowed for the occasion from her friend.

They drew up at the grand entrance to a large hotel. The door was flung wide by a flunkey in braided uniform and breeches. Vinnie stepped out with an assured air but Sophie hung back, overawed by the splendour of the setting.

She found herself in a sumptuous hall gilded with golden plasterwork, huge floral displays, lavish velvet curtains, draped and with gold-tasselled fringes, just like the stage of the Grand Theatre. Everywhere she turned candles shimmered by gilt-framed mirrors amongst acres of starched linen and cut flowers in silver vases. From the ceiling hung a glittering crystal chandelier; at her feet was carpeting as thick as a mattress. This was a world of wealth and privilege which would have Bert and his cronies high on their horses with indignation.

She smiled at the thought. Eeh, Gran, if yer up there watchin' . . . a right Sodom and Gomorrah is this! Poor Bert, he'd never cope wi' this lot, but there's no one to stop me stuffin' meself fit to burst like Lady Oftenbroke. It won't happen again. This thought gave her the confidence to stride forth and meet the waiting party.

A group of women held out their arms to welcome

Vinnie: an elegant older lady in an amethyst guipure lace overcoat worn over a gauzy straight gown as smooth as a gull's wing; a younger woman in pale green tulle with a choker of pearls mirroring her perfect complexion; and the plainer-faced woman, wisps of hair straying from her bandeau, who flung her arms around Vinnie with delight. The Pankhursts. Sophie almost curtseyed before them.

Vinnie turned in her direction as an afterthought. 'I would like to introduce my friend, Sophie Seddon Knowles, one of our representatives in the North-west district, here for a briefing. Sophie was one of my fellow hunger strikers in Preston Jail.'

One by one Sophie was presented to Mrs Pankhurst, Sylvia, Adela, to Emmeline Pethick Lawrence and lastly to Christabel.

'Charming, my dear, delighted to meet one of you at last.' Miss Pankhurst spoke as if they were old allies, as if she knew her, as if for a second she were one of them. Then the woman's gaze flitted to other new-arrivals and she glided away.

They were placed like honoured guests at a table under the chandelier. Overwhelmed by the glamour of the company and the setting, Sophie watched nervously as the endless courses were presented on gold-rimmed plates, holding back until she observed which fork or spoon was the right instrument with which to attack a dish, fixing her gaze on Vinnie's movements across the table.

The woman next to her smiled warmly, and to Sophie's surprise winked. A girl with golden hair and twinkling blue eyes, she had a sharp face which reminded Sophie of Grace's in her younger days.

'Bit different from yer snap in the mill?' the woman whispered, stretching her hand forward to grab a crusty dinner roll. She was missing a finger tip and Sophie realised she was talking to Annie Kenney, the famous millhand from Oldham. 'What a show, eh?' Her accent was thick and unaffected. 'Women gone up in t'world, that's thee and me.' She laughed at herself. Sophie relaxed immediately and they chatted about Churchill's visit and Sophie's efforts to fly the flag. Annie knew all about life in the North of England and was not in any hurry to return there.

The meal seemed to go on for hours and Sophie was thankful that there was no waistband to her dress. She had eaten enough grub to last a week and felt herself nodding off from the effects of real wine. How these ladies managed to stay so slender on such a diet! Then she remembered that every one of them had been on hunger strike and probably would be again.

Soon enough they were out in the chill November air, making their way back to apartments close to Clement's Inn. In a vast drawing room, its doors securely shut, Christabel Pankhurst revealed her plan to attend the late-night sitting of the newly recalled Parliament. This was to mark an end to their truce; signify their protest at the chucking out of the Suffrage Bill once again.

'Do we go back to get changed?' Sophie whispered to Vinnie, conscious they were all dressed in beautiful evening gowns.

'Oh, no! That's the hoot! We'll spring out and catch them unawares. If not, well, it's stone-throwing time again . . . usual stuff.'

They were ushered secretly down the back stairs and through the servants' quarters like thieves in the night. The maids stood back dumbstruck at this procession of glamorous ladies squeezing inelegantly into covered wagons and carts outside. Mist curled around the back streets as the horses plodded over the cobbles and the rich dinner churned in their guts. Sophie felt a twinge of unease. 'What's goin' to happen, Vin?'

'We rush out of the cart and in through the gates if we can, push the guards out of the way. Lots of screaming and noise, lots of publicity. Stick close by, but if you get clobbered, well, it's each for herself. You should know the score by now.'

I know the score all right. The pursuit, arrest, hunger strike, prison. Sophie felt sick, all the fight draining from her. A surfeit of rich food hung like lead in her stomach, burning against her ribs. Try as she might, she could not raise her spirits. For once she was shivery scared. Here I am, sitting on makeshift benches with the greatest women in the movement – a privilege granted to only a few – and all I can do is tremble like a bobbin, all of a spin! Suddenly it all felt unreal: the restaurant, the elegant company, a grotesque parody of what she was fighting for. What am I doing here? What am I fighting for? Is it just for the right of ordinary women to manage their own lives and to have some say in the government of their country, a chance to rise up from the drudgery of daily life, to rise like bread? She looked around them all. How many of them had ever baked a loaf of bread in their pampered lives? What did these women know about her bread and butter world?

A suffocating panic stirred inside her, not unlike the emotion she had first felt in prison and that same feeling of foreboding from her nightmare. 'It'll all end in tears.' Bun Gran's warning whispered in her ears. There was hidden danger in this strange territory, the menacing misty streets. She was far from home and those who would be anxious for her welfare, from Bert and Grace, Ada and Phyllis; all those whom she had so thoughtlessly abandoned.

Bumping over the cobbles there was plenty of time to bring each one yearningly to mind. Into her dark thoughts came the fear that she would never see them again; that prison walls were beckoning, and the torture chair. Wake up, you dozy brush! What have you been dreamin' of? she asked herself. This was not her fight. They had different rules here. She would not be missed.

Her mind was razor sharp, focused on only one dreadful fear. The tally man was coming to call for his dues, for all her selfish gadding about of the past three weeks. Now was the hour and there was no escaping this engagement. Funny how she no longer cared whether Vinnie was embarrassed by her presence here or not. She would see it through to the bitter end, no matter what. Her only hope was to slip away unscathed when it was all over.

Where have I been these past months? Floating about like soapsuds in the breeze, so busy I've not even been bothered about my friends, not even opened their letters. She felt the rustle of envelopes in her pocket. If I get out of this in one piece, it's time I went home and bottomed out my life. Time to be honest with myself. Back to plain clothes and porridge, and time to repair the Bread and Roses Society once and for all!

They were waiting in the shadows long before the Houses of Parliament: waiting with reinforcements, Black Marias, foot soldiers. Not polite policemen from the 'A' Division but burly dockside troops, sons of the East End, who would stand no nonsense from a bunch of hysterical women. Waiting with tracker dogs and truncheons, waiting with flares down the escape routes, waiting to attack.

The exercise was doomed before it began; a futile gesture to storm the blue wall of well-entrenched enforcers of law and order. Christabel charged ahead, her cream hat bobbing aloft. A soap box was found for her from which to address the crowds. Rising like Venus from a sea of dark uniforms to inspire her troops: 'Rise up, women! Rise up for your freedom! Let us charge forth like Boadicea in her chariot. Right is on our side. The brave deeds done this night will be tomorrow's headlines. Forward! Votes for Women!'

'Votes for Women!' echoed the crowd as they pushed forward. Vinnie and Sophie were squashed in the fray, hordes of shoving, sweating bodies pushing them back and forth like waves hurled against a harbour wall. Stones from the back landed not on the wall but on the heads of the frontliners, a line of bloodied women crushed front and behind. The police wall broke and regrouped, separating and encircling groups of Suffragettes, engulfing them tightly. They were outnumbered and overpowered.

'Use your hat pins, stupid! Prick your way up front! Get stuck in there, gels!' came a rallying call from Vinnie.

Sophie was hatless and defenceless as four policemen circled her, cutting her off from the flow, pushing her into a corner against a wall, away from the main débâcle into a group of excited onlookers.

The rest was a blur of panic and fear as she smelled the booze and the sweat and felt the hands pulling at her skirt; roars of laughter as they yanked it higher up her thighs, over her face. 'Take a picture of her drawers. Let's have'm off her!' She fought like a wild cat, suffocating in the heat and the shame as she felt the hands groping her legs, pulling down her garters. Someone pinned her arms behind her back and grabbed at the front of her bodice, ripping it open in the attack. Then she fell forward on to the pavement and tasted the dust in her mouth and the smell of blood in her nose. There was a sickening thud of a boot against her ribcage and she blacked out with the pain. Someone was touching her, feeling her body, and she kicked out instinctively, crying out to curse them, but no sound would come out, only a searing pain in her ribs.

'Gerrof me, you animals!' she cried out at last.

'It's all right, ducky.' A strange face hovered over her, trying to pull her gently from the mud. 'In here, quick! Come on, before you gets arrested!' The woman in a poke bonnet half-dragged her through a door into a church hall where other wounded women lay gasping, bleeding, crying on the pews. They were inside the citadel of the Salvation Army. Another officer in uniform examined her and smiled.

'You'll live, but we can bind up your ribs in case they are cracked. You've lots of bruises but no damage, me duck.'

Sophie sipped some water, watching the woman move over to a frail lady who was semi-conscious, lying on a makeshift stretcher. Her face had once been beautiful but now was merely silver skin stretched over bone. 'Get her to hospital. Look at her. If she survives the night it will be a miracle.' Sophie sat transfixed by the sight of the woman's bleeding face, white hair tumbling down like cotton threads, breasts exposed and bruised.

'Who could do this to an old woman?' Her own strength ebbed and flowed through the long night. With aching weariness, she tried to rise but staggered a few paces only. Her instinct was to get out of this hideous place, this whole alien city, but in her more lucid moments she realised she had neither money nor support. All her belongings were in Vinnie's flat and Vinnie was sure to be behind bars now with the Pankhursts. As she struggled up, a Salvation Army woman held her hand.

'Stay a while, dearie. Your friends will know to collect you here. It's safe here.'

She waited in vain for any message from Vinnie. The pain in her ribs was growing worse and she lay down in defeat, watching the dawn through the windows. It was a room full of memories of her own childhood: the rows of chairs and the hymn books, the smell of polish. Memories of St Anselm's, Plover Street, and that first meeting with Grace, assailed her.

Sophie felt over her aching body and wept for her humiliation at the hands of the ruffians who had played with her body like a toy. She fingered Grace's dress in disbelief. All that was left of the garment were torn muddy rags, covered in blood, lumps of black oil splattered across the hem. The dress given with such love and worn with such pride was beyond repair, a tawdry rag hardly covering her decency. She blamed herself for its destruction. How would it ever be replaced? How could she ever admit to Grace how careless she had been?

Then she felt the crumpled envelope still deep in her pocket seam and drew it out. She recognised the spidery scrawl of her oldest friend and tore it open in relief.

My dear Sophie,
You are very much missed at home. Come home, please, I think you are much needed here. By the time you read this letter, God alone knows where I will be. Although we have had our differences recently I just want you to know it was not I who told the newspaper of the protest in the Town Hall Square. As God is my witness, I would hate you to think me a traitor, a spy or an informant. The blame for that lies firmly at the door of the proprietor of

Mullarkey's fisheries who wanted to save his shop windows from any damage.

I will never forget the joy of our friendship, how close we once were. Perhaps all would have been different if Lavinia had not decided to return and spoil things between us again. Ask her about her first visit to my house with Dora.

I have no time to be bitter and mean to make the most of my short span. You know how fiercely I value my independence. I don't intend to be a burden to anyone.

Please take up the case of Mary O'Flynn when you return. I can see you as an excellent Poor Law Guardian one day. Remember me with kindness to Phyllis and Bert.

Aye your bread and roses friend,

Grace Thompson

The pages swam before her. The letter made no sense. But the nightmare insect rose out of it, dancing across the handwriting, flapping black menacing wings.

I must get back and see her. We can sort it all out then, Sophie decided.

The journey back to the flat in Trentham Gardens was a blurred nightmare. She somehow begged lifts, a sorry sight in her bloodstained outfit, claiming she had been knocked down accidentally. Some spat at her, recognising her as one of the Panks; others propositioned her to pay in kind for their helping hands. Weak as she was, she was in no mood to humour them.

Sophie found the spare key behind the loose brick in the

porch and let herself through the front door. Vinnie was not at home but there was a short letter and a pound note pinned with a Holloway brooch to her old hat.

Hope this finds you unscathed. The newspapers are calling it Black Friday! We are going to sue the police for use of undue force and improper attacks on the marchers. Am lying low with Sylvia. We may nip over to Paris for a short break out of the hullabaloo. Go back North and keep up the good work, old girl. Deeds not words! Leave key in the porch.

Last night seemed a thousand years ago as she washed, painfully and slowly, and gathered her bags, closing the door on the note and the money in disgust. She limped her way back to Euston Station, fingering Grace's letter.

Please God, let me not be too late. I must get back and sort out this mess! Panic rose in her again. The train seemed to stop at every station. She had no money for food or drink and her thirst was like a raging fire. Her head was throbbing and sometimes she saw the world as if through a thick veil of mist. She slept fitfully and woke only when a woman nudged her. She dragged her bag across Manchester to Victoria Station, using up every ounce of her strength and will to find the right platform. There was so much damage to repair.

If Grace was sick then she must nurse her back to health as her friend had once so generously done for her. How selfish I've been dumping Phyllis on Ada, so ungrateful and unthinking, she realised.

Once the grey moors overlooking the town came into view, clouded with rolling mizzle and gloom, she could relax for a few seconds. Her spirits rose with the sight of each familiar landmark: the Bee Hive Mill Chimney, the footbridge at Rose Hill, and the Town Hall clock. The pain in her ribs made her double up, sticking into her like a knife. She would go to Ada first and give them all a surprise. Funny how reluctant her legs were to climb the station steps out on to the Brow. She clung to the rail, forcing herself forward in one last effort. At the top of the stairs was a man selling the *Evening News*. By his side was a billboard. The headlines in bold black letters caused her knees to buckle under her as she crashed to the floor with a scream. 'Oh, no! Dear God, no!'

Into the Fire
1910

Chapter Sixteen

Grace Thompson paused at the doctor's gate, clutching her handbag to her chest. It was far too bright an autumn day to sit in his waiting room, then be prodded and examined like a fish on a slab. She did not want to see the look of disguised alarm, the pitying glance at the sight of her decomposing flesh, the flaring of his nostrils as he sniffed the sweet distinctive odour of death.

My breast is not for display. How could anyone want to touch such an odious object? The moment of weakness was passed and she turned briskly into the living day, along familiar pavements, scrunching the rotting leaves underfoot. This was a day for visiting friends, for walks in the country, for fresh air and exercise to calm her restless spirits.

She called first at Dora Wagstaff's residence but the maid said her mistress was out of town. So she strolled through Queen's Park to admire the autumn bedding, watching nursemaids wheeling sturdy baby carriages towards the swings. Then on impulse she hailed a cab for the ride to

Plover Street and knocked on the door of number nine. No one answered. She ploughed through the washing lines in the back alleys, remembering fondly all the secret schemes of the Bread and Roses Society. She wandered aimlessly up to the recreation ground, sitting on a bench in the rose garden, watching the park keeper prune overhanging branches.

It was going to be one of those days when nothing would turn out right. You're alone with this one, old girl, she thought. There's no one around to care what you do or where you go, so you'd better show them you can take care of everything yourself. You've always been alone, come to think of it, and everything you ever loved seemed to disappear the minute you reached out for it. Mama, Sophie, marriage hopes. They all left you to it. Grace smiled with relief. That was it. There was no one left who really mattered. No one at home. Even Papa had a nurse to care for him.

What's the point? Who cares? Why not show them you can enjoy what's left of your day? Grace jumped up with renewed energy and took an omnibus to the railway station.

She stood on Blackpool Promenade facing the offshore breeze. This is lovely, just the ticket! She found herself skipping and remained oblivious to the funny looks she was getting from passers by and their curious dogs. She found the exact pavilion where Bun Gran had stuffed herself sick with tubs of Morecambe Bay prawns, an Italian ice cream pokey hat and a bag of chips. What a day that had been, the donkey rides and roller skating! She dug deep into her lucky bag of memories but found it sadly unsatisfying.

You always were the hanger on, the maiden aunt, the pitiable object, she thought. Sophie always went home to Bert and Phyllis, leaving you alone.

Then she remembered the shopping expedition. Oh, the fun of buying that secret dress! Perhaps if she went back to the gown emporium in the Arcade and bought one for herself?

Grace strode back towards the town, to the very same shop window, pressing her nose against the glass. It felt cold and the shop was dark and shuttered. Trust her to come on their half-day closing.

Buying another dress would solve nothing. When would she ever wear it? When, for that matter, had she ever seen Sophie wearing the first?

Bright colours were not for Grace. She preferred sludgy safe tones which merged into the social scenery. Her friends would be perturbed to see such a dowdy spinster bedecked in a gaudy gown. She'd be out of place as Sophie must have felt in her rose velveteen. Poor Sophie! No wonder she had never worn the dress. How foolish Grace had been to foist it upon her. Oh, Sophie, how has our friendship come to this? she wondered. I do hope the letter will resolve matters. Perhaps if I climb the tower again and remember the giddy days . . .

Grace retraced her steps once more. She lingered along the edge of the sand, picking up smooth pebbles which she placed in her coat pockets, examining each one for colour and texture, rubbing her fingers over the cold stone as she stared out to sea. The beach was almost deserted, only a few bodies like herself bending into the wind. She peered up at the iron frame of Blackpool Tower and smiled.

It was closed for re-decoration but it was easy to persuade the attendant that she had an appointment in the Palm Grove Restaurant, that she was part of the renovation team. There were workmen going further aloft and she spun them a tale of wanting to see the very top before it became dark, and they were happy to oblige such a sensible lady. They left her on the landing by the railings, peering through the telescope and searching the scudding clouds for answers.

It was not the same, climbing those last steps alone, without the warmth of her bread and roses friend. 'Never go back', people say, and they were right. Without friends life was a stale crust. Without hope for the future what was the point? She felt like an eagle with telescopic eyes, soaring high above the world, round and round in a mindless circle with wearying wings, a watcher at the edge of the earth, tired.of the same sights and sounds. What was the point?

I might as well . . . Grace broke off. I'll show them! Why not? This is the place; at one with wind, sea, sky. Her heart thudded as she pinned the note to her lapel. Now was the time. She scrambled over the railing, opened her arms and prepared to fly.

The Coroner dutifully recorded yet another verdict of unlawful suicide. Another mind disturbed by over taxing of the brain and recent ill health. It was the second such finding that season and he made yet another plea to local officials to enclose the turret. It was becoming too convenient a departure point. Grace's defiant public exit sent shock waves throughout the town and the network of women's organisations across the Lancashire plain and beyond.

Ada read the subdued obituary in the *Evening News* but the reality of Grace's death would not sink into her skull. The small paragraph, tucked discreetly among reports of autumn bazaars and fireworks, concentrated on her charitable works in the community. The salacious details of her impulsive departure were left to the less respectful accounts in the national press: HEIRESS JUMPS OFF BLACKPOOL TOWER.

If only, wept Ada to Dora Wagstaff, we had noticed something and got her to talk to us.

If only, declared the Board of Guardians, she'd been less intense in nature this need not have happened.

If only, confessed Bridie Mullarkey, I had told them all sooner about Frank's treachery, no one would have accused Grace.

In a trickle then a stream and then a flood, all her quiet acts of kindness and generosity poured out into the open; a life lived for others at the expense of her own well-being. News came of her bequest to the female wing of the Union Workhouse, to ensure more amenities and better conditions. It was rumoured that Mary O'Flynn was to be moved to a private institution for reassessment and the possibility of release with an annuity. There was a generous bequest for Phyllis Knowles's education and a donation to the Women's Suffrage Society.

How little we know about other people, even our closest friends, thought Ada sadly as she cast her eyes over the latest occupant of her spare room. For in the wake of all this sorrow had come the burden that was Sophie Knowles, broken in spirit, standing on the school house doorstep like a rag dolly, so distraught by guilt and remorse she was unable to move, think or speak. Deep in shock, heavily sedated, she lay upstairs semi-conscious in the spare room. Once more the Knowles family was dependent upon her healing ministrations, trusting that somehow Ada would bring Sophia Seddon back to life.

Everyone came to pay their last respects to Grace: the nosy parkers and the ghouls alongside genuine mourners, official representatives and duty attenders in black ties and armbands. Ada sat with Phyllis and Dora, each wrapped up in their own thoughts and memories. On the coffin was placed the last bud of the season's *Rosa graciae* and a wreath of laurel entwined with Suffrage-striped ribbon: green for hope, white for purity and red for sacrifice. Or was it rage?

Ada was not sure what the red stood for now. Phyllis sat silently observing the rituals, frowning with concentration. She tugged at Ada's sleeve. 'Why did Auntie Grace go and leave us? Was she cross with me mam 'cos she wouldn't play out with her anymore?' Ada shook her head.

'Well, I'm vexed with her, Auntie Ada, for sneaking off

like that so I can't say tarrah or sorry for what Mam did, goin' off an' all. It's not fair, is it?'

Ada clasped her hand and whispered, 'No, you're dead right. It's not fair. But then life's not fair either.'

That's a lesson it is never too soon for you to learn, she thought to herself.

Sophie was woken by the lighting of the gas lamp outside her bedroom window. For the first time in weeks her sleep had been sound; the deep refreshing sort, not the frenzied thrashing and twisting of sheets she had hitherto endured. Nor had she fallen fearfully into a whirling abyss of nothingness, watching in terror that black bird hurling itself over the ridge, spiralling down clumsily, flapping broken wings to try to regain height – only to flop down like a spiked umbrella, bouncing on to the rocks below. How she feared that nightly journey into a hell where strange creatures leaped from the shadows.

With the dawn had come fear of familiar objects; the paisley shawl draped over the bedpost contained dragon figures dancing menacingly towards her. She had screamed at each chime of the clock and it had had to be removed. Then came the drugged sleep with a tiredness which encased every limb in lead. Her mind was misted with a veil of forgetfulness. Then came fear of venturing further than the little bedroom with its borrowed safety, plain walls and creaking bare boards. Here she was safe, behind the crocheted curtains of cream cotton lace.

She drifted in and out of a curiously comforting

acceptance that at last she had gone do-lally, 'daft in th'head', as Bun Gran had always predicted. Her brains were worn out and she no longer cared one jot or tittle what might happen next. I'm safe out of it all. No more up and doin' for me. They can certify me for all I care. What's the point? She cried into the pillow but could not remember why the tears were rolling down her nose.

Some nights, in the twilight between sleep and waking, the old fears had returned; gagging and choking against the tubes, the taste of rubber piercing her throat, flailing against violent bodies as she fought her way back to consciousness, feeling the bruising tightness of the binding across her ribs where those bastards had kicked her to the floor. Am I paralysed? She had checked out each reluctant limb, forcing it to obey her orders and move, sinking back with relief into the hollow she had moulded into the mattress. I will not think about any of that stuff again, she vowed.

Now she waited for the knocker-up to tap his pole tipped with brolly wires along the windows. There was only silence. Perhaps they had put straw down outside the house? She listened for the clatter of clogs, the morning trek to the mill gate, but all she heard was the clop of a horse's hooves and the rattle of bottles. Sophie searched through her cluttered mind. Where was she? There was a fire glowing softly in the bedroom grate. What an extravagance, to have a fire in a bedroom. She must be ill. But where was she? A familiar shape, silhouetted against the door, placed a water jug by her bedside.

'Good! You're awake, Sophie. I have a young visitor for

you. Let me freshen you up a bit and straighten the counterpane. I'll send Phyllis up and bring you some tea.'

Sophie smiled at Ada as a myriad questions rattled around her brain but remained unspoken. How strange to have no memory of how she came to be sleeping in Ada Norris's school house high on the edge of town. The past was a confusion of voices and echoes. Who was Phyllis? A young girl popped her head around the door.

'Mam? Feeling better now?' said the child in a white pinafore, starched and pleated, with black stockings and shiny boots; a girl with a side parting and thick black plaits braided loosely, strands of hair straggling across her brow. This girl reminded her of someone and Sophie smiled as if she knew who this creature was.

Phyllis? Phyllis? She scratched round desperately inside her head.

'Mam, wake up, don't doze off again. I can't stay long. I came on Mullarkey's fish and chip cart, delivering in the village. Missus Bridie sends her love. I brought you the newsletter. Miss Pearson, my teacher, gave it me to show you. It's got a picture of Miss Shaw in London. See, in the dock. She's done it again, putting tar in a pillar box. In the first division this time, in Holloway Prison.

'Look, and there's Miss Pankhurst with her, coming out. Miss Pearson says . . .' The child bounced eagerly on the bed springs.

'Put it by.' Sophie shoved the paper away.

'But, Mam! I thowt you'd want . . .'

'Put it in the bin!'

'Miss Pearson's joined the Suffs meetings at Mullarkey's, just like you and Auntie Grace.' The girl drew back, seeing the strange look on her mother's face, eyes screwed up tightly as if to blot out her words. 'Sorry, Mam, I forgot.'

Grace? Grace? Another name from the back of her mind. Phyllis fingered the patchwork quilt, tracing the circles of quilted scrollwork on the coverlet. 'Auntie Ada's dead good with her fingers but she's a right stickler for stitches at school. When I were staying here, did I tell you what she did to poor Elsie Greenhalgh?' whispered Phyllis. There was no interested reply. 'Do you know, Miss Norris made her bring her sewin' from the back row where she and Louie Liptrott were gassin'. Made her hold up her french seams on the drawers she were stitchin'. She dangled them for all the lads to see and shamed her rotten!

' "This won't do, Elsie Greenhalgh. Go back and unpick every stitch." Bright pink Elsie went. The lads call Auntie Ada The Major behind her back. She's right handy wi' the cane. No one believed I lived at her house and she read stories to me.'

'She was my teacher first in Plover Street, remember? Me and Annie Pilling were her favourites.' Sophie smiled weakly. It was no use pretending she did not recognise her own daughter who was now sprouting up like a beanstalk. She was on the mend.

Phyllis stood staring at the shrunken woman in the bed, with her white hair and startled expression. This was not the mam who'd stood on carts and shouted down hecklers. That mam had vanished to London and this one didn't seem to know who she was, so Phyllis reached out a hand cautiously. 'You won't go off and leave us again, Ma, will you?'

'Never, our Phyllis,' replied her mother with all the strength she could muster.

'I'll make you better. I've made you a special cake, boiled it all up in a pan. Dad says it's that clarty you could lay bricks with it! Would you like a piece?'

Sophie shook her head.

'Not yet, love, but I will try some later.'

'Me dad says yer to gerrit off yer chest, spit it out. Stop hugging it all round yersel'. What's he on about? Come home and we'll make you better. He's brassed off with doin' for himself. Come home.'

'I can't, not yet.'

'Dad says you can't stay here forever. It's not fair on Auntie Ada,' said the child.

'She's not complained,' replied her mother.

'Dad says she wouldn't say owt,' came the reply.

'I'll think about it,' was the compromise. The clatter of cups on a tray heralded Ada with the tea. Phyllis wolfed down the parkin and the lemon crusty sponge slice.

'The cart'll be passing the door soon. I've got to go back in time for Dad's tea.' She turned accusingly to the figure in the bed and then peered out of the window, hesitating. 'It's grand sleepin' in this room with all them sheep and cows up in the back fields. That peaceful you can hear yourself think!' Everyone laughed politely. ' 'Bye, Mam. Think on what me dad says,' was Phyllis's parting shot as she thundered down the stairs. Sophie raised herself, heaving her legs out of the bed.

'I must get up and see her to the cart.' She paused, testing her legs. 'Am I too much for you, Ada?'

'If you were, I'd tell you. You're doing nicely.'

'I feel guilty about Phyllis.'

'That's a good sign.' Ada smiled with relief. At last her friend was looking beyond her own feelings to the needs of her child. 'You just need time to build yourself back up again slowly. Lots of walks and good food. Plover Street will be waiting for you when you're well.'

Clinging to Ada's plump arm, she shuffled over to the stairs with head as light as cotton fluff, lowering her disobedient limbs, one by one, down the steps on her bottom. Only in the lobby with its cold tiled floor did she stand upright unaided. The air outside felt damp and December-cold. Taking a deep breath to steady herself, she waved the cart down the town road, surprised at the satisfaction this gave her. Ada was right. It was time to get on her feet, time to shake off the dusty covers and give all the dark corners of her life a fright.

Sophie stepped slowly off the bus as it stopped below Plover Street. She looked around, expecting somehow that everything would be changed; new colours perhaps, new residents, different paintwork. But it was all comfortingly familiar; shabby, shrunken in size even, but unchanged. The same lonely women peered through shining windows. The pigeons roosting in St Anselm's bell tower still splattered the flagstones from a great height.

It was Saturday afternoon and the streets were empty of men who would be cheering on the Wanderers from the terraces. The pavements were edged with black frozen snow and the sky slate-grey and menacing. A few children chased each other around the lamp posts, muffled in scarves and woollen tammies. Phyllis started with surprise and dashed up to greet her. 'Mam! Mam! Yer back. Wait till I tell me dad!'

'No, love, leave it to me. Stay outside a while longer. Me and him have a few things to sort out. Don't look so worried, I'll not be flittin' off again. Or if I do, you'll be comin' with me. Let me give him a turn.'

Phyllis ran off again, leaving her mother time to reflect, to survey the front doorstep. No one had donkey stoned it for months. It was a sorry sight and no mistake. Bun Gran would be dying of shame up there.

This was no front doorbell sort of entrance, more of a creeping through the kitchen homecoming. Quiet, cautious, assuming nothing.

Sophie's hands were shaking. What if he showed her the door after all these months and chucked her out on to the pavement for all of Plover Street to nod their heads at? What if too much had been torn to pieces ever to be mended and darned back together? Those last few steps were the hardest to take; all the 'sorries' and 'what went wrongs' dancing in her head, making her feel dizzy. She looked up at the back walls, the plain bricks and shabby paintwork. Not much of a dwelling after London drawing rooms and Queen's Park villas but nevertheless a warm glow of satisfaction comforted her, seeing it. This is my home, where I belong. Here be my roots and my world.

Sophie pushed against the sneck. The door opened. She threw her bonnet into the room. It skimmed over the table and landed on the chair where Bert was snoozing, the *Clarion News* draped over his face. The paper slipped down and a voice said, 'What's this then? The rover's return?'

'Aye,' she replied, sliding through the door cautiously, embarrassed and uncertain.

'Well, we are honoured. Mrs Seddon Knowles has come to pay us a call.'

'If yer goin' to be like that, I'd better go.'

'Stay, lass. Nay, yer know I'm glad to see you. Come here and let's have a sken at you. Sorry about the mess but me and Phylly did our best.'

'It looks fine to me, Bert Knowles. I think you did a grand job under the circumstances. It's a darn' sight cosier than some of the places I've sat in,' she replied shyly. He took the kettle to the slop stone tap and filled it, placing it on the gas ring.

'We couldn't manage the oven so I bought us one of these gas cooking rings. It's a champion time saver.'

Sophie stretched out her fingers to examine the taps but Bert grabbed her hand and kissed it.

'What were all that in aid of?' Sophie felt tears welling in her eyes; tears of guilt, and of surprise at his warmth.

'Good to have you back in the houseplace. We've

missed you summat rotten. Besides, I've been that cold in bed with no one to warm me toes on!'

'So I'm nowt but a hot water bottle, am I?' Sophie laughed.

'Welcome back, Phia. Don't ever leave us again.' She buried her head in his waistcoat and sniffed tripe and onions, boiled cabbage, and the smell of her man.

Chapter Seventeen

'It's the first time I've felt like baking for months.' Sophie stood at her own kitchen table with arms dusted in flour, bashing down the dough as if her life depended on it.

Thump! That was for all the knocks she'd taken. Thump! That was for Grace Thompson, for not letting her make up and be friends properly, for abandoning them all and giving her no chance to make amends. Thump! That was for Lord Asquith and yet another General Election with yet more promises, promises and no action. Thump! That was for the terrible Pretoria pit disaster two days before Christmas which left a thousand orphans and widows, three hundred men entombed after the blast under Hulton Colliery. Sadness hung like a pall over the town, putting Sophie's own sufferings into perspective.

No longer would she allow herself the indulgence of giving into the black dog days of despair, shrouding her mind with morbid thoughts of punishment. The days when she feared her own loved ones would be harmed in some catastrophe, the worst fear of all. She saved the biggest bashing down to the last. Thump! For the Pankhursts and Vinnie Shaw. Thump! Thump! For all the letters of encouragement and condolence, all the gifts and comforts they could well have afforded to supply, but never bothered to. Thump! For their reproachful silence after she tendered her resignation. Not one of her so-called Suffragette mates bothered to look the road she was on! Not a bleeding word from any of them. She wanted to bash their snooty heads in! So much for the individual in the Suffragette military campaign. It was as if she had never existed. Just gun fodder, easily replaced. No time to pick up the wounded from their battlefield. Oh, no! After such treatment she was happy to turn back to the local Suffrage group and stay law abiding again, if they would have her. Thump! From now on I'll labour in my own vineyard, keep my own counsel, and Vinnie Shaw can jump in the canal for all I care, she vowed.

Anger made her hungry and she knocked up bread, meat and potato pies, beef pasties and Chorley cakes. In her own kitchen she felt Queen Bee, keeper of the kingdom. Soon she was baking for half the street, selling her surplus to the corner shops. Nothing was too much trouble: home-made toffees, cough candy and gobstoppers, mint balls and treacle jaw crackers, cinder crunch and fudge tablet. It kept her busy and the dragon of sadness at bay.

Soon spring burst into colour and the sap rising lifted her spirits. The time for introspection was over and she lost herself in a frenzy of cleaning, sorting out the grime of

Plover Street, visiting old friends to repay their gifts and kindly acts. There was so much to be thankful for. Bridie had brought her fish every week for she was convinced it was good for tired brains. Dora Wagstaff took her out into the country in Dr Wagstaff's automobile which chugged and banged over the ruts and seemed to need its tyres replacing every mile down the road. She walked with Ada for miles over the moors, filling her lungs with sharp moorland air and her head with new ideas.

The first broken fence to mend was her marriage and she climbed shyly back into Bert's bed to give him her warmth again. They talked long into the nights, to reach some understanding of what had gone wrong. Then she repaired the broken bridge over the Guild and Suffrage rift by promising to run a cake stall at the local carnival to raise funds. She ate humble pie when they asked her to promote the *Suffrage Cookbook* again. True to her word, she pestered everyone to distraction with requests for recipes and ideas to make the book worthy of their aims.

It was Ada who came up with the idea of adding quotations about the domestic virtues of women at work and home to spice up the recipe collection and add some bite to it. This idea was pounced on by Sophie with an enthusiasm bordering on obsession. The pamphlet was in danger of becoming a weighty tome rather than a bit of fun.

She picked up the threads of her everyday life again and on the surface made a full recovery, except in one tender compartment of her heart. She would never talk of Grace Thompson. If she cropped up in conversation at the Guild,

Sophie would leave the room. The words in her friend's last letter were branded deep inside her head. She could not even touch the envelope without shaking and trembling with guilt, but nor could she bring herself to destroy this last link with her friend.

As the weeks turned into months this feeling grew no easier. Was there no one to absolve her from this terrible sense of remorse? She no longer believed any priest had the power to take the pain away. Yet part of her knew she must make her peace or it would burn inside her like a bitter acid and spoil the rest of her life. It was time to seek penance.

One afternoon late in the March of 1911, when the first crocus heads poked warily out of Lord Dunscar's flowerbeds, overlooked by the brassy trumpets of haughty daffodils, she found herself at the door of St Stephen's Vicarage, hands trembling at this impulsive act.

On receiving her name the housekeeper ushered her into a dreary hallway and through to a cramped room full of papers and books. Sitting in a wicker bath chair by the fireside, reading a book through a magnifying glass, was Grace's father, Rowland Thompson, now an old man.

He was a pitiable sight with white wispy tufts of down haloing his head in the fading light, framing a face yellow with age. His faded eyes were surrounded in loose, sagging skin; his hunched shoulders wrapped against the draughts in a tartan blanket.

'I don't know if you remember me, sir? I was Grace's friend, Sophia.'

'Old Wilf Seddon's daughter from Plover Street – as if

I could forget. Sit down, child. How nice of you to call. Will you take some tea?' Sophie sat down, relieved at this unexpected welcome.

How could this wizened old man, with his croaking voice and trembling limbs, ever have been the Vicar who had frightened her as a child with his stern warnings? Here was the man who had discouraged her friendship with his daughter; once so aloof, so above her station, now he seemed grateful for her company. His genuine warmth took her by surprise and she started to weep.

'I came to show you this letter. If only I'd opened it earlier perhaps I might have stopped her. I've been ill but I want you to see it for yourself and make sense of it for me.' Sophie handed him the tattered page. His hand shook as he drew the glass across the letter, examining every word.

'You mustn't blame yourself,' he said finally. 'Grace was very determined to do things her own way. She could be very secretive.' He struggled to hold the magnifying lens. 'She sent all her friends farewell letters and tidied up her legal affairs. That was her way. This fits with the note she left for me.'

He paused, as if deciding whether to go further. 'You might as well know, strictly between ourselves, of course, that the post-mortem examination revealed a growth on her chest. In fact, it was quite advanced. She was very ill. We did not publicise the fact, word of such a disease is better kept within the family. Exactly the same condition as her poor mama and at the same age too. We had always

293

shielded her from such knowledge but children have eyes and ears and no doubt she remembered Margaret's suffering.'

'You're telling me that she knew she had . . .' Sophie did not pronounce the fearful word. 'A growth? Did she not seek treatment?'

'Apparently not. She kept her secret and I blame myself that I was too short-sighted not to notice her troubles,' the Vicar confessed.

'But I feel that I am to blame,' Sophie persisted. 'We fell out as people do, over foolish ideals and political beliefs. I went to London and she wrote me several notes but I was always too busy to reply. I have to live with that for the rest of my life; too busy for the friend who once saved my life. How can I ever make it right in here?' Sophie pointed to her chest. 'It burns away, I can't settle to anything serious. I don't know what to do.'

'You must forgive yourself. Go and talk to her. Get it off your chest. Tell her how you are feeling. She's in the churchyard next door. It's the only way to find some peace. We're often harder on ourselves than others would be. Believe me, my dear, talk to her. I promise it will help. I often wheel myself there and share my thoughts with her.

'I'm glad you called. She left you all her books in her will. They are packed in a box in her room. Go and see if there is anything else of hers you might like as a memorial.'

'Are you sure? I don't feel I deserve anything,' said Sophie, wiping away the tears.

'You might also consider continuing her work in some

way. Perhaps doing what she asked of you in the letter? Look after the women of the Workhouse. That was her hope for you, Sophia.'

They sat quietly in the firelight, sipping tea, each with their own thoughts; an old man and a woman from different worlds, united by a shared grief.

The room upstairs was cold and musty, the bed made up with a coverlet pulled back as if awaiting its occupant. It was a plain room with delicate wallpaper, maroon velvet curtains and oriental rugs. On the mantelpiece were sepia photographs and postcards shoved behind the candlesticks, alongside a faded Palm Sunday Cross. The wardrobe was the same one from St Anselm's days, with the mirror on the door where they had pulled faces at each other as children. Sophie flung open the door and buried her head in the clothes. The smell of Grace was still undisturbed, the lavender soap and attar of roses. She rocked back and forth as memories flooded over her.

By her bed was a small bureau and a writing case embossed with the gilt initials, G.M.T. Inside were envelopes tied up with red ribbon, old letters well-thumbed. Sophie recognised her own scribbled notes. As she lifted the vellum pad, she touched the crinkled, desiccated petals of a pressed flower. Dropping the pad, she gasped. Oh, surely not the same rose? She fingered it reverently as she placed it carefully back in the case. This was what she must take home for remembrance. She paused for one last look. How quickly a room became lifeless without the warmth of living flesh to move the air. It felt like a mausoleum and she an intruder.

Sophie drew back the curtains to view the garden; already the lawn was greener and the trees sprouting buds. How cruelly the seasons follow each other, mindless of our suffering.

Quietly she closed the door and saw herself out of the back door, through the garden gate into the churchyard; to the corner verge where they had discreetly buried Grace, away from the rows of headstones. Propriety did not allow a headstone so Sophie sat by the mound and poured out her thoughts, oblivious to the chill north-easterly which whistled around her battered bonnet. Was the Vicar right after all? Did it help to open her heart, to talk to the dead?

Chapter Eighteen

'Stand still while I measure up your Coronation costume again,' said Ada, on her knees, trying not to swallow a mouthful of pins.

'Why must I be Joan of Arc? This helmet sits on my head like a pea on a mountain. Surely you could have got someone younger for the job? Not very original, is it?'

'Stop wriggling. You're worse than Phyllis . . . ants in yer pants, madam. You'll do as yer told for once! All that cooking has put some flesh on your bones at last. I'm going to have to let out the waist – or have you and Bert something to tell me?' laughed the teacher.

'Not on yer Nelly! One scallywag is enough for us.' Sophie tousled her daughter's hair.

'But I don't want to be a page boy in the procession.' Phyllis shook her head. 'I want to wear a white dress when we all go to London, not boy's clothes. Why do I have to wear lad's stuff?'

'If you keep on mitherin', we'll leave you behind in the

left luggage compartment and march in the Coronation Procession without you. So there, Phyllis Millicent. Just shut yer gob!'

'Will we see the King and Queen?' asked the excited child.

'I doubt if they'll be watching a girt big Suffrage Procession.' I'm not sure I want to be back there again with all the crowds either, she thought privately. Sophie was not at all convinced that a pilgrimage back to the capital would lay her bad memories but she was not going to spoil it for her kiddie or her friends by being a misery guts. This time others must come first.

'How are we going to carry all yer cookbooks?' Ada smirked.

'Well, if everyone carries a few in their bags, we'll get by. It's to be hoped we'll have none left to bring home. Dora says we can rent a stall in Hyde Park after the march. She's booked the tickets for the train and organised everything. Do I have to wear armour? Can't I just pin a notice on my back saying "Joan of Arc"?'

'Where's yer sense of occasion? If you think you'll be hard done by, think about poor Dora decked out as Gloriana, waddling through the streets in a farthingale and ruff. We're giving the costumes a try out on Saturday at the Whitsun Carnival.' Ada was in no mood for shirkers.

They duly assembled for the procession of floats around the town streets, wobbling on the back of a decorated mill cart as Famous Heroines of the Past. The rain stayed away long enough for the carnival stalls to be set out on the Bee

Hive sports ground. As the queue of floats waited for judging, the heavens opened and down poured buckets of Lancashire's best over the crowds, soaking off tissue and crêpe paper, drenching the bookstalls and displays, sending the sodden crowds scurrying for cover in the tea tents. Joan of Arc's helmet disintegrated into a soggy, sorry sight.

In the distance a small bookstall was hurriedly packed away by a group of women in familiar green and purple colours. Sophie shot a quick glance across at them with mixed emotions. Had things gone differently she would have been with them, selling badges and booklets. Strangely she no longer felt guilty or embarrassed. Mrs Seddon Knowles belonged with the law abiding 'Suffs' from now on. Militancy was over for her. When she went to London for the big procession she would be wearing red not purple on her sash.

Vinnie Shaw strutted around the office like a peacock. 'No Vote, No Census, girls! That's the plan and so far, so good. On the night of the second of April, 1911, we'll hit the town for the biggest all-night party in the country and the census forms will become a farce. Why should we bother to register if we don't legally exist?

'All over the country our sisters will open church halls and theatres, meeting halls and schoolrooms, to play all night. What a hoot! Plays, tableaux, revues and concerts. And we, the women of Clement's Inn HQ, will be hiring a West End theatre for our very own theatrical evening. Three cheers for the Pankhursts!' The office rang with excited shouts and keen anticipation of the mass act of defiance.

Already there was great secrecy and rivalry about the productions. Who would produce the wittiest sketch, the most lavish display, or give the best performance with dancers, actresses, opera artistes and concert pianists offering their services to the Cause, free of charge? Tickets were selling fast for dress circle seats at the most glamorous venues.

Vinnie was one of those selected to devise a fill-in sketch for the 'Census Revue'. Something quick and witty; an in-between-the-acts sketch, to distract the audience for a second or two. Everything comes to she who waits, she thought as she flounced around the corridors.

Since that spell in Holloway with the Pankhursts and her new posting in the publicity department, she felt herself at last invincible, indispensable and inseparable from those at the top. Every day was chock full of meetings with the press, orders to pass down the ranks and parties to attend. Hardly time to rehearse the *pièce de résistance* which would win her a share of the limelight at the Census show. There was too much to sort out: scenery to be painted, costumes to be scrounged from somewhere, and secret rehearsals to be held out of the office to make sure the sketch ran slickly.

'Who Killed the Conciliation Bill?' sung to the tune of 'Who Killed Cock Robin?' had been discarded in favour of a scene with St Peter's wife waiting outside the pearly gates of Heaven.

Now she must muster, bribe and cajole all the art

students she could find to finish off her three ornamental arches. It was going to be a show stopper.

To the left of centre was the exit arch to the fiery furnaces of Hell; all flames and torments. To the right of centre would be the trumpeting white angel of the heavenly archway, and through the central archway was to be the Throne of Heaven itself.

As she stood in the wings on the night of the performance, watching the tiers of gilded rows filling up with women in glittering tiaras, she saw a myriad jewels flash in the soft gaslight. Many were wearing emerald, amethyst and diamond brooches, seed pearl chokers and white satin evening dresses. Behind her came a hubbub of excitement from backstage where the bustling artistes chatted like starlings at nightfall. The orchestra in the pit tuned in their instruments to the A note, while in the dressing rooms singers warmed their throats and checked their opening notes. The gang was all here on the front row. All the Pankhursts and their retinue. This is going to be a wonderful evening of fun and frolics, wit and repartee, and here I am at the centre of it all, where I belong, she thought smugly.

The programme was running to time and as she gathered the performers for her sketch, Vinnie felt a surge of energy buoying her up. The arches were in place, glittering with tinsel and shimmering in the footlights. St Peter's wife stood in her green overalls with 'Votes for Women' splattered over front and back, standing sentry with her sweeping brush in the central arch. The curtain went up and the audience laughed at her antics. First to arrive was a woman in prison-striped garb who came to the gate.

'What did you do for the Vote?' asked St Peter's wife, barring the entrance.

'I went to prison for the Cause.' Cheers from the audience as she was ushered through the angel gate. Then came a caricature of Mrs Partington, the Anti-Suffrage Campaigner, which had the audience hissing and booing. Same question, different destination, again amid cheers. The next on stage was a girl in clogs and a woman chained to a pretend lamp post. They managed their lines clearly. Then came a woman dressed in uniform padded up to look like General Flora Drummond, the Scottish leader and another dressed to look like Lord Asquith. He was sent to Hell fire.

Then St Peter's wife addressed the audience directly. 'What are you lot out there in those posh seats doing for the Vote? Rise up, women!' This was to be the high point, the punchline of the sketch as the lights dimmed to leave one lone figure approaching the centre arch, dressed in barrister's robes and a huge hat swathed in Suffrage stripes – bearing an unmistakable likeness to Christabel Pankhurst herself. The light went up and St Peter's wife bowed low, ushering her through the central arch to the heavenly throne itself. 'Welcome home, your worship. I was just sifting a few out for you.'

The curtain fell to a trickle of polite applause. Nothing more than that. The women in the wings huddled together, nonplussed. 'They didn't see the joke?' whispered Vinnie in surprise.

'Oh, I think they did, dear, and were not amused. I always thought it a bit risky, making fun of Miss Christabel,' said a helper as she tore down the scenery. 'Did you warn her beforehand?'

'Why should I need to do that? It was a compliment I was making, likening her to God Almighty, not a criticism.' Vinnie felt sickening panic flooding her limbs. 'Surely she would not take offence?'

'Only time will tell you that,' came the cautious reply. Already the moment was passed and the curtain raised on the next item, the stage lit once again. Vinnie turned slowly from the brightness and the warmth, stepping backstage into the cold.

'When are we there?' squirmed Phyllis, peering out of the carriage window a minute out of Manchester. 'Is that London?'

'Settle down, we've hardly got going yet. Play with yer magic colouring book,' sighed Sophie as they sat hunched up together, squashed in a line of carriages crammed with hundreds of other Lancashire 'Suffs'. They were off to the Coronation Procession on a fine June morning, the sun rising before them with the promise of blue skies and dry feet.

'Can I take me pinny off? I'm boiled,' whined the child.

'No, you just keep yer white frock clean for the marching, after Auntie Ada was up all night treadling our dresses together on her sewing machine. Poor soul's worn out already.' Sophie smiled at Ada who was curled up by the window fast asleep, totally oblivious to the chatter of smartly bedecked women in white cotton outfits and Suffrage sashes; their wide-brimmed hats balancing at precarious angles, weighed down with ribbons, flowers and borrowed plumage.

They'd gathered on the platform before dawn, like a sea of white foam amongst the soot and steam. Once conveyed to Manchester the separate groups were linked with coaches from all over the North-west. An army of excited women and children with baskets brimful of pasties and sandwiches, bottles and flasks, off for the day trip of a lifetime. Already faces were soot-smutted as the temptation to hang out of the window got the better of the curious. Once they reached the grey London suburbs, the chatter rose to a roar of anticipation as everyone scrambled for baggage and clothes, lost children and squashed picnics.

Euston Station was awash with many such groups from all over the country: children with labels round their necks, women ushering, counting and recounting their offspring and groups, yelling instructions, issuing maps, pouring out of the station under its imposing arch.

Ada was in charge of her silk banner, Sophie the picnic box and cookbooks, Dora Wagstaff gathered up the stragglers while Phyllis tagged along with Miss Pearson's party of teachers and students. Sophie was familiar enough with her bearings to direct scores of nervous parties on their way towards the Embankment and the start of their bit of the procession.

The sun blazed down from an ink-blue sky on to a dusty city. Hungry and excited, they ate their crumbled sand-wiches while watching boats scudding by on the River Thames. Phyllis and Dora's daughters raced in and out of the gathering groups of excited women.

'Don't get dirty! Don't get lost! And keep your hat on!' yelled their mothers.

How different it all felt this time to be amongst ordinary folk like herself, day trippers in awe of this sophisticated metropolis. How Grace would have loved to be here, sharing the occasion and the fun. The memory of her own last day in the city flooded over Sophie. How quickly the tide of sadness could ebb and flow in one year.

The parade began to assemble according to the marshalling instructions; other parades were joining them from all over the city. In the side streets were wagons loaded with tableaux, lavish displays by professional soci-eties, depicting great events in the lives of historical women. Joan of Arc, Good Queen Bess, the Lady with the Lamp, Elizabeth Fry. In fact Sophie counted six Joan of Arcs and was glad they had managed to change Dora's mind about wearing costumes. Theirs would have looked so homespun alongside these elaborate creations displayed on flat-topped lorries, bedecked with bunting, rosettes and Coronation regalia. The poor participants stood sweltering in their heavy costumes in the noonday sun; behind them a river of white dresses flowed as far as the eye could see.

'As long as I live, Ada, I shall never forget being part of this.' Sophie found tears filling her eyes.

For one brief day all the Suffrage Societies had forgotten their grievances and were uniting for this Coronation extravaganza in all its greens, purples and reds, marching if not side by side, then in one continuous line. Women proudly proclaiming their power and position for once. Their sheer numbers brought the city to a standstill and a reluctant admiration of their obvious determination to have a voice.

Suddenly it seemed as if all their separate societies, like little buckets of water, had pooled together to form this huge flood tide. Sophie felt so proud she was bursting for Phyllis to mark the scene, but typically she was off playing tag with the other girls, being a pain in the neck.

It was going to take hours for the procession to move down Victoria Embankment and across the river bridge at Waterloo and back over Westminster Bridge in a loop to make its progress towards Trafalgar Square, to assemble in Hyde Park for the rally. Sophie could hear a drum band and pipes leading the procession. There were four-in-hand coaches with famous dignitaries riding open-topped (be blowed if she recognised any of them), waving to the crowds who had gathered for the spectacle on the pavements in their straw boaters and bonnets.

There were eight hundred women in academic gowns and mortar boards, and a thousand carrying silver arrows glinting in the sun – the women imprisoned for the Cause. Indian women in golden robes glided gracefully in saris, representing the Empire, with banners of velvet embossed with elephants. Then came the Trades Union banners and the Union representatives – teachers, doctors, nurses in uniform – on and on came the streaming banners, tilting and swaying.

Sometimes, as they marched past under Ada's banner, the crowd to either side fell silent, as if the grandeur and dignity of this procession, the simplicity of the women in their bridal white, overwhelmed the onlookers. Hoisting up their local banner, linking arms as they stepped out along the route, past the grey grandeur of state buildings, palaces bedecked with flags and bunting and the tall ships' masts, was a moment for each to savour. Any doubts Sophie had had about bringing herself and Phyllis evaporated amongst the warmth, pride and gaiety of the atmosphere around her.

A strange glow of certainty burned within her. The Vote would come. It would have to come after this show of strength. Perhaps by the time young Phylly came of age the franchise would be hers. No one could ignore the dignity and splendour of this peaceful occasion. It would live in their memory forever.

But will having the blessed Vote change much in our lives, I wonder? she thought. Our victories will be small ones, steady, slowly grinding down prejudice. It won't be easy for men to yield up their positions, jobs, power; to share with the sex they still call frail and inferior. But just for today I feel hopeful.

Even the sight of the militants in their dark green

battledress did nothing but enhance the total show of strength. 'We mean business. Take us seriously or else,' they seemed to declare.

The ice cream cone vendors plied soft cooling pop and refreshments to the wilting walkers; the crowds encouraged them with cheery cockney banter; organ grinders and barrel organs filled the air with jaunty music. Phyllis disappeared several times, causing panic as Sophie and Ada held up the line to yank her out of the crowd where she stood gawping up at all the buildings with fascination. 'It's a grand place, is London. Why can't we come and live here?'

'Never mind grand place, madam, one more step out of line and you'll get a grand clout!' warned her irate mother as she yanked Phyllis back to her side. 'I'll have to pin a label on yer back if you don't stay by.'

By the time their part of the seven-mile-long procession reached the gates of Hyde Park, the first rallies were over. For Ada's group there was only one destination. They had just about enough energy to collapse under the shade of the nearest tree and soothe their swollen feet.

The springtime cherry blossom had long since floated down and shrivelled into a dusty pink carpet. They lay back in the dappled shade, enjoying the fragrance of new-mown grass and the promise of high summer, savouring their satisfaction in the day and the rightness of making the effort.

'If I don't find a quiet bush somewhere, I'll burst! Are you coming?' said Ada to the group.

'You know me, I'm a camel, I can last for hours. But take Phyllis and we'll find the stalls. As I've lugged these ruddy books around all day, I'm not goin' home with a single one. Catch me up over there.'

Sophie rose reluctantly and gathered all the booklets from the others. So much effort had gone into getting all their recipes into type, never mind chasing people to donate funds to set it up. She followed a group of women carrying embroidered sashes to a marquee and dutifully waited under the tent until a space was found for her to set up her stall.

Glad of the shade, women drifted through the Exhibition Hall examining goods, strolling in groups in elegant tea gowns, bedecked with medals and brooches. Others like Sophie herself were in simple shifts of cotton sheeting made on the cheap from offcuts. What a mixture they all were: different shapes and sizes, young and old, rich and poor. Somehow today it did not seem to matter; the barriers of class and rank had disappeared, replaced by a mutual feeling of pride and confidence. All women together.

'Roll up! Roll up for your *Suffrage Cookbook*! Selling like hot cakes, specially prepared for this occasion by Lancashire women. Buy our recipe book. Every one tried and tested by my own fair hand. Come buy! Eccles cakes and Wet Nelly, tattie pie and hot pot. Get your cookbooks here and support the Suffrage cause in the North!'

Sophie forgot her embarrassment and started to shove the books out into the crowd like pamphlets on a street pavement. She was a dab hand at that. Her eyes took in a group of noisy Suffragettes with green and purple sashes just entering the marquee. They looked in amusement at her wares and walked on by. A lone woman picked up the booklet, looked at it and put it down, eyeing Sophie almost with contempt. She walked on without comment. Sophie stared at her face, one she would recognise anywhere with its slightly bulging eyes and frizzle of fine pink hair piled under an enormous wide-brimmed hat; they were the unforgettable features of Lavinia Shaw. Sophie turned to Dora Wagstaff who had just arrived.

'Did you see that? Did you see who I just saw?' Dora looked puzzled. 'Here, mind my stall . . .' Sophie shot off through the crush, watching Vinnie's hat bobbing on its way out into the park. Once outside she spun the woman round roughly. 'Hang on a minute, missy . . . Wait yer sweat, Vinnie Shaw. You don't just walk past me and mine as if we were dog dirt. How dare you stick yer nose in the air at my cookbook, after all we've bin through?' Vinnie stepped back with genuine surprise.

'I didn't recognise you. It's been a long time . . .'

'Too bleedin' right! Not a word in nine months. Not even a letter of sympathy about Grace. I know you know what happened, Ada wrote to you, so don't come the innocent with me. You Panks don't care for anyone unless they come with a lah-di-dah title these days. I bet you'd not leave yer precious Sylvia Pankhurst high and dry if she'd been stranded.

'Where were you when I needed you? Not a word. Left me to pick mesen off the floor. I could have been dumped in the Thames like a sack of kittens for all you cared! All for one and one for all? Hah! Selfish biddies! It's everyone for themselves more like. And now you try to walk past me. How dare you? If I could turn the clock back . . . Grace warned me about you but I never would see it. I thowt she were jealous but she had good reason to doubt you after you stole her bloke. She never said owt but Ada told me yon mucky tale.'

'That's not exactly true. She got that wrong.' Vinnie stood back, uncomfortably aware that all her friends were moving closer to see what the fuss was about. 'I have been rather busy myself. In prison, you know. We all have to make sacrifices for the Cause.'

'Oh, aye? And what sacrifices have you ever made? It nearly cost me my home, my health, my marriage. No Cause is worth that.'

'But that's where you're wrong, my dear. That's woolly thinking. The Cause comes first, above all else,' replied Vinnie with a false smile.

'Pull the other leg, dearie, it's got bells on it! *You* come first to you, your belly and your comforts, and then your precious Pankhursts. Out of all the thousands of women here, I have to bump into you – but I'm glad to be able to say it to yer face at last. Get out of my life and good riddance! Your sort aren't worth botherin' with. You don't care about us lot, us plain folk: real women with working lives, balancing the pennies, making do and getting by. It's all jolly hockey sticks to you, all a big game with yer green army, tartan generals and fancy friends!'

Vinnie turned to walk away, her face puce with rage at

this scene, but Sophie followed behind mockingly, refusing to be ignored. 'Not so fast, milady. I've not said my piece. You were never fit to wipe Grace Thompson's boots. She tried to make change quietly, by changing conditions for downtrodden women.'

'We are all working for change, Sophie, believe me,' replied Vinnie as she straightened her gloves and fiddled with her hair. 'I am sorry about Grace naturally, but every battle has its casualties. Things have not been easy for me recently. In fact I am wondering whether or not . . .'

'Tough! Can't you hear what I'm saying to you? You don't just blow hot and cold with friends to suit yoursen. I shall have to live with what I did for the rest of my life. So help me God, I'll not do again to anyone what you did to me and I to Grace. No wonder our Phyllis calls you the Vinegar Lady! Maybe one day even *you'll* catch a cold and need a friend or two to lean on. But if you were on fire I'd not spit on you! How can you keep a friend if you treat them like paper doilies? Use them once and then dump 'em in the bin? Think on!'

'Oh, Sophie! Don't take everything so seriously. I'm sorry you're taking this attitude.' Vinnie backed away, looking to her cronies for support, but they had all walked away. 'Now look what you've done!'

'Oh, go and boil yer head. Come on, ladies, let me past. I need a breath of fresh air!' Sophie swung round and made for the tent with a spring in her step.

'Where've you been? We thought we'd lost you,' said Ada anxiously.

'Just finishing off some business long overdue with Vinnie the Vinegar Lady.' Sophie smiled with satisfaction at having said her piece.

'Poor old Vinnie, she's got a lot to learn,' said Ada.

'Why did I go along with her? Why didn't you tell me she was nowt but candyfloss?'

'Would you have listened?'

'No, I suppose not. But she's left a right nasty taste,' answered Sophie, gathering her baggage.

'Vinegar is sour and sharp, good for pickling and sprinkling on chips but not for drinking on its own. Far too bitter to stomach. You have to feel sorry for her, though,' Ada added thoughtfully.

'Whatever for?'

'Think about it, Sophie. What has she got in her life?' was the teacher's reply. 'Anyway we've sold all your books now. Can we go home, Missus Knowles?'

'Easier said than done, me thinks,' sighed Sophie as they gathered their weary troops together and shuffled through the park, through the dust, horse dung and evening crowds.

She stared around at the dusty city with the eyes of experience, seeing past the grandeur of gardens and statues, porticoes and squares with elegant shop façades, to the squalor lurking in the shadows, to the wandering people, bobbing and jostling aimlessly like flotsam tossed upon the shore; flung by powers beyond their control. For her, the sophistication, glamour and speed of life here held no allure, left no impression other than the strong desire to be safe back on home territory.

There was certainly a confidence in the stride of Southern women, a purposeful brisk walk. For them she supposed this was the heart of things, the centre of action, the battleground. The daughters of the city were brasher, more defiant of convention, forcing themselves on to the open streets. London was their home and the Suffrage women would carve out a niche for themselves here.

Ahead was the distant triumphal arch through to Euston Station, like a welcome beacon guiding the way forward to trains loaded with welcome flat vowels and burring Lancashire chatter.

Sophie sat tired but content. Here was just as much kindness, tolerance, courage and purpose, at a pace she could follow. Their battles were none the less dangerous or exhausting for being fought on Northern fields exposed to damp air. The wind was just as rife with prejudice and pomposity here. Women were still chilled by menfolk mouthing off against equality from Chapel pulpits and Union clubhouses. It was the same struggle on harder, higher ground, without the comfort of numbers or high society support, just a handful of stalwarts, juggling home-care and politics, feminine duties alongside personal ambition; digging trenches and defences with one hand tied behind them all the time.

I'm rooted in millstone grit and blossom best upon heather moors and cobbled streets, she realised. My life is best suited to plain cooking among friends who'll fight alongside me. I can't wait to get home! Then she dozed off with a smile on her face.

The train chugged alongside the platform late that night. Lifting her sleeping child, limp as a rag doll, Sophie stepped out into the damp air, drawing in its sooty sharpness with relish. By the station clock, hands in pockets, pipe in mouth, stood Bert, waiting patiently for their safe return. He gathered up the child and they climbed the steps together.

Postscript
1971

Sophie Knowles was relieved that the stream of visitors was drying up at last. What a fuss over her ninety-fifth birthday! It was tiring her out. Trust Phyllis to want to mark the day. She meant well but it was making Sophie feel like some mothballed relic from a museum, wheeled out on special occasions for closer inspection. What she needed was a bit of peace and quiet.

'I think I'll have a sit in the back garden, Phyllis. I can do a few squares.' She rose slowly, shuffling for her knitting bag.

'Wrap up then, there's a bite to the breeze,' shouted her daughter as she sided all the best china from the table.

Sophie made her escape to the wooden bench by the rose bushes; their buttery petals tipped with pink were full-blown now. Her attention drifted towards the open fields beyond the small garden, to the distant colliery shafts and the speeding traffic tearing down the motorway towards Manchester.

Knitting Oxfam squares with clacking needles was soothing, rhythmic, repetitive; the softness of wool across her papery skin comforting. Knitting gave her time to rummage inside her head, time to crochet pieces of her life together on nights when sleep was impossible.

If only life were as simple as knitting. Pity it took a life-time of mistakes and dropped stitches before you got it right with friends. There were none of the real ones left to blow out the candles on her cake; just a few puffing oddballs like herself, hanging by a thread, and faithful Phyllis who still remembered the old days. Let's face it,

319

Sophie Seddon, you're archive material now judging by the number of students who come knocking on yer door with their tape recorders and notepads!

Why had friendships been such a blessing and curse to her? The oldest ones, forged in fires of suffering, were the best, however short-lived and stormy.

The roses caught her eye again with their battered velvet petals and rusting buds. *Rosa graciae* gave value for money and no one else in the fold could sport a bush named after their oldest friend. She nodded off, smiling with satisfaction.

The rustle of a breeze, cold on her cheeks, stirred Sophie awake. For a moment she was poised between two worlds, past and present fused into a confusion of memories. The Bread and Roses Society – was it really so long ago?

Before the war that changed everything. Before Bert volunteered with his Pals' Brigade to be blown to smithereens in a crater somewhere. Only his name remained, etched on the Menin Gate alongside that of half the able men of Plover Street. Before the queues and rations and droves of sullen silent ones returned half-dead from their trenches. Before the 'flu bug picked off the weak-chested from the mines, mills and cold houses. Before the depression damped down smoking chimneys and emptied full bellies, preparing the way for yet another war.

There were no spares left for Phyllis to dance with or make a brew of tea for. Hers was to be a generation without a regular supply of eligible men; too many mown down by two world wars. All she got was the Vote in 1928 – and about bloody time after all the hard labour the women took over in 1914! Oh, and the right to wear trousers without shame or comment.

Ada Norris popped her clogs quickly once she retired, out cycling one afternoon and dead in her chair by teatime. That was the way to do it, not hanging on each week reading the Obituaries to see who the lucky ones were.

I've had enough, she decided. I've done me bit for this town, flown the red flag on the Town Council, argued budgets late into the night, fought planning applications, canvassed on every doorstep in my ward like the stubborn old cow I am. How much I've achieved I'll never know, and for what sort of Socialism I'm no longer sure. There were too many power cuts and cold suppers. Warmth comes before food when yer my age.

So much change in a lifetime: fancy cars, telly, coach trips abroad. Yet she felt like a stranger in her own town. Every year mills closed and turned overnight into empty shells with broken windows and cracked clock faces. No lunchtime rush to the corner chippy, no women in head-scarves and curlers, sunning themselves on the Lodge wall, whistling at the fellas, mee-mawing to each other. Half her world was pulled down for redevelopment and slum clearance. Plover Street was levelled by bulldozers and now St Anselm's was demolished and a shabby park full of litter stood in its old place. All in the name of progress.

'Time for yer trip, Mother, or are you too tired?' Phyllis

brought her a welcome brew. 'I'll just get the car out of the garage while you pick a few blooms for your friends.'

Dear Phyllis. She means well but she talks to me like I'm a kid. God knows I've tried to shove her out of the nest but she's always been content to be a homebody with just her Choral Union and Townswomen's Guild and Saturday afternoon at Burnden Park. But the Wanderers aren't what they were, not since Nat Lofthouse hung up his football boots.

Every month they crossed the town up Dunscar way to the cemetery to take a bunch of fresh blooms. Phyllis sat in the car listening to 'Woman's Hour' while Sophie tottered down the path past rows of old friends to pay her respects.

Even the graveyard looked neglected. The young didn't keep their relatives up to scratch these days. She divided the last of the *Rosa graciae* between her friends, Grace and Ada. Grace now had a proper headstone, thanks to a donation from the Suffrage Society when it closed its books in 1930.

She paused as she arranged the flowers in the urn; bending down was a creaky business these days with no guarantee of not ending up U-shaped.

'I've looked at all the names in here, Grace. Not one worth writing down like we used to, but I saw a beauty in St Michael's Great Lever the other day: Lemody Rebecca. We must have missed that one.

'Would you believe, slap bang next to a Lavinia – but not our Vinnie! Last time I heard anything about her she'd taken up with Olive Baden-Powell and was high up in the

Girl Guides, trooping all over the globe, bitten by some snake on a safari apparently. I bet it were the poor snake what died though!

'I had another visit from a student wanting to know all about the Votes for Women business. Quite a blether we had. I told her bits but not all. It wouldn't be right going into all of it.

'I must be off now. Phyllis'll be waiting. Got an appointment at the chiropodist. Nice lady, sorts me bunions out a treat. Turns these owd pins into velvet cushions for a few days. Still, what's the fuss? Be down here soon enough and then we'll give 'em such a turn.'

Sophie smiled. 'You and me together again, bread and roses . . . just wait on.'

LAW-ABIDING LANCASHIRE WOMEN WORKING PEACEFULLY FOR THE VOTE, PRESENT OUR SELECTION OF RECIPES

PLAIN AND FANCY

A CELEBRATION OF COUNTY COOKING

We may live without poetry, music and art,
We may live without conscience, and live without heart,
We may live without friends, and live without books,
But civilisation can't live without cooks.

Price 6d.

*A good dinner sharpens wit
and softens the heart.*

Lancashire Meat and Potato Pie
Serves 4

450 g (1 lb) best stewing beef, cut into chunks
1 medium onion, peeled and cut small
3 good sized carrots, peeled and cut into chunks
salt and pepper
900 g (2 lb) potatoes, peeled and cut into small chunks
enough shortcrust pastry to cover top of pie dish
Oven: 375°F (190°C) Gas Mark 5

1. Place the meat, onion and carrot in a saucepan, and cover with 1.2 litres cold water.
2. Add salt and pepper to taste.
3. Bring to the boil, remove scum, cover and simmer for 2 hours.
4. Add the potato and more salt, and bring to the boil again.
5. Transfer to a deep pie dish (earthenware, and 10 × 18 cm/4 × 7 in in diameter).
6. Cover the dish and cook in the preheated oven for 2 hours until the meat is tender.
7. About 15 minutes before serving, remove the cover, and grease the top of the pie dish.
8. Roll out the cool shortcrust pastry, and place over the pie. Make a criss-cross air hole in the centre. Raise the oven temperature to 400°F (200°F) Gas 6.
9. Return the pie to the oven until the crust is golden, about 10–15 minutes.

Serve with pickled red cabbage and black peas

They talk about a woman's sphere
As though it had a limit
There's not a place in earth or heaven
There's not a task to mankind given
There's not a blessing or a woe
There's not a whispered yes or no.
There's not a life, or death or birth,
That has a feather's weight of worth,
But has a woman in it.

Wash-day Savoury Pudding

Serves 4

2 onions, peeled
salt and pepper
1 teaspoon dried sage
175 g (6 oz) plain flour
2 eggs, beaten
600 ml (1 pint) milk
25 g (1 oz) dripping or lard
Oven: 350°F (180°C) Gas Mark 4

1. Boil the onions until tender, about 20 minutes, then drain, cool and chop.
2. Mix salt and pepper to taste and the sage with the onion.
3. Put the flour in a bowl, and add the eggs and milk gradually to make a smooth batter.
4. Finally mix the onions and seasonings into the batter.
5. Melt the dripping in a medium-sized baking tin (10"–25 cm) and pour in the batter.
6. Bake in the preheated oven for 40 minutes.
7. Slice into chunks and eat with chips and peas. (Like Yorkshire Pudding.)

Ladies who wish to keep their spouses
Content and happy in their houses,
Must learn that food to be a blessing
Must not be ruined in the dressing
It's nice to be good looking
But that will not excuse good cooking;
And men have got such funny natures
They'll judge you by your beef and 'taters.
So if you want to rule and lead 'em
You'll do it if you nicely feed 'em.

Brain Cakes

It's difficult to be specific about quantities for this recipe: use your commonsense!

sheep's brains, washed and blanched
milk
sheep's tongue (pre-cooked)
breadcrumbs
chopped parsley
salt and pepper
beaten egg
some plain flour
a little dripping

1. Boil the sheep's brains in milk until tender.
2. Skin the tongue and then chop it up small. Chop the cooked brains as well. Place in a bowl.
3. Add a cupful of breadcrumbs, some chopped parsley and salt and pepper to taste.
4. Moisten with some of the beaten egg and form the mixture into flat cakes.
5. Dredge with flour, dip into the remaining beaten egg, and then into the remaining breadcrumbs.
6. Fry in the dripping until golden brown on both sides.

Serve with winter vegetables, pickled red cabbage and jacket potatoes.

A contented mind is a purse well lined,
And a purse well lined is a contented mind.

Tripe and Onions

Serves 8

900 g (2 lb) tripe, dressed and washed
100 g (4 oz) onions, peeled and sliced
900 mls (1½ pints) milk
50 g (2 oz) butter
25 g (1 oz) plain flour
freshly grated nutmeg
salt and pepper

1. Cut the tripe into narrow strips about 5 cm (2 in) long.
2. Simmer the tripe and onion in the milk until tender, about 60 minutes.
3. Melt the butter in a pan, and stir in the flour for a few minutes.
4. Gradually add the milk from the tripe, and stir into a thick sauce.
5. Bring to the boil, then season with nutmeg, salt and pepper to taste.
6. Add the tripe and onions to the sauce, heat through and serve with mashed potatoes. Or transfer the tripe and sauce to a flameproof dish, sprinkle with Lancashire cheese, and grill before serving.

*Copy the kettle; though up to the neck in hot water
it still continues to sing.*

Traditional Lancashire Hot Pot

Serves 4

900 g (2 lb) middle neck lamb cutlets (about 8)
25 g (1 oz) lard or dripping
900 g (2 lb) potatoes, peeled and thinly sliced
4 onions, peeled and sliced
4 carrots, peeled and sliced
salt and pepper
1.2 litres (2 pints) stock

Oven: 325°F (160°C) Gas Mark 3

1. Trim excess fat from the meat.
2. Heat the lard in a frying pan and lightly brown the cutlets on both sides.
3. In a large ovenproof casserole or a straight-sided dish, layer the potato, onion, carrot and cutlets, finishing with a thick layer of potato to form the crust. Season lightly as you go.
4. Pour over the stock.
5. Sprinkle salt over the top layer of potatoes, and brush with the lard from the frying pan.
6. Cover with a lid and place in the oven. Cook for 1½–2 hours.
7. Remove the lid and continue to cook for 30 minutes to brown the top layer.

Serve with pickled red cabbage and garnish with parsley for a Suffrage coloured effect.

Better a dinner of herbs where love is,
than a stalled ox and hatred therewith . . .

Herby Pudding (for end of week)

Serves 6

100 g (4 oz) wholewheat flour
100 g (4 oz) oatmeal
50 g (2 oz) spinach, cabbage, young nettles, or any greens
available, chopped
100 g (4 oz) shredded suet
50 g (2 oz) chopped mixed herbs
milk and water

1.   Mix all together with a little watery milk to make a stiff dough.
2.   Put in a well greased pudding basin (medium 7"–17 cm), and cover with greaseproof paper or muslin cloth.
3.   Steam in a steamer for 3 hours.
4.   Turn out and cut into wedges to accompany cold meats and leftovers.

Can be sliced cold and fried in dripping!

*Let plain living and high thinking go
hand in hand.*

Wet Nelly (A Lancashire Bread Pudding)

Serves 6

a knob of butter
225 g (8 oz) fresh breadcrumbs (e.g. left over
from bread sauce)
150 ml (¼ pint) milk
2 teaspoons mixed spice
grated rind of ½ lemon or orange
100 g (4 oz) shredded suet
100 g (4 oz) soft brown sugar plus some extra

Oven: 350°F (180°C) Gas Mark 4

1. Grease a 20 cm (8 in) square roasting tin with a little of the butter.
2. Soak the breadcrumbs in the milk for 30 minutes.
3. Stir the mixed spice, grated rind, suet and sugar into the bread and milk. Mix thoroughly.
4. Turn out into the greased tin and smooth the top.
5. Dot with butter and sprinkle the extra sugar over the surface.
6. Bake for 1–1½ hours until firm and golden.
7. Cut into slices and serve hot or cold.

Delicious with a serving of cream.

To all the prize is open,
But only she can take it
Who says with Roman courage:
I'll find a way or make it.

Eccles Cakes

Makes about 8

225 g (8 oz) prepared puff pastry, chilled
50 g (2 oz) butter, melted
175 g (6 oz) currants
1 teaspoon mixed spice
25 g (1 oz) soft brown sugar
a little milk or beaten egg white
some granulated sugar

Oven: 450°F (230°C) Gas Mark 8

1. Roll the pastry out thinly on a floured surface, and cut into 10 cm (4 in) rounds.
2. Mix the melted butter, currants, spice and sugar together.
3. Put a generous dollop into the centre of each pastry round.
4. Dampen the edges of the pastry rounds with water and gather into the centre like a bag, enclosing the currant filling.
5. Turn over and carefully flatten a little.
6. Make three slits across the top of each cake (for Father, Son and Holy Ghost).
7. Brush with milk or egg white, and sprinkle with sugar.
8. Place on a greased baking sheet and bake in the oven for 15 minutes until golden.

Bible Cake for Sunday Tea

1. 225 g (8 oz) Judges V, 25
2. 225 g (8 oz) Jeremiah VI, 20
3. 1 tablespoon I Samuel XIV, 25
4. 3 of Jeremiah XVIII, 11
5. 225 g (8 oz) I Samuel XXX, 12
6. 225 g (8 oz) Nahum III, 8 (chopped)
7. 50 g (2 oz) Numbers XVII, 8 (blanched and chopped)
8. 450 g (1 lb) I Kings IV, 22
9. Season to taste with II, Chronicles IX, 9
10. a pinch of Leviticus II, 13
11. 1 teaspoon Amos IV, 5
12. 3 tablespoons Judges IV, 19

Oven: 325°F (160°C) Gas Mark 3

Beat Nos 1, 2 and 3 to a cream;
Add 4, one at a time, still beating.
Then add 5, 6 and 7 and beat again.
Add 8, 9, 10 and 11, and mix well.
Lastly add No. 12.
Bake in a slow oven for 1½ hours.

May the Lord have mercy on your efforts!

She who would eat the fruit must climb the tree.

Hedgerow Cheese

Makes about 8 jars

1.35 kg (3 lb) wild blackberries,
damsons or elderberries
1.35 kg (3 lb) cooking apples
water
sugar

1. Wash and drain the soft fruit, and wipe the apples. Chop the apples thoroughly.
2. Place all in a pan with sufficient water to cover.
3. Cover with the lid, and cook gently to a pulp.
4. Rub through a sieve.
5. Return the sieved pulp to the open pan and cook further to reduce the pulp until thick. Weigh the pulp.
6. To each 500 g (1 lb) pulp add 500 g (1 lb) sugar. Cook over a low heat to dissolve the sugar, then continue simmering until thick and gooey.
7. Draw a spoon across the base of the pan. It should leave a clear line if the cheese is ready.
8. Pour into prepared moulds or cover as for jam in small jars.
9. Turn out and cut into wedges. It can be used as a relish.

Lemon Dainty

Serves 4

1 cup granulated sugar
50 g (2 oz) butter
2 eggs, separated
2 tablespoons plain flour
1 cup milk
juice and grated rind of 1 lemon

Oven: 350°F (180°C) Gas Mark 4

1. Beat the sugar and butter to a cream.
2. Fold in the egg yolks and the flour, then the milk.
3. Beat the egg whites to a soft peak, and fold them into the mixture after adding the juice and rind of the lemon.
4. Pour the mixture gently into a greased shallow oven-proof dish. Set in a roasting tin of hot water. (Size 9" glass dish.)
5. Bake for 1 hour until golden on surface.
6. Serve with cream.

Bonfire Parkin

100 g (4 oz) brown sugar
50 g (2 oz) lard
50 g (2 oz) butter
225 g (8 oz) black treacle, warmed in the tin
1 egg, beaten
150 ml (¼ pint) milk
225 g (8 oz) medium oatmeal
225 g (8 oz) plain flour
1 heaped teaspoon ground ginger
½ teaspoon bicarbonate of soda

Oven: 350°F (180°C) Gas Mark 4

1. Melt the sugar, fats and treacle over a low heat.
2. Add the egg to the treacle mixture with some of the milk.
3. Put the oatmeal, flour and ginger into a bowl, make a well in the centre, and pour in the treacle mixture. Beat well until smooth.
4. Add the bicarbonate of soda to the remaining milk, stir, then add and mix well.
5. Pour into a greased tray about 28 × 23 cm (11 × 9 in) and 5 cm (2 in) deep. Cook for about 50 minutes until firm. Leave to cool in the tin.
6. Cut into squares and store in an airtight tin. The parkin is best left for two to three days before eating.

Do what you can, being what you are.
Shine like a glow worm if you can't be a star.

Clarty Cut-and-Come-Again Cake

175 g (6 oz) dark brown sugar
400 g (14 oz) dried fruit
100 g (4 oz) butter
1 heaped teaspoon mixed spice
1 teaspoon bicarbonate of soda
250 ml (8 fl oz) water
2 eggs, beaten
225 g (8 oz) wholemeal flour

Oven: 350°F (180°C) Gas Mark 4

1. Put the sugar, fruit, butter, spice, bicarbonate of soda and the water together in a pan and bring to the boil for a few minutes.
2. Allow the mixture to cool, then beat in the eggs and flour.
3. Turn into a greased round tin, 18 cm (7 in) diameter.
4. Bake in the oven for about an hour.
5. Cool in the tin. The cake keeps well.
6. Serve in wedges with Lancashire Tasty cheese or a creamy Wensleydale.